THE FROGMAN OF LOVELAND

A NOVEL
by
Paul Edward Morris

with artwork by
Dagna Majewska

Copyright © 2022 Paul Edward Morris

All rights reserved.

No part of this book may be reproduced or used in any manner without written permission of the copyright owner, except for the use of quotations in a book review.

An Important Note to the Reader:

This book is a work of fiction. Names, characters, places, and incidents are the product of the author's imagination or are used fictitiously. Any resemblance to actual events, locales, or persons, living or dead, is coincidental.

ISBN: 979-8-218-08332-8 (paperback)
ISBN: 979-8-218-08886-6 (ebook)

Thefrogmanofloveland.com

CHAPTER ONE
A New World Order

Late October 1978 - North Pole, The Arctic Ocean

A pretty, winged girl with owl-like features and a tattered white dress knelt at the feet of Santa Claus, shaking. She knew her future rested upon her absorbing every word the imposing bearded man was about to offer, but her nervousness made concentrating impossible. After all, he was the most famous person in the entire world, at once both magical and powerful. So she kept her head lowered and made sure to take deep breaths, something still within her control.

Santa, accustomed to sharing his kingdom's lore with exacting verse, opened a thick, leather-bound book and began to read in his booming, trademark voice:

> *"'It was the winter of 1946. Mankind's Second World War had just ended, lifting the cloak of doom that had covered the earth for so long. Like twilight, the peace had brought about the promise of a bright new day, and overnight life had changed from something merely survived to*

*something coveted, its wondrous gifts too bound-
less to not be shared with others.*

*And just like that, the world exploded, growing
as never before.*

*A renaissance, and yes, a time of promise, indeed.
But to me, also one of grave concern. I had but a
single workshop on a frozen island, a thousand
miles from civilization, and a hundred years
behind it. The future was clear: man would soon
outgrow our way of doing things.*

*Never before had I even considered shutting
things down, but our creed was that if we
couldn't reach every child, then we shan't reach
any.*

So it was into this abyss that I stared.'"

At this, the winged girl looked up and locked eyes with
Santa for the first time. She sensed a tiny sliver of vulnerability
way down deep, which soothed her ever so slightly.

Santa continued:

*"'One morning, I went out to feed the reindeer.
It was usually quite the chore for me, moving
from feed stock to feed stock and then from pen
to pen, making sure that each got their fill. But
this particular morning, my bones were aching.
So I sat on a stool instead, placing their bowls
at my feet, giving each a nice filling of feed. And*

sure enough, the boys hurried over and pushed their way in, just as happy with this morning's feast as with any other.

Then it hit me like a hoof to the head: the children didn't care where their toys were built, or who built them, or what blasted steps we took to get them under their tree. The insatiable little bundles of joy only cared that they got them!

And thus, the plan was born.

Mini workshops would be sprinkled throughout the entire world, so I could simply go about my route, scooping up toys from each and dropping them right back down to local children, before they even settled in my sack.

Speed would rule the day, and no matter how fast the world grew, I could keep pace.

To get it done, I first chopped the world into bite-sized chunks called Territories. Then I set about to cut a devilish deal with a group called the Polies, egotistical little toy-making machines who would serve as my supply line.

Now, of course, Polies being Polies, I knew they'd want a dollar for nine dimes. So I made them an irresistible offer. They would be given total autonomy to create the finest toy production network the world has ever known. And in return for their toil, they'd live like princes and

*grow old like kings, set up for life in a castle to
call their own, filled with anything their hearts
could conjure up!'"*

Santa closed the book and took a good, hard look at the girl.
She seemed a bit anxious but also determined, and a certain
glow radiated off of her, emanating a warm calm. Her presence
touched Santa's heart, melting his voice into a softer tone.

"Please, remind me of your name again," he said.

The winged girl cleared her throat. "Um, it's Flats, sir," she
replied.

"Very good. So, Flats, for thirty-two years, my plan has
worked to flawless perfection. Until this moment. A matter
has surfaced, one most grave, that standeth to take down the
entire operation. A Polie, one of the originals, has deserted
his post, leaving the entire Territory in the hands of what is
considered by many to be a most heinous creature: *a frogman.*"

"A frogman?" Flats asked, willing her voice steady. "Is that
something you find heinous as well?"

Santa realized that he had been misunderstood. "Goodness,
pardon me. Absolutely not! All of the earth's creatures are
treasures to me, even frogmen. But most other humans have
an entirely different perspective on those they see as *unique*,
and the phrase 'leaving well enough alone' just doesn't apply to
them. So go forth and bring this matter under control, doing
whatever you must, and when you return, the key to our world
shall become yours. But I shall also caution you. Should you
fail, there is no sense in returning."

Flats swallowed hard, having no idea what she was getting
into, but also knowing she had no say in the matter. "This
place, sir, where is it?"

Santa leaned in closely, his voice hushed. "It's called *Loveland*. And here, let me introduce you to the purported menace you shall be bringing under rein!"

Santa stood tall and swept his arm out, theatrically gesturing over to a crystal ball. Within it, a boy could be seen lying in a deepened sleep. His face had been badly beaten, and his heavily bandaged hand rested limply at his side.

"But sir, why does he look the way he does?" Flats asked.

Santa studied the boy, grasping for an answer. "I can only surmise that the trauma of his injuries must have been so severe as to have rendered him green in tone," he said as he lowered his towering frame back down into his chair.

Finding this reasoning curious, to say the least, Flats nonetheless nodded. She rose from the ground and curtsied, then quickly ran toward the door.

Just about to the exit, she saw Spiro, a sixteen-year-old elf with whom she shared a foul bit of history, brazenly barging into Santa's office. Flats realized he had been listening outside the door the entire time, and even this briefest of encounters made her stomach turn, making her dash all that much more desperate.

As Spiro stormed up to Santa, the bearded man let him have it.

"Have you taken leave of your senses, boy? You should know better! No Polies, not even the Elder, are to set foot in my chambers without a formal, embossed invitation. Ever!"

But the words didn't seem to register with Spiro one bit. "Sir, the winged girl, she needn't go anywhere! I shall go in her place, as I would be most honored to slay the gruesome monster!"

Santa eyed the elf closely, sensing the violent storm brewing within him. "Son, this is not a matter of slaying. It is a matter of a whole other sort, one foreign to both you and your people. *A matter guided by love…*" he said, his voice wistfully trailing off to a near whisper.

He placed his hand firmly upon Spiro's shoulder. "You see, this sacred order was formed by the original Saint Nicholas seventeen hundred years ago as a way of spreading joy, love, and goodwill, principles that continue to serve as our guiding light, shining upon all that we do. And I sense Flats has the purity of heart to resolve this matter in a way that honors those principles. Now, I have no doubt you Polies could resolve it as well, but I'm equally certain that your resolution would come through the barrel of a gun. So, my good man, you shall maintain a goodly distance from it and all those involved."

"Oh, yes, sir, most certainly," Spiro replied, oozing sincerity.

He turned away from Santa and headed for the exit, a slippery smirk snaking out across his face.

Meanwhile, Flats made her painful way across the frozen Arctic tundra, the jagged ice cutting into her spiny feet with every step she took. The icy pain, along with her unnerving encounter with Spiro, suddenly lit a flame. She took off running, faster than ever before, leaving every hint of pain and despair, isolation, and Polie disdain behind in her wake. Then, leaping crazily into the air and flapping her wings wildly, she became airborne.

Though low at first, she quickly ascended, rising up and soon soaring high into the sky. Exhilarated, she let out a wild call, a cry of freedom from the harshness of the earth below, emboldened by the possibilities of a new life in the great big world now unfolding beneath her.

Against all reason and logic, Flats was certain she heard a response. She imagined it came from the boy in the crystal ball, beautiful but different, like her, his eyes pleading up to the heavens for help and his palms stretching upward, with his entire world hinging solely upon catching her fall.

And everything was different now.

CHAPTER TWO
The Beast You've Feared

A few days earlier - Loveland, Ohio, U.S.A.

One hot Indian summer day, Frenchy the frog, aged to the equivalent of fifteen human years, stood stone-still on the front porch of the Loveland Amphibian Orphanage. He was desperately trying to make his four-inch body appear even smaller than it already was. Frenchy listened silently as Tante Frog, the house mom, was tearing through another of her infamous drunken rants, spewing hurtful invectives, laying into anyone unlucky enough to get in her way.

"You lazy little good-for-nothing toads! I have half a mind to swing open these doors and let the river hawks have at every last one of you! Believe you me, I'd do it if it weren't for the fifty bucks a month the state pays me to house your sorry asses. Now get a gosh-darned move on and go fetch your dinners!"

Closing his eyes, a familiar movie began to play in Frenchy's head. He watched himself gliding over the hillside as effort-lessly as a butterfly, hand in hand with a beautiful, angelic creature, her clutch emitting an otherworldly warmth.

The screen door slammed angrily against the wall, bringing the daydream to an abrupt halt. Frenchy opened his eyes to find Tante, a bullfrog twice his size, towering over him.

"And you, out here sulking about like a salamander! Time to face the music, boy, and get over it. It was nobody's fault but your parents'. Too dull to keep their distance from that menace Johnny Deere!"

Tante knew how to cut deeply, but the comment was brutal, even for her.

"God, how can you be so cold?" Frenchy asked, stunned.

"Because the world is cold, boy. Sear that into your head now, and you won't be let down later. Life sucks, then you die."

Frenchy swallowed hard. He knew any additional commentary would be met with violence of some sort, but he also knew he had to say *something*. Letting such vile, mean-spirited comments go unchallenged always seemed to Frenchy to give them life, like she actually had something to say. She didn't.

"Just because you gave up doesn't mean that everyone else has to. You can bet your ass I won't."

"You foulmouthed little snot!" Tante Frog raged.

With that, she picked up her broom and smashed Frenchy over the head with it, hard. She then reared back and swung it like a hockey stick, sending Frenchy flying off the porch and tumbling head over heels onto the hillside.

He picked himself up and walked off, not giving the old woman the pleasure of knowing how badly she had hurt his head. Nor would he ever show the internal pain inflicted.

"Washed-up old croaker," he muttered. "She's wrong. Wrong about everything. Life doesn't suck. Not even a bit. You just gotta find the right person to share it with."

Hopping off along the hillside, Frenchy's thoughts drifted

from Tante's bitter words to his empty stomach, which he realized hadn't been fed for a good twenty-four hours. And, feeling a little rebellious, he had an idea about where he'd like to fill it: a place he'd often heard about, but one that he had never actually visited. Until today, he hadn't dared.

Of course, the rational voice in his head was screaming that he shouldn't set foot anywhere near the ammunition factory. Everybody knew it was a dangerous place, where machines and men cranked out the instruments of war with neither time nor tolerance for anything that got in their way.

It was a positively absurd notion, going hunting there.

However, the dark-hearted fortress was also rumored to host the biggest insects in Loveland. So he paused still to mull it over.

After a few moments, Frenchy sprang up excitedly, then issued his fateful decision. "If I'm going to become a legend, I gotta start doing legendary stuff," he said to himself.

So, having arrived at the Little Miami River, he jumped in, the factory's tall smokestack and clocktower rising up ahead, serving as clear navigational beacons.

Reaching the opposite riverbank, Frenchy spotted an acquaintance from the orphanage, a dry, dour lizard named Izzy. Both avid bug hunters, they occasionally kept each other company during their daily outings for food.

"What's up, Izzy?" Frenchy called out, spicing his greeting with a little extra enthusiasm, hoping to get the conversation off to a cheery start with a guy who was usually anything but.

"Same shit, different day," replied Izzy, perfectly in tune with his personality.

"Goodness, Sunshine!" Frenchy said, laughing. "Come on,

let's go find some food. And how about you try not to be such a wet sandwich, if just for today? Life's too short to go through it with a sour puss all the time!"

"Whatever," Izzy said, without any more inflection than his previous offering.

So off they went, hopping and slithering along the riverbank toward the factory.

After a few minutes of silence, Izzy spoke up. "You know what's annoying about you, frog?" he asked, apparently still agitated about the wet sandwich crack.

Frenchy had never really given thought to what, if anything, was annoying about himself. "Um, no, I sure don't," he said.

"You're too goddamn chipper!" Izzy replied, his words finally finding some life. "I mean, hell, we're all stuck in that shithole orphanage, under the boot of that bitch, so what's there to be chipper about ever, let alone all the time?"

Frenchy considered the inquiry, looking to provide a thoughtful answer to what Izzy clearly meant as a rhetorical question. "You know, Izzy, the future's unwritten, so I'm determined to write my own. The way I look at it, if I don't, it will be left to write itself, and I might not like the way that story turns out," Frenchy said, pleased with the way the words sounded when hearing them aloud.

But those same words didn't sit well with Izzy. "Uh, yeah. Sounds like some kinda new age hippie bullshit to me. I mean, we're in a totally hopeless situation. Dead broke, without a soul in the world that gives a rat's ass about us. So what could you possibly want to find in this wonderful future of yours?"

Frenchy stopped dead in his tracks and looked squarely into Izzy's bulging eyes. "What do I want? To be lifted up by the most powerful force in the world: *love*. I know that it's out there, and I'm certain it will find me."

Izzy laughed derisively. "Love? Life's great fugazi, a binky for those unable to survive this world on their own! But suit yourself. I just hope your little frog heart doesn't break too badly when the story doesn't have a happy ending."

Izzy's negativity only strengthened Frenchy's resolve. "Well, Sunshine, I look at it this way. I'll take the risk of my heart getting shattered to pieces, just so long as something wonderful fills it, even if but for a moment beforehand!"

With Frenchy's words hanging in the air, they arrived at the factory door, finding it cracked open just enough to ease through. They pushed inside and were immediately knocked back by the roar of guitars and drums blaring through large speakers, the sound so loud as to have taken on physical force. An eerie smoke hung in the air, covering the walls with a thick black tar, as surly human men busily packed boxes marked "DANGER" with menacing-looking cargo.

Suddenly, one of the humans spewed a missile from his mouth, drilling Izzy dead-on, drenching him with the sticky brown goo of chewing tobacco.

"Aghhh! You see?!" cried Izzy in a hushed tone that was, luckily, undetectable by the humans. "Seriously, you see?! Surely a wonderful goddamn future lies right around the corner!"

Shocked by how huge the humans looked up close, and thoroughly disgusted by the gooey brown mess, Frenchy headed back toward the door, motioning Izzy to join him.

Hopping a few feet outside, Frenchy noticed an old barrel rusting beside the river, its guts oozing out the bottom and forming into a bright green pond underneath. Bugs of all types blissfully hovered about, fully unaware that they would soon be at the bottom of both boys' bellies. And what easy hunting it would be, for not only were the bugs fat and slow, but also glowing green, fully void of stealth.

"Well, this should make up for it!" Frenchy called out excitedly.

So Frenchy and Izzy went to work, their long, elastic tongues making quick work of the bugs, so many quickly turning into too many.

Trouble set in as soon as the first bugs started reaching Frenchy's belly. A fire sparked to life inside him, its flames spreading as though the bugs fluttering within his stomach all had little gas cans, and they were purposely rendering as much destruction as possible.

Frenchy's eyes shot over to the barrel. He could make out the human word NAPALM, but what really caught his attention was the photograph, showing a huge plot of farmland engulfed entirely in flames. "Christ!" he gasped.

He tried to burp, thinking it might relieve some of the pressure, but instead a little burst of flame shot out, rendering him the world's first fire-breathing frog.

Panicked, Frenchy looked over to Izzy. His already bulging eyes were getting larger and larger, looking like they were ready to pop. And then they did. Well, actually all of Izzy popped, exploding him into vapor. He was simply *gone*.

"Bloody hell!" Frenchy shouted. Knowing that he somehow had to douse his internal flame, fast, he took off toward the river, hopping like mad.

With the heat inside him growing more intense with each

hop, he could see the water up ahead, quickly nearing. Finally, three feet away, he made a crazy last leap, emitting a trail of smoke out of his butt as he blasted through the air.

To an observer on the riverbank, Frenchy would've appeared a sure goner.

Then, with one sharp splash, everything changed. At once there was the darkness of the river bottom, and Frenchy's mind filled with a restful peace, a warmth washing over him as though he'd been wrapped in a big, cozy blanket.

Moments later, a white light burst to life around him, snatching Frenchy out of his restful state. The light then dimmed, revealing in its place his grandfather, Pappy, walking toward him with a warm look on his face, kindly shaking his head. Pappy had raised Frenchy, and they had been close right up until Pappy's passing about two years prior.

"Good to see you, Pipsqueak," said Pappy. "But they sent me out to tell you that it ain't your time yet."

Before Frenchy could say a word, Pappy was gone along with the light.

The next thing Frenchy knew, he was sprawled out on the riverbank as though he had been brought there by a force other than himself. He started to rise up, looking on in astonishment as he did so, his eyes rising up and up past their usual place, two inches above the ground, to now over five feet in the air.

Terrified, Frenchy turned to the water. But he was too afraid to face his reflection, instead clamping his eyes shut tight.

Digging into his reservoir of courage, he recited the words Pappy had told him to say whenever he was afraid: "The beast you face is never as bad as the beast you've feared."

When Frenchy forced his eyelids open, his gaze locked onto

a reflection of himself in the water, that of a singularly unique creature, a crossing of a human boy and a frog.

He found himself by no means unpleasant looking; in fact, he thought his new features were quite attractive. But with slightly green-tinted skin and fully webbed hands and feet, there was no denying the fact that he was now quite *different*.

He had become the Frogman of Loveland.

CHAPTER THREE
Salvation

Still gazing into the river's surface, Frenchy gave himself a good slap across his face.

"It's just a dream," he said aloud, on the brink of slipping into shock. "I'll wake up, and I'll be normal again."

A brutally cold wind blew across his wet, naked body, snapping his mind back clear. Frenchy noticed his little red beret floating atop the river's surface, so he scooped it up and placed it on his head. It was now ridiculously small, not even covering one-tenth of his head's surface.

The sky had turned a dull gray, ushering in nightfall. Odd, since it had been midday only moments ago, hadn't it? Regardless, it was very much time to get moving.

Clutching his little beret, Frenchy started walking along the riverbank, wide-eyed at how the world moved beneath him, his perspective so much higher than what it used to be. Rocks and tree roots, once mighty obstacles, were now just little bumps along the way, suggesting that the human way of walking might not be such a bad way to go.

But Frenchy's new view of things had also created a serious problem: He was too high up to see the markers that had always guided him around the hillside. His tried and true directional signs—the shiny black rock, the slimy patch of moss, the line of spore-filled mushrooms—were all gone, concealed and distorted by the colossal shift in vantage point.

In fact, he couldn't find a single thing that looked even remotely familiar, feeling as much a stranger in this place as he'd have felt on a distant planet.

Making matters even more unsettling, Frenchy sensed that he was being watched. Wherever his eyes darted across the river valley, he saw a set of eyes peeping right back. But when he'd try to lock in on them, they'd slip behind a tree, seemingly wishing to remain undetected.

Distracted by the ominous peek-a-boo, Frenchy hadn't been paying attention to where he was going, and he now found himself just a stone's throw from a group of human boys. Clad in blue uniforms and little yellow scarf-ties, they looked harmless, just kids being kids, poking their long sticks with puffy marshmallows on the ends into a smoldering campfire.

Frenchy noticed a backpack stuffed with clothing, which would come in quite handy considering his current state of nakedness. He snuck up and snatched it, then took off running.

Catching sight of the naked, green creature streaking away, three of the boys froze in fear. But the fourth boy wasn't fazed at all. Instead, he calmly sized up the situation, taking inventory of his men and their weaponry.

He began pointing to the other boys one at a time, assigning them their weapons of war. "Thompson, slingshot! Robby, axe! Slim, knife! Now let's let that slimy creature know he stole from the wrong Scouts!"

The little warriors grabbed up their weapons and took off after Frenchy, whooping and howling as they ran.

Terrified, Frenchy ran as fast as he could. Seeing the underpass of a bridge ahead, he thought he could momentarily escape their view, then lose them for good by scurrying up the embankment on the other side.

Seconds later he had made it to the darkness of the underpass, and his plan appeared to be working. Two of the boys had fallen back, and the other two had disappeared altogether. Taking a quick breath, Frenchy eyed his path to freedom.

But as soon as he started up the embankment, his plan unraveled. Two of the boys dropped from the bridge, landing right in front of him and blocking his exit. Then the other two closed in from behind, having sprung a perfectly executed trap.

Cornered by the crazed little soldiers, Frenchy trembled with fear. He searched his mind for the right human words, picked up by listening in on the campers hanging out in the river valley over the years. "Here's your stuff back. I'm sorry," he muttered softly, laying the backpack down on the ground. "Please, just don't hurt me."

Just then, an inexpressible low murmur sprang to life in the distance, quickly growing in force and speed, the sound heralding the pending arrival of a rather vast number of some type of creature. In fact, it sounded like an advancing army of them.

"What's that sound?!" the group leader, clearly spooked, shouted into Frenchy's face.

"I don't know!" Frenchy, just as rattled, replied.

"The beast is lying!" the boy declared. "Robby, quick, split its head open!"

Robby raised his axe overhead, readying to slam it right down onto Frenchy's crown.

With no time to spare, a large group of peculiar-looking,

rat-like elves surrounded Frenchy in an instant, buffering him from his would-be assailants. Though they didn't say a word, their large eyes bored into the boys, announcing that neither they nor their adopted charge were going to be messed with. It was quite clear that Frenchy was *their* captive.

The boys, now staring at not one but two very unique types of otherworldly cryptids—including one with his green junk hanging out—took off running without another word.

Alarming as the new creatures were, Frenchy's first order of business was to put some damn clothes on. Dumping the contents of the backpack on the ground, he snagged a tee shirt and shorts and pulled them on. While they didn't fit very well, they were quite better than the alternative.

"Um, thanks. Thanks a lot, guys," Frenchy then offered to the elves.

He took a moment to study his saviors. There were too many of them to count, and each practically identical. They were around two feet tall, with little potbellies and vaguely human forms, insomuch as they stood upon two legs. They had distinctly rodential facial features and long, pointy ears, rendering them rather jarring on the eyes.

The creatures didn't respond with words. Rather, they formed a circle around Frenchy, locked hands, and proceeded to walk along the riverbank with him as their captive, repeatedly chanting what sounded like "speshelwon" as they went. This totally spooked Frenchy, who peppered the creatures with questions about who they were, where they were taking him, and what the hell it was that they were saying. But language was futile. They didn't even acknowledge the words.

After many turns along the riverbank, the oddball ensemble soon stood in the shadows of a building so huge and ornate,

Frenchy at first thought it to be make-believe. But as he examined it closer, he could see that it was in fact a very real medieval castle rising up from the edges of the river, straight from the pages of a fairy tale. And there was a man coming out of its main entrance.

Two of the rat-elves' hands parted and created an opening, enabling the man to enter the circle. For the most part, he looked human, and was close to Frenchy's size, with long, pointy ears, just like the rat-elves. He was shoeless, which, along with his sun-drenched beard and long, tangly hair cascading about in every direction, gave him a rather wild appearance.

The Admiral

Having just fended off a maniacal cast of characters, Frenchy swallowed hard, hoping he'd find better luck with this bunch.

CHAPTER FOUR
The Special One

Thankfully, Frenchy quickly realized that the elf-sized man was different, in every sense of the word.

Smiling warmly, the man pulled a little metal tin from his pocket and opened it, exposing a wonderful assortment of salted dried flies. With his stomach painfully empty, Frenchy tossed the entire tin's contents down in one gulp, comforted by the fact that food still tasted good in his new form.

The man nodded and made a walking motion with his fingers, pointing toward the castle as he did so. Frenchy nodded in return, cheered by the thought of getting out of the elements and their unfriendly winds. The pair walked across a courtyard, almost junkyard-like in its unkempt condition, with dead trees lining the pathway and garbage strewn about. They then proceeded up a set of dilapidated stairs and into a circular area, which seemed to be some sort of Control Room.

Through the room's glass walls, Frenchy could look down on a cavernous factory floor, abuzz with a great many more of the rat-elves, each hard at work.

The man walked over and joined him in peering down below. "Woodsman Scandies," he said finally, in the same human language as the campers. "Ugly little Appalachian rat-elves. They're dumber than a box of rocks, but they work hard. And unlike the Polie apprentices they used to send down here, they don't stand around bitching all day," he said with a shrug of his shoulders, apparently believing he had summed up all that needed to be said about them.

Woodsman Scandie

Frenchy felt entirely unsettled. Trying hard to nudge his brain back toward something that felt the least little bit like normal, he went to lick his forehead, a weird, comforting tic he had turned to since he was a toddler. But this only disoriented him further, since his new tongue couldn't even make it as far up as his nose.

His eyes darted around the room, landing upon two photographs. One showed the man in his younger days, working on the same floor as below. He wore a green shirt, a fresh version of the one he had on now, and a dour expression, as though the weight of the world rested upon his shoulders.

Frenchy went over and picked up the other photo. It showed the man freed of his shirt, standing at the helm of a speedboat. He appeared to be dancing across the water, his long yellow hair flowing in the wind, his eyes aglow. The same person in both, but somehow very different.

Suddenly, the man was right beside him, studying the photo intently. "Christ, I'd do *anything* to feel like that again," he blurted out, his words cracking with emotion.

Embarrassed, the man turned and paced about, composing himself. "My goodness, I'm sorry. Nothing hits a duller note than an old sailor's tale of regret, so let me instead introduce myself. I am Admiral Ulf Saueskinn, Special Administrator for the Territory of Ohio, which used to actually mean something thirty-two years ago, back when that fat bastard charlatan started up this whole racket. Now we're all just slaves to the North Pole, me and all the other Polies, running to stand still."

The man waved his hand dismissively. He seemed distant, *off*. "'Tis all just a fairy tale now," he continued. "But be that as it may, my friend, you can simply refer to me as the Admiral. I got the name since I command an army of pirates, a good fifty of them. They're stationed down on the riverbank, anxiously awaiting my next command!"

Frenchy thought that commanding an army of pirates sounded kinda cool, and he figured he must have somehow missed the armada on his approach to the castle. After all, he had been rather preoccupied.

The Admiral extended his hand, which Frenchy reached out and shook.

PAUL EDWARD MORRIS

"Nice to meet you, Admiral. I am Frenchy," he replied.

"I am well aware," the Admiral said, without further explanation.

Frenchy was puzzled. "But how could you know?"

At the same time, a big yawn snuck up on Frenchy, bringing a smile to the Admiral, and allowing him to dismiss the question as if it had never been asked.

"Goodness, it looks like someone needs to put his day behind him. Please, my friend, won't you stay as my guest?"

Frenchy, freaked out and discombobulated, but also afraid to be out roaming the hillside amongst the humans, had no better option. He nodded appreciatively.

The Admiral started down a hallway, summoning for his guest to follow. "Excellent. Your quarters are this way," he said. "I think you shall find them quite fitting."

They proceeded down a hallway, its walls a marshy shade of green, its ceiling twinkling with little lighted stars. A warm breeze began to blow, bringing with it the familiar fragrances of summer. The breeze picked up as they made their way, and by the time they reached the guest room, it felt as though they'd stepped full-on into a midsummer's evening down on the bog.

The Admiral snapped on the light, revealing a sweet suite for one of amphibious leanings. Lily-pad-shaped rugs floated atop a soft blue carpet, while firefly lights hung from the ceiling, the low murmur of crickets humming in the distance.

A red beret with an *F* on the front sat propped up on the bed, along with a fresh shirt, vest, and pair of pants, just like Frenchy had always worn, but fitted perfectly for his new size. Puzzled, he looked over to the Admiral. "Okay. Come on. This is totally creepy. Please, tell me, how could you possibly have known to arrange this stuff ahead of time?"

The Admiral smiled. "Tis known as the Scandie Prophecy. I hear those little critters reciting it every Sunday at their Gatherings. A brief passage in the early pages of the enormous tome goes like this:

'Into the murk He fell for one day, then two.
On day three He arose, fully born anew.
He is the Special One, once low, into great He grew.
And if you believe in Him, you will be special, too!'

"Take it for what you will. Lord knows those Scandies sure believe it!" the Admiral concluded.

The odd riddle was more than Frenchy could even begin to wrap his brain around. In fact, this entire bizarre day had been so otherworldly that he was now certain it was just an elaborate dream. Surely, when he awoke, he would be back at Tante Frog's, and things would all make sense again. So he laid his head upon his pillow and quickly surrendered to his fate-twisting day.

Turning out the light, the Admiral whispered softly, "Welcome home, Special One."

CHAPTER FIVE
Someone Take the Wheel

Frenchy awoke the next morning feeling totally confused by the previous day's events, and hiding his head beneath his covers was only making matters worse, filling it with puzzling questions that found no answers. It was now clear that none of this was a dream. But nor was it necessarily a nightmare, for he still essentially felt like himself, and his new physical form was starting to grow on him. Plus, the roof currently over his head was a significant upgrade from the orphanage's.

But still, it was all just so flippin' *weird*.

With Frenchy not being big on introspection, he opted for motion instead. Popping out of bed, he hurriedly put on his snappy new clothes and took a quick peek in the mirror. Liking what he saw, he bolted from his room, retracing his steps from the previous night and quickly arriving back in the circular observation area. The Admiral was already there, pacing excitedly. Newly clad in a red shirt, the elfin-man was quite twitchy, and his eyes were wide with frantic anticipation.

"Good morning, my friend. It's about time you're up. Quickly now, there are a few things I must tell you, and then I need to be on my way."

Frenchy looked at him inquisitively. "On your way?"

"That's right. My destination"—the Admiral handed Frenchy a snow globe with a miniature castle inside, on its bottom a little bronze plate with "HAMMERFEST" etched upon it—"the single most difficult place on earth to reach."

He handed Frenchy an airhorn, along with a book titled *Bavarian Phrases*. The Admiral then reached into his pocket and pulled out a piece of paper, slowly unfolding it and holding it out for Frenchy to see. It depicted a crudely drawn picture of a very large human, with a face like that of a bull.

"The Wursties," the Admiral continued. "Descendants of Bavarian lumberjacks, their headquarters are in a wretched place called the Festhaus, over in the Black Forest section of the compound. They're said to love three things: ale, sausage, and, ehem, the local area's livestock. Kind of adds up, since I've never actually seen a female Wurstie, and they do have a slightly bovine quality about their features."

Frenchy squished up his face, bewildered.

The Admiral chuckled, finding something amusing in his own curious tale, then proceeded with his ramblings. "Communicate with the Bavarian beasts only if you must. To roust their leader, sound the horn four times, and be sure to learn some of their nasty guttural phrases. Most importantly, never show them any weakness. If they even sniff it upon you, they'll tear you to pieces!"

Frenchy eyed the book for a moment, utterly confused. With so much bizarre information being hurled his way, he was having difficulty taking any of it in. Attempting to draw a distinction between the beasts and the little guys in the giant room below, he pointed toward the factory.

"So these beasts, they're totally different from those guys?" Frenchy asked.

"Bloody hell, boy!" the Admiral shouted, quite angrily. "Stop being so obtuse! And enough with the ridiculous questions! Wursties! Giant cow-screwing ale guzzlers! Scandies! Two-foot-tall rat-elves, screwing not much beyond themselves! Now, does that sound different to you?!"

Without another word, the Admiral abruptly turned and ran out the door, setting off at a dead sprint.

Caught off guard, Frenchy ran out after him, but he couldn't keep up, falling a good distance behind as they raced through the castle and then out the back entrance. In fact, by the time Frenchy reached the riverbank, the Admiral had already scaled the ladder to his sailboat, and he was now sitting in the captain's chair, furiously scribbling something on a piece of paper.

The boat was docked all alone on the Little Miami. It kept company with no armada, and no pirates. In fact, the little boat didn't really even appear to be seaworthy, with its shoddily painted name, *Freedom*, having just about totally faded away.

After a few moments the Admiral turned back to face Frenchy, holding out the note.

Frenchy walked up to the boat, his eyebrows arched in the hopeful anticipation that whatever was on the piece of paper would help make some sense out of this most bewildering of situations.

He studied the paper. It read:

"I, Admiral Ulf Saueskinn, Special Administrator for the Territory of Ohio, do hereby bequeath and bestow onto Frenchy, the Honorable Frogman of Loveland, the Loveland Castle and the Territory of Ohio over which it presides. And for a certain red-suited, fat-bottomed one of you sitting in your velvety, pillowed chair at the North Pole, squinching up your nose and wondering how one could do such a thing, ask yourself this: Is it more ignoble to give over that which was rightfully promised, or to dim lifeless the soul of the one to whom you had entrusted it all, without so much as a tinge of remorse? Regardless, what's done is done, and it shan't be revoked. Up Yours Truly, The Admiral."

The Admiral then put an exclamation point on whatever point he was making. "That jolly fat bastard snatched thirty-two goddamn years away from me! For what? To carry on some silly Sacred Order of Saint Nicholas? Goodness, he stepped on so many of us on his path to worldwide fame and adulation. So, while I hope you fare well with this place, I shan't be giving it so much as another thought. And as for Santa and his magical ho-ho-ho line of bullshit, well, let's just say he can stick it all right up his big fat sack!"

Frenchy shook his head. "I don't understand," he said softly. "What am I supposed to do with this place?"

"Holy Toledo! Kinda late in the shipwreck to be worrying about the deckchairs, now ain't it, laddie? But just to shut ya up, here's a quick, three-part crash course into your mystical new world. One, don't trust the mysterious winged girl. She's a puppet, her strings tethered directly to the North Pole. So when she tries to cast a spell on you with her charm and beauty, it must be met solely with your total and absolute silence. Remember, the darkest of demons sometimes come shrouded as angels."

A gust of wind blew in and billowed out *Freedom*'s sails, pushing it out into the Little Miami. The Admiral quickly checked her course before turning back to Frenchy.

"Two. Those Scandies, they worship the ground that you walk on, so don't hesitate to turn to them for help. You're sure as shit going to need it."

Seeing that his time with the Admiral was quickly nearing its end, Frenchy blurted out the one question he simply had to have answered. "Please, you have to tell me. What's the deal with those guys! Why do they have such reverence for me?!"

"Christ, you and your endless bloody questions!" the Admiral snapped back.

He turned on a dime and grabbed a hockey stick, a rather curious accoutrement to have on a boat. Holding the end of the stick's shaft, he pointed its blade up to the heavens, at the same time thrusting his other arm wide out to the side. Balancing on the little boat's bow, he looked full-on like he was attempting to part the Little Miami River.

But nothing happened.

The Admiral turned back to face the shore. His eyes wide and wild hair blowing in the breeze, he looked every bit the madman. "Don't you see? *They were there!* Just as it's written in Chapter One of the Prophecy! They watched as you entered the water as one form and stayed down for three days. And they watched as the light brought you back up, fully anew, and watched still as you walked across the water's surface as casually as one strolls down the street. They believe that you were brought back here to perform three miracles, and your little walk on the water was number one. So they await to see what numbers two and three bring."

The Admiral paused, as if experiencing a moment of clarity. "I've never bothered to read it all the way through, but supposedly the last chapter is already written. I hope it goes well for you, laddie!"

Frenchy again shook his head, trying to straighten his thoughts. "Everyone around here is off their freakin' rockers," he whispered to himself. Then he continued, loudly enough for the Admiral to hear. "Um, that's not really what happened, I don't think."

The Admiral shrugged. "They had many eyes upon it, and you apparently had none. So who are you to say?"

The Admiral then fixed his gaze forward, with *Freedom* fully pulling away from the shore and becoming one with the current.

Drifting far downriver, the Admiral abruptly turned back toward the shore, realizing he had forgotten to offer the third lesson. "Oh, and number three, stay totally invisible to the humans," he shouted. "You'll never be anything but a monster to them, and trust me, you're gonna rue the day if those maniacs ever catch wind of you!"

The Admiral spun back to face forward, and he wasn't to look back again.

As the boat disappeared into the horizon, Frenchy took in the vastness spreading out in every direction, from the river ripples to the hilltops, from where the sun awoke to where it went to sleep. He felt a lonely chill, realizing that the humans, or really anything roaming this hillside, for that matter, could freely walk in and confront their town's very own monster, at any time of their choosing.

Frenchy

CHAPTER SIX
A Really Rough Joint

The following morning, Frenchy had a scheme running around in his head. It involved heading back into human territory, which was quite the daunting thought for him, since his previous encounter with the humans had gone so incredibly wrong. But he needed allies, and scoring some human bounty might help him to get on the good sides of those Bavarian beasts, the Wursties.

His first order of business was to come up with a disguise that enabled him to move freely amongst the humans, undetected. So he raided the Admiral's freshly vacated quarters, finding them perfectly intact. A lucky break for Frenchy, indeed, as the full closets and dresser drawers provided him with a wealth of cool fashion options.

Rifling through various items on hangers, he settled on a pair of pants, oddly tight around his nether regions yet flaring quite widely at his ankles, and a brightly checkered shirt, which he buttoned midway up his chest. Checking his reflection, he sensed there was a little too much green showing, so he added three thick gold necklaces and a pair of mirrored sunglasses, topping off a rather head-turning look.

Thinking he now stood a solid chance of blending in while out amongst the humans, he headed out the back of the castle, just your average, everyday green-tinted dude sporting some seriously pimped-out duds.

Strolling across the courtyard, he saw a Scandie off in the distance. Wanting to give his disguise a test run, he snuck up on the little guy and tapped him on the shoulder.

Turning and taking a look at Frenchy, the Scandie at once froze in place. Then, overwhelmed to see Him so up close, his eyes rolled back in his head and he passed clean out, falling to the ground like a plank of wood.

Frenchy drew a quick conclusion. "Ha!" he said. "I look so groovy, the little fella must have confused me for a human. Just about scared the pants right off of him!"

Now fully confident he'd remain undercover, he set out through the woods, soon approaching a big steel bridge that spanned the river. Resting at its base was a windowless brick building, with a flapping flag overtop identifying the confines as The Monkey Bar. Having never before conducted trade with the humans, this seemed as good a place as any to start.

Frenchy made his way up the embankment and into the area where the humans parked their transportation machines. He watched as a tall, long-haired human unloaded boxes from his machine onto a metal pushcart, which he would then roll over to the back of the building. Then he'd disappear through the rear door, come back out after a moment, and do it all over again.

Frenchy tracked him going through the process three times, each time counting off the seconds he spent inside. He sprang into action as soon as the man went inside for run number

THE FROGMAN OF LOVELAND

four, knowing that he had about thirty seconds to do what he needed to do.

Frenchy jumped up into the open back of the transportation machine and grabbed two boxes marked "RHINELAND DARK ALE" lowering them down to the pavement below. He then snatched two packs of Bavarian bratwurst and shoved them into his pockets. Removing one of the gold chains from around his neck, he left it where the ale had sat, figuring it was a fair exchange for his haul.

As he jumped back out of the machine, his eyes darted over to the building entrance, and that's when he first saw it: an actual live monkey in an elaborately decorated cage, smoking a cigarette and drinking a bottle of beer.

Locking eyes with Frenchy, the monkey blew a big puff of smoke, then began shrieking in the loudest, most grating tones imaginable.

"Shit!" Frenchy exclaimed.

Hoisting the heavy suitcases of brew, he went to take off running, but all the weight made moving with any speed impossible. Even more concerning, a new kind of transportation machine was now speeding across the parking lot, this one with red lights flashing atop. Its wailing siren, combined with the cries of the crazed monkey, created an unholy racket that rattled Frenchy's thoughts and rendered him unable to think clearly.

The machine came to a screeching stop, and an agitated human jumped out, aggressively waving what looked like a curved metal tube in Frenchy's direction.

"Officer Shockey! Loveland Police Department!" the human shouted. "Hands up!"

His mind snapping back clear, Frenchy remembered what

the Admiral had said about the humans, and he knew better than to be captured. So, terrified, he decided to make a run for it.

In one quick motion, he tucked a box of ale under each arm and launched himself backward toward a line of trees at the top of a steep hill. Two quick blasts rang out as he did, crisp explosions louder than anything he'd ever heard. Adrenaline pulsating, his desperate dive's momentum propelled him down the hillside, rolling both him and his ale down to the bottom of the river valley, right up to the border of some type of farm.

Though now out of view of the shooting human, a new problem arose: He couldn't go back to the castle via the route he originally took. Instead, he'd be forced to take an unfamiliar shortcut.

Little did Frenchy know, but he had stumbled upon a huge weed-growing operation in full bloom, its property borders lined by a fence so badly in need of repair that it had far more gaps than slats. Nor were there any noticeable lights or sensors, or really anything to keep out visitors—well, except for the sign warning any trespassers that they would be cut to pieces, which, unfortunately for Frenchy, had long ago fallen face down to the ground.

And there was something else ominously notable about the property, or, more precisely, four things: the flags flying above the property's corners, each showing a ghoulish figure atop a motorcycle, captioned with the words "SATAN'S FURY."

Frenchy eyed the three very large, very hairy humans working up near the top of the hillside. They were clad in blue jeans and black leather, with lots of flashy silver chains hanging about, and they were busily cutting down trees near the top of the hillside.

From the looks of these guys, their chainsaws, and those damn flags, he started to have serious doubts about passing through. But as he edged all the closer to the property's boundary, he could see that their backs were to him. Further, with the tremendous noises blasting out of the saws, he knew they couldn't hear him either. This had to be a safer bet than going back to where a crazed shooter lurked.

"Screw it," he said to himself. "I'm faster than those fat bastards!"

He took off, his very first step tripping a wire sensor on the property border, bringing to life an extraordinary array of strobes and sirens that lit up the hillside like the Fourth of July.

"Holy shit!" Frenchy yelled, coaxing his feet to go as fast as they could.

In an instant the three men disappeared over the hillside, and seconds later they reemerged atop incredibly loud transportation machines. And, being that these machines had only two wheels, the men were able to barrel down the hill at breakneck speed, immediately surrounding Frenchy and proceeding to ride a tight circle around him. It was clear that they weren't happy about having had a stranger witness whatever nefarious business they were up to.

Even more frighteningly, they each had one hand on their handlebars and the other on their still-running chainsaws.

Terrified, Frenchy attempted to turn and run, but there was no way to break free, the wall of engines and blades now fully encircling him.

One of the men, the largest and hairiest of the three, leaned into Frenchy's face, spitting his words. "Ya know, ain't no visitors ever lived to tell about this joint, boy. And a slimy green one sure as shit ain't gonna be the first!"

The men roared with laughter, their perimeter getting ever tighter as they rode around Frenchy, so close that he could smell the weedy stench upon them.

The extra hairy man tossed his chainsaw aside, and with his freed up hand he grabbed a billy club out of his motorcycle's saddlebag. When he next zoomed by Frenchy, he reared back and smashed him squarely across the side of his head. Then, seemingly enjoying the first whack, he circled back around and gave him another.

The blow felt like it had caved in the side of Frenchy's face, leaving a deafening high-pitched ringing in his ear. He wanted to hit the ground and cover himself, like he would have in his old form, but he knew if he did, the crazed men might stomp him to death. So he forced himself to stay upright and find something to say, anything, to at least buy him some time.

"Please, just take the beer," he said, his jaw no longer moving properly, causing the words to come out slurred and barely audible. "Trust me, I'll never tell a soul about this place."

The men threw their heads back and laughed like crazed lunatics, evil-sounding and shrill. Two of them then hopped off their bikes and stood on both sides of Frenchy like bookends, and they began to play a terrifying game, alternately taking turns swiping at him with their saws, getting progressively closer to his fingers with each attempt.

"No, please!"

Seconds later, Frenchy heard the quick burst of a bone being severed, followed by a sickeningly demented cheer. And then he watched helplessly as his bloody right pinky fell limply to the river valley ground.

Strangely, he didn't feel any pain, and all hints of fear

vanished as well. Time slowed down and he was now able to think clearly, much more so than the weed-skewed maniacs.

He calmly thrust his mangled, webbed hand out in front of his chest, holding it perfectly steady, giving the saws a clear opportunity to cut it cleanly off. "Are any of you cowards tough enough to try it again?!"

"Holy shit," one of the bookends declared. "Freak boy has messed with the wrong bikers!"

The man let out a rebel yell, quickly lunging at the target with his saw. But just a blink before it connected, Frenchy snatched his bloody hand back, at the same time grabbing the man's wrist with his good hand and yanking him a clumsy step forward. The man's saw was thrust forward as well, sending it cleanly into the other man standing right across from him. The blade entered his stomach just above his belly button and ran all the way up to his throat.

It was a sight Frenchy hoped to never see again, that of a human zippered open. But the grotesque scene also gave him an escape hatch, as each of the men were now quite busy, with one of them having been sawed open and the other two bent over, violently throwing up.

Frenchy grabbed the suitcases of ale, which now didn't seem quite so heavy, and took off in the direction of the castle.

Needing a serious buffer from such a violent species, it was high time to cut a deal with the Wursties.

CHAPTER SEVEN
The Wall

Having struggled his way back to the castle's courtyard, Frenchy paused a moment to catch his breath. His mangled hand tucked inside his vest in an effort to slow the bleeding, he set down the ale and sausages, then blasted the airhorn four times, looking to summon the Wursties. With the Admiral's over-the-top depiction of this supposedly motley crew still fresh in his mind, he was nervous to meet them. But he knew he must.

Off in the distance, the unmistakable clatter of boots snapped to life, quickly growing to a loud click, measured like the cadence of a drumbeat.

In just a blink, an army of hairy, broad-shouldered men had fallen into tight military formation, twenty across, two deep. A single Wurstie stepped forward and held a sharp posture, his arms crisply at his sides. Almost twice Frenchy's size, and resplendent in formal military dress, the leader waited for his visitor to speak.

Frenchy frantically paged through the Bavarian phrase book, first working to locate the proper word for "please." Then, noticing the leader's name emblazoned upon his chest, he winged the rest.

The Commandant

"Sir Commandant, builden me das wall. Uh, bitte!" Frenchy said, reaching his hand up as high as he could.

"You hide from enemies?" the Commandant asked, clearly able to speak at least a bit of English.

"Yes! Yes, sir! I got enemies. Lots of 'em. The freakin' humans. They're all crazy, bloodthirsty maniacs!"

The raw emotions of his encounter with the biker gang suddenly fell upon him. The fear, the anger, and the fact that he'd just had to fight for his life boiled over into a single wicked force that spewed out all at once. He started spinning wildly, gesturing emphatically across the compound's grounds like a madman pointing out ghouls unseen.

"Wall that up! And wall that up over there, too! Wall it all in! I don't care how you freakin' do it! Just make sure it's tall enough to keep out all the hatred in this world!"

The Commandant nodded thoughtfully, weighing Frenchy's emotionally charged request. Then he pointed to his men. "Und fur them?"

Frenchy nodded back, then proudly walked over and handed the ale and wurst to the Commandant.

As the pair approached one another, for the first time the Commandant noticed just how brutally battered Frenchy's face was, as well as the tremendous amount of blood caked all over his clothing. Filling with respect for the tough little soldier standing before him, he snapped off a sharp salute.

Frenchy returned it with his good hand, the other still tucked gingerly into his vest. He didn't know it yet, but it was to become a hiding spot his newly mangled hand would often seek for solace.

The Commandant summed up their bargain in broken Germ-lish. "Yes, mein friend. You bringen das ale und wurst. Und we builden das wall!"

Frenchy smiled. He couldn't help but think that the Commandant seemed like a really solid dude, a sharp contrast to the nut job he'd previously met out on these grounds.

They shook hands, consummating their deal.

The Commandant looked down at Frenchy, an intensity now filling his eyes. "We keep you safe, at any cost!" the Commandant declared, speaking as though someone's world depended upon it.

"Why, um, thank you, sir. Danke. Like, of course I really appreciate it, but why would you do that?" Frenchy asked.

"Das Special One, wir das Wursties, no worse enemy, no better friend! Und wir freundin now, so we keep safe," the Commandant replied.

Frenchy nodded. "Why yes, we certainly are—freundin. And I really look forward to getting to know you guys. But right now, I gotta get inside. It's getting dark out here and this thing is really starting to throb," he said, waggling the elbow of his wounded hand in explanation.

"Ja, the rat-elves, they fix."

They exchanged one last salute, and Frenchy managed a weak smile, then he turned to head back inside the castle.

Just a few steps into his journey, his world went pitch-black, and he fell with a hard thud, face-first to the ground.

• • •

A full twenty-four hours later, Frenchy awoke in his bed, his wounds having been tenderly washed and bandaged. Grateful for the act of kindness, he arose and began to walk through the castle, looking to identify the responsible party and thank them. Yet, eerily, for the first time since he had arrived, he found the enormous building totally empty. With the Admiral long gone, now so too were the Scandies, giving the castle a rather spooky aura, one that grew more so by the second.

Needing a fresh change of scenery, Frenchy jogged out into the courtyard.

Once outside, he paused and looked up, his painful jaw dropping fully open. He was astonished by the structure rising in every direction, an impenetrable wall that now encircled the entire compound. With but a single entry point, already manned by an army of Wursties, there was no way the humans' vile hatred could reach him now.

Taking it in, he reflected on all that had happened over these past three extraordinary days. His life had been turned upside down for reasons he couldn't fully grasp, and he'd inherited a magical place with which he had no earthly idea what to do. At the same time, he seemed to keep stumbling upon groups of humans intent on ending his days.

All the while, all by himself. As he had been seemingly forever.

A couple of tears snuck out, tickling his cheeks as they made their journey down. He thought about the wall and its protective embrace as well as the isolation that was sure to come with it. Realizing now that Cupid would literally have to shoot his arrows down from the heavens in order to find his heart, he hoped with all hope that he had made a wise choice.

"Safe from all the ugliness and hatred this evil world has to offer," he whispered. "But what also of its beauty, and its love?"

Chapter Eight
The Future Is Unwritten

The first night within the walled fortress was a painfully dark one for Frenchy. Being lonely was one thing—hell, he had experienced loneliness in spades back at the orphanage—but being *alone*, entirely walled off from anyone like his kind, that was something altogether different. And what even *was* his kind? What was worse, the thoughts only deepened the more they bounced around in his bruised head, their weight taking on physical form, a toothache of the heart.

The morning's first light brought no relief, as Frenchy's world had become one of solid gray, muted of all color. No birds chirped, and no breezes blew. Lying there, it was as though his entire world had been smothered over by a thick blanket of sadness.

Trapped in the gray dungeon, Frenchy's mind searched for something bright, or perhaps a happy melody, anything that might awaken just a tiny bit of pleasure and get him moving. But nothing came.

Then, as the sun began to rise up further, mysteriously, so too did a cheerful little song from beyond Frenchy's window.

Low at first, it rang out once, and then repeated itself, louder each time, ten, then twenty times.

"*Frenchy is the Special One, ate some bugs and then He grew. Now if you'll be Frenchy's special friend, you will be special, too!*"

Frenchy wasn't sure what to make of it. "Kinda sounds like the nonsense the Admiral was spouting," he said to himself. "But these guys seem to have it basically right. I ate some steroid-laced bugs, and they made me grow. And that's that."

Stretching his neck, he took in a good view of the courtyard below. There was an enormous group of Scandies assembled, at least a thousand of them amassed together and singing with all their heart.

Their song soon built to such a roar that it began to bounce the bed up and down. Being thrust about like a kernel of popcorn, a giggle hopped upon Frenchy, soon giving rise to another, opening the door to laughter and eventually ushering in the gift of song.

He joined the wondrous voices for one final round, singing as loudly as he could. As the words rang out, the birds joined in, the breezes began to blow, and then, like a beautiful magic trick, a switch flipped, turning all the vibrant colors of Frenchy's world right back on.

"If they repeat it enough times, maybe they'll even have me believing it," he said, laughing.

He hopped out of bed and made a beeline out to the courtyard.

Approaching the crowd, Frenchy looked around for whoever might be the leader. He quickly identified a likely candidate, a singular Scandie facing the rest of the crowd, standing behind an elevated podium next to a microphone stand.

Frenchy approached him. "Hey dude," he called out.

The Scandie was rattled at first, seeing Him walking directly toward him in the flesh, and appearing to want to chat! To his credit, the Scandie leader kept his cool. "Hello, sir," he said quietly.

"Hi there. I'm Frenchy. What's your name?"

A perplexed look came over the Scandie's face, and he responded in the only manner he knew. "Well, I'm a Scandie."

"Yeah, I know that," Frenchy replied. "But you have to have a name too, right?"

"Um, no, we don't have names," the leader replied. "That would make each of us unique, which would inevitably lead to some of us being more unique and others being less unique. And that doesn't work, since we strive to all maintain the same level of uniqueness!"

Frenchy pondered this for a moment, then allowed the comment to stand without further discussion. The Scandie seemed quite at peace with his answer, so why challenge it?

"Okay. Whatever you say," Frenchy said. "So, I gotta ask you something that's really been bugging me. I just heard you guys singing about me eating some bugs and then growing all big. Which is exactly what happened. But the crazy Admiral, when he was leaving, said something about you guys also thinking that I'm some kind of deity, and that I was, like, *gone* for three days. And then I came back. Now, y'all don't really believe that too, do you?"

The Scandie moved to within a few inches of Frenchy, gazing deeply into his eyes. "With all our hearts," he replied dreamily.

The Scandie's certainty made the first little dent in Frenchy's ironclad view of the whole bug-eating incident, which he regarded as strange, but not, er, *holy*.

"Well, the Admiral said you guys saw the whole thing," Frenchy continued. "Like, did you personally witness me coming out of the water and then walking on it?"

The Scandie laughed. "The Admiral, he certainly liked to play loose with the truth. No, nobody actually *saw* what happened that magical day. But we all know what happened, as the Prophecy foretold it."

Frenchy was fascinated, but at the same time creeped out, as this was beginning to sound very cult-like. Which would make him what, exactly?

"So," he said. "Is this some type of religious thing you got going on here? And, if I can ask, if nobody saw anything, how the hell can you be so sure it happened?"

The Scandie laughed once again. "Religious?" the Scandie replied. "No. Religion is about rules and regulations. Power and position. That is not what we have here. And how can we be sure? Well, what we *do* possess here is one of the most powerful forces on earth, rivaled only by love: faith. An unwavering belief in the unbelievable."

Frenchy took it all in, impressed by the Scandie's reasoning and earnestness. Thinking about it, he really didn't know what had happened in the river that day. And if they knew, or thought they knew, or damn well just wanted to believe they knew, who was he to tell them they were wrong?

"I gotta tell you, you've sure given me a lot to think about!" Frenchy said, reaching out and shaking the Scandie's hand. "Thanks for trying to clear that up."

"Glad to be of service, Oh Special One," the Scandie replied. "And now, may I ask a question of you?"

"Of course," said Frenchy.

"Do you have the skeleton key?" asked the Scandie.

"The key," replied Frenchy, puzzled. "No, I don't have any keys."

"Uh, drats," muttered the Scandie. "Excuse me." He leaned over and turned on the microphone, then addressed the rest of the group. "Boys, there's no key. Everyone can head back to bed!"

A loud, collective groan rose up from the crowd.

"Now, now," said the leader. "Be not dismayed, and taketh with you our morning's message: 'Whilst none of us arrive in the heavens alive, those with faith will arise anew.' With that in heart and mind, what on earth could there be to be dismayed about? Now go forth and be Scandie-like."

The crowd did as told and began to disperse at once, now with an upbeat bit of a bounce in their step.

Frenchy was intrigued by the message and, frankly, surprised by the initial reaction from the crowd. "Geez, disappointed to be given a little extra time in the sack?" he said with a little laugh. "You'd think they'd be happy to have some time off."

"Oh, goodness, it's just the opposite!" the Scandie leader answered. "The making of toys is our higher calling. Unable to do so, a crucial part of the Prophecy would go unresolved, and we'd have no reason for being. You'll understand someday."

Once again, a seemingly straightforward topic had veered uncomfortably toward the Twilight Zone, so Frenchy bailed, setting his feet in motion. "Well, alrighty then. I gotta hit the road," he said over his shoulder. "I'm sure we'll be seeing each other again soon, but until then, take care!"

"Goodbye, sir," the Scandie leader called out just as Frenchy reached the exit.

Once outside, Frenchy decided to put the Scandies and their robust imaginations on the back burner for another day. For, having been sprung from the clutches of the gray dungeon, he had an important mission in mind. It was time to turn a page.

He grabbed a shovel and headed across the courtyard, down to where the wall neared the riverbank. There he dug a shallow grave, gutting through the pain pulsating within his damaged hand, worsening with each shovelful of dirt. Once satisfied with the grave's depth, he pulled the tiny beret he'd worn as a little frog from his pocket—his last link to anything from his past—and chucked it in.

Pushing the dirt back on top, he made a declaration.

"The past is past. I'm big, I've got a screwed-up hand, and I'm alone. I'm also smart, funny, and pretty damn cool. Time to turn this walled-in place into a world of my own making!"

A peace washed over Frenchy, an internal promise having been made to not waste another moment feeling sorry for himself. His future was unwritten, and it was high time he started writing it.

CHAPTER NINE
She's the One

Newly emboldened by the fresh deal he had made with himself, Frenchy began his trek back toward the castle. But just a few steps in, a strange sensation beset him. He began to be tugged along as though he was a chunk of steel and a giant, invisible magnet was pulling him where it wanted. Having never before felt such a powerful force, he resisted mightily, but it was simply too strong. The force won the tug-of-war, sending him head over heels into a forward summersault across the courtyard lawn.

As he stood up to gather his bearings, a loud, fast flutter burst free from the heavens. Frenchy looked up to see a creature tumbling awkwardly through the sky, closing in on him at an alarming speed. With no time to run, he thrust his palms upward to brace for contact, and a second later the creature bowled into him, knocking him right off his feet.

Having first been yanked around and then steamrolled over, Frenchy jumped up hot as a pistol, ready to unleash a solid right hook into whatever it was that had just hit him.

And then he saw her.

She was striking, with rounded, slightly owl-like features and skin the color of vanilla ice cream. Her hair framed her face into the shape of a heart, at its center a cute, petite nose and, just beneath it, an equally adorable pair of red lips. But most striking were her eyes, twinkling like the river at twilight, painting the sun's reflection in a beautiful blue hue.

Flats

"Sorry about the landing. It's a bit of a work in progress," she said crisply, her words confident but softened by a dash of humility and self-deprecating humor.

The girl looked at the boy standing in front of her. He was shivering slightly, and he had one hand tucked deeply into his vest as though he was attempting to conceal it. His eyes were soft and quite beautiful, and, like she recalled from her glimpse into the crystal ball, he was tinted green, which was not at all off-putting. His scent was pleasant too, hinting of almonds and alfalfa. But what stood out most was his vulnerability, complete and pure, as well as charming… and the girl knew instantly that the cut-and-dried mission the North Pole had sent her on was about to turn a good bit messy. For she could see something clearly in his eyes, something to which she could perfectly relate. This was a boy from whom nothing else should be taken.

She stalled for a second, trying to figure out how to ease into the questions she had come to ask. "Well, um, so, hello. My name is Flats. And, uh… I just happened to be in the area, and I couldn't help but notice when I was flying over that you have a rather huge medieval castle sitting over there. Kinda unique for this part of the world, no?"

She paused, continuing to eye Frenchy, who in turn stood in stone-cold silence.

Frenchy had never before heard anything like her voice. She seemed to be speaking, but the sounds didn't come out as words but rather as little melodies, like the cheerful musings of a morning bird.

"I see," Flats continued, regarding his silence as suspicion. "So that wackadoodle Admiral planted the whole 'secrecy' thing in your head. I bet he told you some nonsense about me being a spy too. Whatever. I'm sure his imaginary band of pirates tipped you off to the old man's true mental state. So, how about we try a different route, and start off with a simple, straightforward question: Is that castle over there yours?"

Frenchy was able to distill the words this time, and he replied with a subtle nod of his head.

"Interesting," Flats said. "So how would a kid such as yourself find himself the owner of what is probably the largest castle this side of the Atlantic? I mean, don't take this the wrong way, but you don't seem like the kind to have taken it by force. And, just out of curiosity, do you have some kind of official document that says it's yours, or do you just believe it to be so?"

Up against the beautiful creature standing before him, every piece of advice the Admiral had given Frenchy went right out the window. Looking to get in her good graces, he reached into his pocket and pulled out the Admiral's note, unfolding it and proudly displaying it for Flats to see.

Wide-eyed, she began to read, letting out an audible gasp when she realized that the Admiral had, in fact, legally assigned over not just the castle but the entire Ohio Territory to Frenchy. "Oh my…" she declared.

She continued reading, and when she got to the personal insult about Santa's backside, she became so flummoxed that she actually uttered the words out loud. "Red-suited fat-bottomed one!" she exclaimed. "Oh my goodness! Nobody ever talks about Santa Claus like that!"

She composed herself and made a request of Frenchy, knowing she'd need proof of what she had just read. "Hey, can you hold that out real steady so I can take a picture of it?" she asked.

"Sure," Frenchy replied, pleased to see that his document was being given its proper due.

Flats pulled a Polaroid Instant 10 camera out of her pocket and aimed it at the document. She clicked a button, and seconds later a cloudy little cardboard square crept out the bottom. Miraculously, the image on the square slowly turned from chalky white into a murky image, then continued right on transforming into a perfectly clear photograph of the important paper Frenchy held within his clutch.

Frenchy, without having the first clue about Ohio real estate law, nevertheless offered up his own legal opinion. "Looks to me about as official as it gets. It's signed and everything!"

Having seen it with her own eyes, Flats concurred, and she realized that she'd have to approach this matter rather delicately. Her focus now began to shift to a bold scheme she had hatched immediately following her meeting with Santa. It was fraught with serious risk, hinging on the deeds of two fifteen-year-old boys, the green one currently standing in front of her, shaking, and another, a Polie apprentice considered by many to be totally off his rocker. But it was the best plan she had at the moment.

Pocketing the photo and the camera, Flats strolled over to a window into the factory and peered in. Though enormous, it was also terribly dilapidated, with the critters slinking around inside it moving with neither vigor nor purpose.

She rejoined Frenchy. "Okay, I have an idea," she said. "But first I need to pick your brain about something." Her focus was palpable. "Do you think you could get your giant toy factory up and running well enough to make a toy for every human child in this Territory? There's a heck of a lot of them, and you'd only have about two months to finish."

"Holy shit!" Frenchy exclaimed. "I've been wondering what those guys are doing in there. Honestly, I wouldn't even know where to begin because I don't know the first thing about making toys."

Flats shook her head. "Goodness, what on earth did the Admiral do?" she asked under her breath.

Thrown off, she paused, so many moving parts rattling around in her head. Most of all, she questioned what was really leading her thoughts, her heart or her brain.

A couple deep breaths later, she had made her decision: They were going to take a life-changing leap. All three of them, together.

"Hey, I really appreciate you being so honest with me," she said. "And you seem like a really sweet guy. So we're going to give something a shot. I'll be back here in a few days, and I'll be bringing a very important guest with me, a kid about your age. Now please, listen very carefully to what I'm about to say. It's going to be absolutely critical for you two guys to get along and to do exactly what I ask you to do. And when I say critical, I mean for all three of us, you, me, and the new guy. Because kids like us are lucky enough to ever get a shot in the first place, and we're certainly not going to get a second. So, what do you say? Are you in?"

Frenchy had no earthly idea what Flats was talking about. But, head over heels smitten, what was he going to do? Of course, he just smiled and nodded his head yes.

"Good," Flats said. "I'll see you in a few days."

Frenchy, knowing her departure was imminent, fired off two pressing questions. "Hey, hang on. Can I ask where is this other kid coming from? And who is your boss, like the person in charge of all this?"

"Sure. The kid, he's coming from the North Pole," Flats replied matter-of-factly. "As for my boss, well, it's Santa Claus."

Evidently starting to numb to the insanely strange things popping up all around him, Frenchy could only laugh. "Of course!" he said. "Santa Claus! Who else? And I guess that makes sense, with the toys and all!"

Flats giggled. "Exactly." Then she turned and readied herself for takeoff but stopped cold, suddenly realizing she had overlooked a most important matter. "Oh my goodness!" she blurted out. "I'm so sorry. We got so deep into our conversation that I totally forgot to ask you your name."

Frenchy smiled and extended his hand. "It's no problem. I'm Frenchy."

The two hands embraced, one webbed and the other clawed, and they let them linger like that, just a touch longer than your standard handshake.

"It's a pleasure to meet you," Flats replied. "So, do you share this place with anyone, like family?"

"No," answered Frenchy. "I'm an orphan. The only other beings here are these giants called Wursties and a bunch of those little guys that you saw working inside. They're called Scandies, and they're the workers, evidently. I haven't really gotten to know them too well yet, but they think I'm some type of god. Anyways, how about you? Do you have a family?"

Flats eyed Frenchy with a smirk, the "god" comment taking her mind off the sting of answering a question she had always hated answering. "No, I'm an orphan too. But wait a second, did I just hear you say they think you're a *god*?"

"Yep," Frenchy replied, laughing. "Supposedly walked on water and everything! It's a puzzle I'm still trying to sort out, but I think the little guys might just have vivid imaginations. Or maybe the Admiral filled their heads with so many fugazies they started to believe some of them. Whatever the case, they seem at peace with it, so I've decided to just let it be for now."

Flats smiled. "Well, if it turns out that you're a living, breathing deity, let me know. It's not every day that you get to meet one of those. Besides, I suppose we could all use a little divine intervention at some point, right?"

"Right," Frenchy said, returning the smile. "And yes, I'll be sure to let you know once it gets all sorted out!"

"Well then," Flats said. "It's definitely been interesting. And I'm looking forward to seeing you again in a couple days, Frenchy."

That was it. She had spoken his name, turning syllables into song and Frenchy's legs to rubber. All he could offer in response was a bashful little wave, which Flats returned, and then she was off, casting a most lovely image as she ascended into the autumn Loveland sky.

Twelve hours later, when night had fallen and the huge harvest moon was angled just so, Frenchy returned to the spot of their meeting. Drifting amongst the moonbeams, he thought of her, and he hoped with all his might that she was thinking of him too.

CHAPTER TEN
Hatching a Plan

Flats flew straight from Loveland to the North Pole, so eager to share her news with Santa that she didn't once stop to rest. Arriving at the door to his office, she paused and took a deep breath. She was a tiny bit nervous, but excited more than anything else, and certainly a million times more confident than she'd felt during their first encounter. Some of her ease resulted from the warmth she'd seen in the old man's eyes the last time, but it mainly came from the feeling that she now held a good part of her fate in her own two hands. She was armed with information, and a plan.

She reached up and grabbed an ornate knocker, giving it a good rap against the door. A moment later, Santa's eye peered out through the peephole, then the door swung open, a warm smile spreading across the face of the big man on the other side.

"Flats!" he began. "Back from foreign lands! Please, come in and regale me with tales of your adventures."

Flats couldn't help being taken a little aback by Santa's outfit, a single, bright red pajama-like number stretching from his neck to his toes. Skintight, it definitely showed the full scope of Santa's epic physique.

"Thank you, sir," Flats replied. "It has been a rather long journey. Would it be okay if I sat?"

"By all means!" Santa said cheerfully. "I've made that journey more times than I can count, but the reindeer do all the work. I couldn't imagine actually doing the flying myself!"

Flats smiled. "It wasn't too bad. Lots of gliding. But goodness, it's cold up there! So I'm glad for the opportunity to warm up a little, and I appreciate you taking the time to see me without any advance notice."

"Of course! Consider my door always open for you," Santa said. "So please, tell me of what you found in the magical-sounding place called Loveland."

"Well," Flats began, a little haltingly at first, aware that her opening comment contained a small but very meaningful rebuke of Santa. "The boy we saw in your crystal ball, the one the others so hurtfully call the Frogman, he has a name. It's Frenchy. And he's actually very nice."

Santa eyed Flats closely, and at the moment the word "Frenchy" left her mouth, her color changed dramatically, going at once from her usual whitish hue to the beet red glow of a candy cane.

"Ah, Frenchy," Santa said, allowing the word to linger in the air a moment. "Tis a fine-sounding name, and I promise I shall be certain to forever retire the use of the other f-word."

"Thank you, sir," Flats replied. "So, here's the situation. The guy you originally bequeathed the castle to, the one called the Admiral, built what has to be the biggest toy factory in the entire world, connected right to it. And he actually did what everyone had feared, formally signing everything completely over to Frenchy. I saw the legal document, and it looked official. But you know the craziest part of all of this? Frenchy's never so much as made a single toy!"

Flats knew she was taking a gamble in not pulling the photograph of the document out and showing it to Santa, but she had found its words about his backside so potentially hurtful that she couldn't bring herself to let him see it. Besides, she was confident that an ironclad description of the matter would do the trick.

It became apparent that it had.

"My goodness, an official legal document," Santa said with a knowing smile, moving right past the question of *whether* the castle could ever be reclaimed to instead *what should be done about it?* "So we've lost control of an entire Territory to a boy named Frenchy, who apparently has no training in the toy-making arts, and in a little over two months we're going to have over one million children counting on us to deliver. So, Flats, what do you think we should do, pray tell?"

Flats rose from her chair excitedly. "There's a kid at the Polie Academy, he's sort of a legend, actually. His name is Elvis Parker. Have you heard of him?" she asked.

It was now Santa's time to turn candy cane red. Immediately turning his back to Flats and walking over to the window, he worked to conceal the blushed state of his skin. For while Santa had considered this boy to be a critical cog in his Machiavellian plan since its hatching, hearing his name associated with it nonetheless hit close to home.

"Um, yes," he said, his words coming out muddled. Forcefully clearing his throat, Santa continued. "I've heard tales of the Parker boy. A big kid. As tough as iron. From the lore I've heard, he's fought over half the other boys at the Academy and whipped them all. Why is it that you asked about him?"

"Because he's perfect!" Flats blurted out.

Santa was perplexed. "Perfect? Whatever do you mean? Perfect for what?" he asked.

"For this mission! Paired up with Frenchy, they can save the day! I've asked around about him, and he's both smart and fearless. Plus he's one of the only guys up here that never acted like a creep toward me. But maybe the most important thing is we haven't any time to spare, and I heard he'd leave on a moment's notice." Flats paused, her emotions suddenly acutely in tune with the painful words that were about to come out. *"Because everyone says he'd be leaving nothing behind,"* she said in a whisper.

Santa winced at that last part as though he had just been punched in the gut. Once again, he worked to regain his composure. "I see," he eventually replied. "And you believe that by bringing him down to Loveland and making use of what is now Frenchy's operation, that the three of you can pull off some sort of toy-making miracle?"

"Well, sir," Flats said, "what I do know is that we're in a serious pickle, and if we fail to deliver in Ohio, that means you'll shut it down for the rest of the world. So I understand the stakes. Now can I say with any degree of certainty that we'll be successful? No, I can't. But it's the best plan I have—well, really the only one—and I say we fight like heck to make it work."

Santa was impressed by Flats' confidence as well as the calm she exhibited while under considerable pressure. He went totally still, lost in thought.

"Okay," Santa said finally. "Consider it done. I'll put the wheels in motion."

"Excellent, sir! Thank you so much!" Flats exclaimed. "So, one last thing. What shall I promise as a reward for success?"

"The usual deal that I give the Polies for a successful delivery, and the same offered to you. The Parker boy would have a wish coming to him, for whatever his mind can conjure up."

Flats was about to ask about what would be coming to Frenchy as well, but she paused, not wanting to inject an unconventional twist that could possibly turn the whole deal sideways. Besides, this was freakin' *Santa Claus*, and of course he'd do the right thing when the time came. So she decided to just let it be.

Santa sat down at his desk, pulled out a piece of embossed stationery along with an ornately feathered fountain pen, and started writing out a note longhand. When he concluded, he took a crimping tool out of the drawer and held it up to the paper, putting the indentation of his official symbol, a stocking cap with a little ball at the tip, upon the page. Folding it carefully, he held it out toward Flats.

"Take this to that arrogant little twit the Elder. And tell him to hurry his scrawny butt over here. I structured the directive's prose even more formally than usual to remind both him and his mouthy offspring that they need to be officially summoned in order to be seen here."

"Yes, sir," Flats replied, carefully reaching out and grasping the paper. "I shall take it at once. And tomorrow, I shall be on my way back to Loveland along with my guest."

Santa smiled. "Godspeed and safe journeys, young lady," he said.

Flats rose up and smiled back warmly. "Thank you, Santa. Until next time, be well, sir."

She then turned and strolled to the door with an extra bounce in her step, pleased to have a most critical piece of her plan in place.

Though fully exhausted, Flats knew she had to make one last stop before she could retire for the night. Launching into flight, she flew high up over the North Pole, soon arriving at its largest house, a mansion actually, home to the Polie leader known as the Elder.

She slid the note under the door and gave a good, loud rap with the knocker, then turned and took off back in the direction of her quarters, eager to put this long, eventful day to rest.

• • •

A few minutes later, back at Santa's chambers, there was another rap on his door. He had changed into his most formal attire, complete with an ornately adorned sack thrown over his shoulder, to convey that the meeting that was about to go down was going to be strictly business. Passing a reflective window, he knew he had accomplished his objective.

Santa Claus

He walked over and cracked the door open ever so slightly, making it abundantly clear that his visitor, the Elder, was not welcome to enter.

Santa looked down at the old elf, a prickly, dour-looking specimen not even half his size, and barked out several crisp sentences. "Let's forego the small talk. Effective eight a.m. tomorrow, the Parker boy is to be placed in charge of Ohio, fixing what you people have broken. And consider this an order, not a request."

Santa paused for effect and then continued, his voice now rising. "And while I have your attention, I would like to make it abundantly clear that the little barge-in stunt your offspring pulled the other day shan't happen again. In case it has slipped your elixir-addled mind, let me provide you a reminder: I created the world you and your kind so lavishly inhabit, and I can do it all over again with freshly hired help."

Adding a most abrupt exclamation point, Santa slammed the door with full force, causing it to latch shut just an inch away from the tip of the Elder's nose.

The Elder, stunned to have been spoken to in such a manner, stared straight ahead at the door knocker for several long seconds. Then his eyes dropped down to the letter he held in his hand, which formally summoned his presence like a haughty diner impatiently clicking his fingers at a waiter. Slowly, methodically, he began to tear it into tiny pieces, pacing with his breathing, which was getting heavier with each rip. "The bloated one's day of reckoning is coming," he whispered through gritted teeth. "At which time he will learn once and for all that the delivery boy is beholden to those who produce the goods, and not the other way around!"

Then he tossed the pieces high into the air like confetti, at the same time turning on his heels and heading back in the direction of his mansion.

Chapter Eleven
A Pack of Polies

Later that same night, Spiro and several of his fellow Polie Academy classmates shared a high-backed booth at the Arctic Public House, a popular North Pole drinkery. As usual, they were enjoying the house specialty, ice-cold Christmas elixir sucked down through the hollowed-out core of a candy cane.

Spiro was busy holding court, and with just a moment's listen it was evident that he loved the sound of his own voice.

Spiro

"That smelly, senile, bearded fat bastard," he exclaimed loud enough for the entire bar full of fellow Polies to hear. "Where does Santa get the gall to butt into the business of running a Territory?! He knows for the last thirty-two years, and forever after going forward, that the Polies run this thing. He just does the deliveries, like a glorified mailman, and nothing more!"

Spiro took a long drag on his candy cane, adding fuel to his fury. "I just heard it firsthand that he intervened on behalf of that headcase Elvis Parker, and he's sending him down to run that Territory where the crazy old coot deserted his post. At least the hothead will get a good ass-chewing tomorrow before being cast off to the nether regions!"

The other boys at the table shifted in their seats, wondering if the rant was over. Apparently, Spiro was only getting started.

"But what really pisses me off is that the fat bastard is sending the winged girl down there with him! Like he's trying to turn one of our Territories, *one of my Territories*, into some sort of land of misfit pet projects! But whatever. I have bigger issues to concern myself with than that stuck-up little tease."

An uncomfortable quiet fell over the table, as everyone present had heard the rumors about Spiro's unrequited interest in Flats and how he had once gotten handsy with her. And also of how she'd sent him to the hospital with a broken nose as a result.

But any unease was lost on Spiro, who, being Spiro, managed to kick the awkwardness up to a new level. "And speaking of Elvis Parker, I heard it through the grapevine that Santa might have a special reason for keeping such a watchful eye over him. Like, Father Christmas just might be father to someone else! And that's all I'm saying about that subject."

Even deep within a Polie bar amongst nothing but Polies, talking about Santa like this was *way* over the line. Save Spiro, everyone at the table looked around uncomfortably, checking to see if the comment had drifted beyond their little group.

His guests fidgeting, Spiro continued firing away, his voice now rising. "Elvis Parker and Flats the winged girl, flying down to save the day. Makes for quite a rich story, even if it's destined to end up as a big old mess, and one that I'll eventually have to clean up. But at least it'll humble Fat Boy, showing up in Ohio on Christmas Eve only to find his outpost in tatters." He laughed, finding himself quite amusing. "At least there's a silver lining: when this is all said and done, it'll bring about a return to the good old days, when he and his type minded their own goddamn business!"

The others at the table, holding out hope that Spiro might be running out of steam, traded rolled-eyed looks, each one of them wondering if they'd be sitting there if the blabbermouth didn't have an unlimited open tab at the pub.

A slight Polie named Theodore finally managed to shift gears, bringing up a topic that was bound to send the rant machine off in a new direction: "But what about that frogman that everyone's been talking about? I mean, I heard that it actually eats human children! Wouldn't you be afraid if it was still lurking down there and you were forced to pay the Territory a visit?"

Spiro made an obnoxious noise, something like a laugh, perhaps, but more like a snort. "Good god, did someone sneak up while you slept and sprinkle pixie dust on you? What do you think, I sit around gnashing at my nails, fretting that something might be lurking under my bed? Because most assuredly

I do not! Trust me, if that thing so much as hiccups too loudly or causes a moment's disruption to our business, I promise that it'll never be heard from again."

Spiro threw his head back and laughed, and the other boys joined in too, the price to pay for free elixir. Disturbingly, they knew Spiro, and they knew he wasn't joking.

CHAPTER TWELVE
Elvis Has Just Left the Building

The next morning, across the railroad tracks that cut a distinct divide across the North Pole tundra, another fifteen-year-old kid was about to experience his own life-changing twist of fate.

With much of the world still enjoying the colorful autumn days of late October, in the Northlandic Region of the Polie Empire, winter's white death had already taken grip. And with temperatures inching beneath the zero line at night, it was enough to make the insides of an unheated metal mobile home feel like a walk-in freezer.

Elvis Parker coaxed himself out of his doubled-up sleeping bags and rose up off the floor. Walking out of his frigid bedroom, he didn't have to look far to find his mother, who lay passed out on the trailer's kitchen floor, half-smoked heaters and empty bottles of elixir strewn about.

"Christ, Tracy," he muttered, bending down to scoop her up into his arms, amazed at how light she was. Walking over to a lumpy couch, he gently laid her down and covered her with a blanket.

She was pretty but aged well beyond her thirty-three years, as though her youth had been rubbed away. He tenderly pushed the hair off her face and whispered, "One of these days, whatever's chasing you is gonna finally wear out."

He then retreated to the bathroom to ready himself for the day's battles.

Staring into the mirror, Elvis first ran some goop through his hair, making sure it was just the right mix of sculpted and messy. He slid on shredded jeans and scuffed black Dr. Martens, then a green shirt, a circular "POLIE" patch sewn onto the right sleeve. Pulling on the finishing touch, a denim jacket with "ELVIS" blaring across the front, he gave some encouragement to the scarred face staring back.

"Hold your head up high, boy. This is the last time these pricks get to call the shots."

Elvis

He went to the fridge and grabbed a bottle of orange Fanta soda, then set out for the brutally cold seven-block walk to the Polie Academy.

Upon arriving, he made a grand entrance, bursting through the front door like he owned the place. The hallway was abuzz with elf-kids, each one dressed just like the others: brown shoes, beige pants, and crisp green Polie shirts, all neatly tucked in. But Elvis' distinct fashion sense wasn't the only thing that set him apart. He was also a good twelve inches taller than all the others, and his ears, rounded at the top, appeared much more human-like than elfin.

The mass of bodies seemed to magically part as Elvis began his walk down the hall, cutting a clear path for him. It was as if the other boys were repelled by an unseen force, like the same-poled fields of a magnet. But make no mistake: there were scant similarities between Elvis and the rest of this group.

Soon, he arrived underneath a sign welcoming visitors to the Office of Polie Disciplinary Affairs. With Elvis now a good distance away, several of his classmates suddenly grew brave, shouting out catcalls and assorted slurs, most of which were about his ears.

He turned back to face the crowd, which he knew was watching his every move. "To the few of you that were actually cool to me through the years, thanks, dudes, I appreciate it. Stay strong. And to the rest of you miserable bastards, you're lucky they're probably gonna throw me out today. Otherwise, I would've eventually kicked every one of your sorry asses!"

To drive his point home, Elvis jumped up and slapped the sign, knocking it out of its supports and sending it crashing to the ground. This brought about a huge roar, a mixture of cheers and jeers, just as he pushed his way into the office. The commotion was not lost on the eight old elves already sitting around a long boardroom table, each with their hands folded in front of them, silent.

A single ancient elf, brimming with pomposity, stood at the head, impatiently smacking his palm with a long wooden pointer.

The Elder

Elvis had experienced more than his share of run-ins with this guy, known to everyone as the Elder, and he held about as much disdain for the old man as one could. In fact, he often daydreamed about what he would do to him if they ever crossed paths outside of the Academy.

"So gracious of you to join us, Mr. Parker, albeit a little late. So let us waste no more time. With haste, boy, get your snotty little behind up here and present yourself to me."

The crack caused Elvis to adopt a snail-like pace, and he took several deliberate moments to walk to the front of the room, swigging from his orange Fanta as he made his way.

The Elder grew agitated. "Goodness, fellow! You've never respected the rules of this Academy, but I demand you at least respect this esteemed committee, if but only for your few remaining moments here."

Elvis smirked. "Dude, chill. What, you get some kinda bonus if you throw my ass out quicker?"

The Elder shook his head. "A petulant little twit right up to the end. So be it then. Committee, we have before us one Elvis Aaron Parker. While a gifted toy-maker, Mr. Parker has over fifty disciplinary marks for a litany of matters, including truancy, smoking, public drunkenness, and having a total and complete disregard for the official dress code of the Academy."

Elvis laughed. "So I'm busted for not wanting to look like a dweeb?!"

Elvis' every word, his every breath, *his being*, aggravated the Elder further, and the old elf's speech grew clipped and loud to the point where he was now practically shouting. "But his most egregious offense is his extraordinary number of fights! Ten incidents just this year alone. Shameful! Mr. Parker, what do you have to say for yourself?"

Elvis shrugged his shoulders. "Why don't you ask the punks that took the beatings? They heard what I had to say."

The Elder angrily fired his pointer up against the wall. "Remorseless and darken-hearted! Well, seeing that you have nothing intelligent to offer, come here and relinquish your patch. In the olden days, I'd have also taken a piece out of your backside, and believe you me, your little bad-boy smirk would be no more."

Elvis took another long drag on his soda and then did as directed, ripping the Polie patch from his sleeve and nonchalantly tossing it onto the table in front of the old man.

The Elder smiled smugly. "So there we have it. On this day, the Royal Order of Polies does hereby downgrade the status of one Elvis Aaron Parker to Expelled, Pending Reinstatement, effective immediately. He shall serve his probation in the Territory of Ohio, being escorted there at the adjournment of these proceedings by the winged girl. Of course, Mr. Parker, upon satisfactory completion of his probation, may return and seek readmission to the Academy, the chances of which I shall peg to roughly that of pigs taking to the sky!"

The Elder threw his head back and laughed, emitting a wheezy, foul-smelling stench.

Apparently succumbing to his emotions, Elvis bent over and began to shake.

The Elder's face brightened with gratification, and he nodded, pleased to see that after so many scores of run-ins with the boy, he had finally broken him.

But hidden from everyone's view, except Elvis' own, was a three-foot-long stream of gooey orange Fanta mixed with a thickened goober he'd coaxed up, stretching from his mouth to the top of the Elder's shoe. Elvis cut the goo loose with his tongue, sending it on down and turning the Elder's shoe into a disgusting orange mess.

Sensing the glob hit his shoe, the Elder came unglued, sending any remaining decorum and snooty pretense flying out the window. "You snotty little piece of trailer trash! So Santa stuck up for you yet again, the crazy kid with the strung-out mom, and found you a landing spot. But know this: you're finished! You'll screw up again, and you'll find yourself out of chances. Your book of days is already written, Mr. Parker, and I know the ending. Just another broken toy destined to be tossed out with the garbage. So off you go, boy. I'm quite certain that your time here is through!"

Elvis took one last draw on his soda, a twisted smile spreading out across his face. Pressing nose to nose with the Elder, he glared, exposing the full whites of his eyes, and cocked his head sideways.

"So shake them bones and let 'em roll, old man," he sneered. "'Cuz me and Santa are bettin' against ya!"

Chapter Thirteen
Boys Will Be Boys

October 24, 1978 - Back in Loveland

Sitting in his room, drawing, Frenchy was locked in a wonderful daydream. He was dancing arm in arm with Flats, fully amongst the humans, just two kids lost in each other's embrace, unconcerned about anyone doing them harm.

Finishing up the drawing, he held it out, gazing at his image of Flats. "She even glows on a piece of paper," he decided.

It had been two days since he'd seen her in the flesh. Two very long days full of hope and doubt and, at times, even contemplation of whether the beautiful creature had really dropped from the sky at all. She couldn't have simply been imagined, could she?

As each minute turned into the next, all that began to matter was that she came back.

A loud, frantic banging on his bedroom door abruptly snapped him out of his trance.

Frenchy hurried over and swung the door open, and

the Commandant, quite worked up, barged in. The sharply dressed Wurstie was apparently taking his newly adopted role as Frenchy's protector very seriously.

"Interlopers! Zwei! Eine frau und ein junge!" the Commandant barked, holding two fingers up.

Rattled, Frenchy grabbed his Bavarian phrase book. "Whoa, Commandant, I don't know what you're saying. Slow... down...!" Frenchy looked up the phrase. "Langsamer. Slower. Langsamer!" He held his hands out, palms down, trying to calm his visitor down.

The Commandant took a deep breath. "Frau." He made a curvy motion with his hands, miming the universal figure of a woman, albeit one with a serious set of hips.

Frenchy got it. "Okay. A girl has arrived."

"Und junge," the Commandant continued. "A boy." He reached down near his fly and stuck his index finger out, which was rather unnecessary of the Commandant, having just gotten his point across in perfect English.

"So a girl and a boy are at the gate, is that right?" Frenchy clarified.

"Ja, at gate," the Commandant said. "Shall we pummel?"

The Commandant then went into full-blown charades mode, bouncing around like a boxer, throwing a rapid combination of punches. Then it clicked for Frenchy: the girl of his dreams was at the gate, and the Wursties were gearing up to beat the crap out of her and her unsuspecting guest.

"No, Commandant! Friends! Freundens! Freindens!!! No pummeling, please!"

Frenchy threw on his beret, and the pair took off for the compound's entry point.

Nearing the gate, Frenchy could see Flats and her guest both being held aloft by the scruffs of their necks by an agitated-looking Wurstie.

Flats was taking it all in stride, a bemused but calm look crossing her face. But the boy was having none of it. He kicked wildly in every direction, trying desperately to render a shot to the Wurstie's nether regions. Fortunately, for his own sake, his legs couldn't quite reach their intended target, and his flailing led to nothing beyond making him look like a tantrum-throwing toddler.

The Commandant ordered the Wurstie to deposit his captives back to earth, and the giant complied, at once setting Flats down gingerly. Then, raising his other arm overhead, he dropped the boy from a good ten feet in the air, high enough to seriously sting his feet.

This totally set the boy off, and he charged headfirst at the Wurstie like a bull seeing red. Snickering, the Wurstie quickly sidestepped and grabbed the boy by his jacket, using his momentum to propel him up into the air and sending him all the way over the top of the compound's wall.

"My goodness!" Flats exclaimed, her head tipping back to track her companion's steep trajectory.

Thankfully, he dropped back down to earth before reaching the rushing waters of the Little Miami.

Laughing, the Commandant and Wurstie said a cheery good-bye to Frenchy and Flats and then went about their way.

A moment later, the boy sheepishly walked back in through the compound's gate, his little flight having apparently calmed him down a bit.

Flats dove right into the conversation. "Wow, charming welcoming committee! Anyway, hello again, Frenchy. So first, let me introduce you two guys. Frenchy, this is Elvis, fresh from the North Pole. And Elvis, this is Frenchy, the guy I told you about that owns that enormous castle over there."

Elvis extended his hand outward toward Frenchy, expecting him to respond in kind.

But Frenchy, basking in the opportunity to once again lay his eyes on Flats, didn't notice the gesture, and he left Elvis' hand hanging there, unshaken.

Thinking Frenchy was acting arrogantly or perhaps even disrespectfully, Elvis glared at him, and if a look could actually burn a hole through someone, this one would have. Elvis then tried a loud, obvious clearing of his throat, but even that didn't draw Frenchy's eyes over to him.

"Jesus Christ!" Elvis finally snapped. "I just flew seven thousand miles on the back of a winged chick, half-frozen and holding on for dear life, in order to try to save your sorry green ass! The least you can do is take a two-second break from checking her out and shake my flippin' hand!"

Frenchy continued to keep his eyes fixed on Flats. Then, if that wasn't awkward enough in the face of having a freshly introduced stranger standing right next to him, Frenchy reached out and lightly placed his palm up against Flats' forehead.

"Just making sure you're real," he said.

Flats let out a bashful little giggle.

"Oh, for Chrissake!" Elvis snapped.

It was Frenchy's turn to shoot a dirty look. "Hey, wiseass, relax!" he said dismissively, feeling his oats a bit in front of Flats. "And watch the green cracks. You've been duly warned."

Now turning fully in Flats' direction, Frenchy spoke as though Elvis wasn't even there. "So this is your big plan?! I'm trying to keep from getting killed by the psychopaths around here, and you bring me this rebel without a clue? Hell, I'd have been better off if you'd just spared the trip to the North Pole and brought me a loaded gun instead!"

Elvis let out a big, over-the-top laugh. "And what am I supposed to do with this shithole of a Territory that the last guy bolted from like it was on fire? Stuck here with a freaky green dumbass that wouldn't know a well-made toy if it sat on his lap!"

In the blink of an eye, Frenchy pivoted around, pulled back, and popped Elvis with a quick right jab.

Unfortunately for Frenchy, however, Elvis clearly knew how to take a punch, and this one did nothing more than royally piss him off. He grabbed the sleeve of Frenchy's punching arm, rendering it out of commission, and turned his other arm into a jackhammer, proceeding to slam it time after time into Frenchy's face.

No stranger to scraps himself, Frenchy wasn't about to back down. He yanked his arm away, freeing up his good hand. Using his webbed fingers to his advantage, he planted them on Elvis' face like a suction cup, fully blinding him. Tucking his right foot behind Elvis' ankles, he pushed his head backward, sending him toppling to the ground with a thud. Then, propelling himself through the air, Frenchy crash-landed right on top of him.

So there they were, less than two minutes into Flats' grand scheme, and the two guys critical to its success were rolling around in the mud, trying to beat the snot out of each other.

Seeing the skirmish, two Wurstie guards came rushing over from their watchdog duties at the entry gate. But before they could reach the combatants and pull them apart, Flats intervened, spreading her wings out to make a screen, impeding their progress.

She shook her head, marveling at her new partners' momentary stupidity, dumbstruck by whatever it was that sometimes made boys act so much like boys.

"Oh my, get a good look at those cavemen!" she said to the Wursties. "And no, don't stop them, let the babies get it out of their systems, and if they don't kill each other, they'll eventually wear themselves out. Then I intend to make my dissatisfaction known in a manner I suspect will have quite a lasting impact."

The Wursties, puzzled, watched Frenchy and Elvis rolling around, trying to do each other serious harm. Then, doing as told, they simply returned back to their post.

Finally, after a few more minutes of punches, slaps, and elbows, Flats' prediction played out, and the two boys lay exhausted on the ground, dirty, bloodied, and gasping for breath.

Flats, her demeanor chillingly calm, walked over to the boys and extended her claw-like hands as though she was going to help them up. Which, technically, she proceeded to do, grabbing each of them by their throats and lifting them to their feet. She then held them that way for several torturous seconds, their pulses beating up against the pointed ends of her sharp, powerful claws.

"So, let this rattle around in your pea-sized brains for a few seconds. A tiny bit more pressure and my talons would sink into your jugular veins. In which case, you'd be dead in about three minutes," she said measuredly, with about the same inflection she might have used for ordering a pizza.

Frenchy's and Elvis' eyes widened with fear, and they both

instinctively stopped breathing, not wanting to risk expanding their necks out even a little.

"Okay, good," Flats continued. "I think I have your attention now."

She released their throats, clearing her own at the same time. "Look, as you're about to learn over the next few minutes, there's an incredible amount at stake here. The next two months are going to change all three of our lives, like, forever."

Flats paused and took a long turn looking into each of the boys' eyes, letting the gravity of the words sink in. "We have one shot. One shot to pull off the plan I'm about to lay out, and it's going to require all three of us to work together. So starting from this moment on, we fight as one, and we stop fighting each other. Can you knuckleheads manage that?"

Frenchy and Elvis, the painful reminder of the death grips still throbbing within their throats, each enthusiastically nodded their acknowledgment.

"Good," Flats said, smiling sweetly. "In that case, I'll retire the jugular clutch."

CHAPTER FOURTEEN
All In

With Frenchy's and Elvis' focus now clearly upon her, Flats launched into her speech, one she had practiced several times in her head on the flight back to Loveland. She was keenly aware that if both boys didn't fully buy in, their efforts would be doomed before they had even gotten started.

"Guys, I'm going to buzz through a ton of information, and hopefully it will all make sense once I'm finished. We'll start with the big picture. It was Santa himself that sent me on this most unique mission, and he's expecting a boatload of presents to be waiting for him here on Christmas Eve, enough for every kid in Ohio. It's on us to figure out how to make, wrap, and arrange all those presents to Santa's exacting specifications. So, faced with this mountainous hurdle, I came up with the idea of pairing you guys up, because together we seem to have all the ingredients to pull this off.

"Now, let's hit rewind and go back to the beginning, starting things off on the right foot." Flats turned to Elvis. "So, Elvis, repeat after me. 'It sure is nice to meet you, Frenchy. I hear you happen to own one of the largest toy factories in the world, and that you have no idea what to do with it.'"

Elvis kicked at the dirt, smiling at Flats' deft touch of diplomacy and humor. "Yeah, what she said," he replied.

"Very well done, Elvis," Flats said, bowing.

She then faced Frenchy, touching his shoulder for a tiny speck of a second. "And you, sir, repeat after me. 'Nice to meet you too, Elvis. I hear that you're one of the most talented toymakers in all the land and that you just might happen to know what to do with this big old factory of mine.'"

Both boys laughed, bringing a fresh breath of levity to the conversation.

"So, dude, is she right?" Frenchy asked. "You'd know how to run a place like this?"

Elvis playfully shot an over-the-top eye roll to the sky. "Yo, what do you think, Ollie Obvious? I just flew in from the North Pole, didn't I? Give me the keys to this bad boy, and we'll be piling up toys in no time. And really, I don't think this is even gonna be all that tough of a challenge. I mean, we still have over two months until Christmas Eve, and how many toys could they possibly ask for? So come on, y'all! Let's roll!"

"Wow, you were sure an easy sell!" Flats said excitedly. "Sounds like we just about have a deal. Frenchy, all we need is your blessing and quarters for Elvis and me. So what do you say, are you on board with throwing your factory into the mix?"

Sensing the deal was about to be consummated, Flats reached out and grabbed both of the boys' hands, and, along with the two of hers, she smashed them all together as one.

But.

Frenchy's feet suddenly went icy cold, spooked frozen on the unfamiliar path he felt he was being rushed down. For the first time since they had initially met, the fireworks that went off every time he so much as thought about Flats had drifted into the backdrop, subordinated to more urgent concerns. Snatching his hands back away from the others, he snapped his words off crisply.

"Whoa! Hang on. This place is *mine*! It's all I have, and it keeps me safe. And I don't know anything about this business of toys and Santa Claus and stuff. If I get involved and something goes wrong and somebody tries to take this place from me, I'm screwed. So I'm sorry, but I think it's best that I just stay out of this, whatever it turns out to be. Yeah, I'm sure of it. I'm not getting involved."

Frenchy looked over at Flats to gauge her reaction, but she averted her eyes, trying to gather the courage to explain the harsh realities of the situation.

"You're already involved," Elvis blurted out abruptly. "As involved as you can be."

Frenchy moved to where Flats' eyes were focused, so that she could no longer avoid his gaze.

She looked at him and nodded, her eyes tinted with regret, and she tried to quiet the nagging thoughts building inside her, reminding herself that she had in no way created this mess. But with Frenchy standing in front of her, his arms crossed tightly and looking totally laid bare, Flats felt a huge jolt of guilt. For she knew he was about to be thrust fully into it.

It was Elvis who plowed onward, determined to lay out the cold, hard truth for Frenchy to digest all at once, ripping off the Band-Aid in a single, painful motion.

"Flats explained your predicament to me during our flight, and, knowing a good bit about the assholes that we're sure to butt heads with down the road, I was able to fill in the blanks.

Those assholes would be the Polies, and they're responsible for worldwide Christmas toy production, including the toys that will be expected to come out of this factory in two months. And Frenchy, what you have to understand about Polies is that you could have all the signed documents in the world, but they won't give a damn. They care about exactly one thing: hitting their toy quota, every Territory, every year. Miss on a Christmas delivery, just one, and they'll be down here to snatch this place back quicker than you can blink!"

Frenchy shook his head, confused, aggravated, and having already heard way too much about these Polie characters. "Christ, we're talking about a bunch of little elves, right? I mean, how tough can they be?"

"We're talking about whole armies of them, Frenchy!" Flats exclaimed. "You have no idea."

"But look at it this way," Elvis continued. "If we're able to meet the toy quota, I think they might just leave us alone. Then we can lay low and continue right on producing next year, and you'll probably be able to keep your castle. But on the other hand, and take this as fact, if we don't produce, it means no Christmas toys for the kids of Ohio. Which in turn would bring all the other toy deliveries across the entire world grinding to a halt. And if that were to happen, as soon as it's discovered that we were to blame, we'll be squashed like bugs!"

Frenchy couldn't believe what he was hearing. "So, out of the clear blue, I have a brand-new enemy?! I've never even heard of these assholes before!" he said, shaking his head. "I don't have anything to do with this stuff," he quietly concluded.

"Unfortunately, you do," Flats replied, almost mournfully. "You very much do. Unless you want to take off now and hide away in the woods, you really need to consider trying to help us with this."

Frenchy's eyes darted around the courtyard, not wanting to even think about what would happen to him if he was ousted beyond the perimeter's protective walls. Feeling like he was drowning, he searched for something to grab onto. "So, what if we tried to make the toys and did pretty well, but didn't quite make it, would that be okay?" Frenchy asked.

"No, it wouldn't be," Elvis replied. "It's an all-or-nothing. Which means if we miss the quota by even a single toy, the Polies will be back to reclaim what I imagine they believe never really left their hands in the first place."

"Holy shit…." Frenchy exclaimed. He paced about, trying to sort his thoughts. "You know, the thing that bothers me most about what you said, Elvis, is that you *think* they'll leave us alone and that the castle would *probably* stay mine. I mean, if we risk everything and pull this off, shouldn't we get a guarantee that those assholes will leave us alone?"

Flats, her disdain of the Polies rivaling Elvis', chimed in. "One can never count on what a Polie will or won't do. They didn't earn reputations as the world's biggest snakes without having compiled the resume."

Out of nowhere, a big smile sprang up across Elvis' face. "Damn! That just gave me an idea! We take the situation out of the Polies' hands and put it squarely into Santa's! Everybody knows that if you run a Territory that meets its quota, you get a wish from Santa. So, Frenchy, if you help us through this, you can use your wish to make sure that you get to keep your castle forever. And since no force can override the power of one of Santa's wishes, the Polies won't be able to say squat about it!"

Elvis locked eyes with Flats. "I'm sure Santa would provide

us with two wishes, since between me and French Fry, well, there's two of us. I mean, you're just like the go-between in this, right? I imagine you have your own arrangement with Santa."

"She's not 'just' anything," Frenchy snapped. Even in his bewildered state, the urge to defend Flats rose to the surface.

Elvis held up a hand of surrender. "Take it easy, Romeo. I didn't mean it like that. I'm just trying to make sure we all know exactly what's coming to us here."

Flats could feel her face heating up and reddening by the second, so she abruptly took off, flapping herself a good fifty feet up into the air. She took a deep breath. It was a slippery slope she was thinking about going down, giving her word for something that would later have to be delivered by someone else. But their efforts were about to implode if she didn't, and then where would any of them be?

Her blushing having subsided, she lowered herself back down to the ground.

Telling herself that Santa would do the honorable thing when the time came, Flats chose what she considered to be the best of two difficult options. "Um, yes," she said. "It's a little unorthodox, but I *believe* that if the two of you are successful, then you will both receive a wish."

"So there you have it, Frenchy!" Elvis said excitedly. "That solves your problem!"

Frenchy was listening closely, taking it all in. Still torn, he walked over to Flats, again looking deeply into her eyes. "I just don't know. If we miss by even one toy. One freakin' toy? Please, be completely honest with me. What do you think?" he asked softly, his vulnerability completely on display, like a small child yearning for the comforting words of a parent.

Flats smiled warmly, and she put her hand on Frenchy's

shoulder. Her voice was now as soft as his, and her own vulnerability peeked out a bit, her usual confident air wavering for a brief moment. "Frenchy, I don't have anything to go back to. Neither does Elvis. And, it stinks, but you won't either if we don't make this work. You know, I'm so, so sorry that you were dragged into this. But we all were. So, since we're all in this mess together, I think we should fight like heck to get out of it together as well."

It was Flats' last sentence that finally began to thaw Frenchy out. Having been on his own for what felt like forever, the word *together* coming from her lips made him feel warm, as though a roaring bonfire had burst to life right in front of him. Suddenly, the weird, scary path from moments ago melted away, an inviting one rolling out right in its place. And since he'd be going down it with *her*, how could it possibly lead him astray?

"Well," Frenchy said. "I guess a long shot is better than having no shot at all."

Frenchy thrust his two hands out in front of him, palms down, and Flats and Elvis did the same, forming a six-hand sandwich.

"So it's a deal, on one condition: I get to name our new crew," Frenchy said.

Flats and Elvis looked at one another, smiling and nodding.

"On three, Ruffians!" Frenchy exclaimed.

The trio pumped their hands up and down, counting off in rhythm. "One! Two! Three! Ruffians!"

They all laughed heartily. The Ruffians. Somehow, it just seemed to fit.

CHAPTER FIFTEEN
Goetta Move On

Frenchy, still standing with his new crew out in the courtyard, noticed a storm moving in across the river valley. "Hey, guys, looks like the weather's about to get rough. Let's head inside and I can show you around," he said.

But before they could set in motion, Flats had another surprise up her sleeve. "Real quick, there's one more thing," she said.

Frenchy and Elvis froze in place.

"The humans in these parts have a strange local holiday," she continued. "It's held on October 28 every year, and it's called Goetta Day. And not only—"

Elvis cut her off. "Yo, what the hell's goetta?"

"That's not important," replied Flats.

"The hell you say! If the humans think enough of something to name a holiday after it, it's gotta be important. So goetta on with explaining yourself!" Elvis demanded.

Flats fumbled around, searching for a logical explanation to something that really made no sense to her at all. "Well, ah, the humans take all the weird parts of the pig, grind them up with oats, form them into little squares and then they fry it."

"And what do they do with it, use it for doorstops?" Frenchy asked.

"Uhhhh, no, I believe they eat it," Flats replied.

Frenchy and Elvis exchanged the most puzzled of looks and then burst out laughing.

"Wait a minute. The humans eat pigs!?" Frenchy asked through his laughter. "Those fat things that roll around in their own nastiness all day? And what do you mean, the weird parts? Like their feet?"

"Dude, I think she means their junk!" added Elvis, laughing even harder.

"STOP!" Flats shouted, blushing like crazy. "Just stop! Don't worry about the goetta. It's not important. What *is* important is that it's a present holiday, one of the few remaining oddballs that the North Pole still handles. So they're gonna need some toys cranked out, fast, and they want us to use it as a practice run for Christmas Eve."

Loud enough to shake the ground, a thunderclap burst from the sky, prompting Frenchy and Elvis to exchange concerned looks.

"So here's the deal," Flats went on. "They're gonna need a toy for every child in Loveland, which is thankfully a teeny tiny dot of a town, maybe a thousand kids in all. One of Santa's drivers will swing by to scoop them up at midnight on the twenty-eighth, which happens to be four days away. Piece of cake, right?"

She handed a thick stack of papers to Frenchy, with the one on top containing a long list of children's names along with details about their desired toy.

He thumbed through the pages, gazing at a wide assortment

of Etch A Sketches, Lite-Brites, and Easy-Bake Ovens, then turned to Elvis.

"Dude, a thousand toys? In only four days? You sure about this?" Frenchy asked.

Elvis grinned. "French Fry, I could do a thousand toys drunk as a skunk and standing on my head! We just gotta get the factory fired up, and we'll need some labor. With that, it'll be a snap."

A smile broke out on Frenchy's face, drawing Flats' attention.

"Frenchy, what's going on in that head of yours?" she asked.

"The Scandies!" he said, excitedly. "We already have a built-in labor supply! There's like thousands of them. Come on, I'll show you."

The Ruffians began their walk back to the castle. Midway there, they encountered two bare-knuckled Wursties, bruised and battered, viciously landing punches upside the other one's noggin.

"Holy moly!" Flats exclaimed. "They're going to kill each other!"

Frenchy laughed. "No, trust me, they won't. They're playing, actually. I see them doing it a couple times a day. Just keep watching."

Sure enough, the Wursties punched it out and then seemed to reach some type of conclusion. They engaged in a congratulatory clasping of the hands, as though they had just been casually hitting a tennis ball back and forth, then each hoisted a giant stein of ale.

"Who are those giants, Frenchy?" Flats asked.

"They're Wursties."

Wurstie

"So what do they do here?" asked Elvis. "They seem like total badasses."

"Yeah, they are. And they're also really cool," replied Frenchy. "They're sort of like my bodyguards, I guess. They protect me."

"Why?" Elvis asked.

"Because everybody around here thinks I'm special," Frenchy said, laughing.

"Oh, you're special, alright," Elvis replied, laughing and yanking off Frenchy's beret, then tussling his hair.

Frenchy snatched his beret back and returned it to its rightful place, then gave a little backhanded slap to Elvis' shoulder, just to send a message about respecting his personal space.

"Come on, time to meet our coworkers," he said, motioning the team inside.

He led them up the castle stairway and into the Control Room. The three of them proceeded to look out the wall of windows onto the cavernous room beneath them, stretching out for as far as their eyes could see.

Elvis' mouth dropped open. "That's the biggest flippin' toy factory I've ever seen!"

"So do you think it will do?" asked Frenchy.

"Will it do?! Hell yeah, it'll do! I could supply the entire world with this joint!" Elvis said, grinning like a kid in a candy store.

Seeing a closed door labeled as the "Material and Instruction Manual Storage Area," he grew even more excited.

"Typical Polie overkill, but I'll say one thing about them: they know how to run an efficient operation. The Academy drilled into our heads that every factory in the world has to have a storage area like that, brimming with every item we could possibly need to make any conceivable toy. With that box checked off, all we need now is our workforce. Speaking of which, where the hell are they?"

"I guess they're all still napping," Frenchy replied. "No, wait a second, I see a few of them down there."

Frenchy pointed at several Scandies down below, doing absolutely nothing.

Laying eyes on the Scandies for the first time, Elvis was taken aback. "They're giant freakin' *rats*!"

"Well, technically rat-elves, according to the Admiral."

"Well, whatever they are, they're weird looking and slow as molasses," Elvis decided.

"All they need is some sort of skeleton key to get rolling," said Frenchy. "And, actually, the Admiral told me they're excellent workers."

"And you took *his* word for it!?" Elvis shot back. "Hell, if you ask me, they're gonna need some serious training, along with an unlimited supply of coffee."

They stood there watching quietly for a few minutes, until Frenchy tossed out an absolute lightning bolt of a comment. "They think I'm a god," he said nonchalantly.

"Oh boy," Flats said, giggling.

Elvis' head shot around ninety degrees, his eyes widening. "Yo, what the hell did you just say?!" he asked, certain his ears must have played a trick on him.

"Yeah, the Scandies, they think I'm a god," Frenchy replied, as though he had just said that the little guys thought he had a cool haircut. Then he elaborated, kinda. "They think I died, came back, walked on water, and here I am. My version is that I was a little frog, ate some freaky bugs, and grew five feet. I guess we're all still trying to hash it out."

Elvis shook his head, perplexed that an entire clan of any type of critter would actually worship the kid standing right next to him. After all, he seemed pretty cool in the brief time he had gotten to know him—but come on, a god? "So, can you cast spells and do tricks and stuff?" he asked.

Frenchy laughed. "No, it's not like they think I'm some kind of teenage wizard. Not even rat-elves would buy that silly premise! They just think I can perform miracles and that I have two more up my sleeve."

Flats' and Elvis' eyebrows arched, and they nodded silently. After all, what does one say to that?

Elvis, having pondered the matter, opted to reset his view

of Frenchy back to the kid he had just started to know a few minutes ago, void of any mystical powers. "So, who'd have thought? Frenchy, Lord of the Rats! I guess I'll have to watch my sinning around you, since I sure don't want to be cast out like a leopard!"

Flats rolled her eyes. "That's *leper*, caveman," she replied. "And you butchered the metaphor. Goodness, what am I saying? There's not a chance in the world you know what a metaphor is!"

They all laughed.

"So, enough about me," Frenchy said. "I've been wondering about something ever since you brought it up, Elvis. You said the Polies are assholes, but aren't you one of them?"

Elvis bent over, gesturing as though he was throwing up. "Christ, don't make me gag. Just the thought makes me sick. I'm 100 percent red-blooded human!"

Fully mindful of the humans' thirst for blood, Frenchy—and Flats—stiffened, both finding themselves fighting the instinctive urge to back away from Elvis.

"The humans, they all seem like monsters, their hearts poisoned by hatred," said Frenchy, his voice filling with a mix of urgency and concern. "But you don't seem like that at all. So you're not like the others?"

"Absolutely not!" Elvis said. "And really, there's a lot more good ones of us than bad. Especially the little ones, because they haven't been taught to hate yet. I think that's one of the unique things about having grown up as isolated as I did. Let's just say there wasn't a whole lot of diversity, and certainly no unique beings like you guys. So I was never conditioned to hate those not like me. Hell, come to think of it, I guess I just developed my hatred of those bastard Polies organically, all on my own!"

They all shared another laugh.

"So how did you end up at the North Pole, mixed up with those guys?" Flats asked.

"My folks married young, and my dad got sent up there for some type of railroad project. He split on me and my mom right before I was born, so we were stuck there. My mom's done her best for us through the years, but... well, let's just say she's tried. I got involved with the Polies when they sent me to the Academy. There were really no other options, since the only other humans up there were Clauses, and they have their own schools. But one cool thing came out of it: Santa learned about me and my mom, and he's paid my tuition ever since. No way we could have afforded it if he hadn't."

Frenchy's curiosity was piqued. "So, all the Santa Clauses, they're humans?"

"Well, yeah, they are. But just to be clear, the small group of humans that live up there are members of a clan called Claus. And of that group, only a tiny, very select few rise to the exalted status of Santa Claus. There's been just seventeen of them in seventeen hundred years, so those cats live long and full lives. They're said to each have had some type of special magnetism that sets them apart from the others, and each can trace at least 50 percent of their blood back to a previous Santa. That way, they keep the throne in the family, which is kinda cool, I think."

Elvis, not really accustomed to talking about himself, suddenly felt as though he had gone on for too long. "Alright, Flats, tag, you're it!" he said abruptly. "Time to enter the Sharing

Circle. I heard of you up at the Pole, but I don't really know anything about you. What's your story, and how'd you get thrown into this mess?"

Frenchy's focus kicked up several notches, as this was a tale he was quite interested in hearing.

CHAPTER SIXTEEN
Head Over Heels

"Well, my people, the Flatwoods Monsters, lived peacefully in the snow-covered mountains of West Virginia for centuries, hidden high up in the pine trees." Flats began tentatively, working to settle into her turn in the hot seat. "But evidently someone had the idea to create a place for humans to slide down those mountains on long strips of wood, so down came the trees, exposing us. Since then, the humans have made a sport of hanging our heads over their mantelpieces. So where once the sky was filled with us, now there's just me. When Santa learned of the slaughter, he scooped me up and took me with him to the Pole, and I've been there ever since."

Flats gently fluttered her wings, propelling herself up several feet into the sky and hovering there for a few seconds, her nerves having been pricked by the pointiest of subjects.

Frenchy watched her ascend, noticing the bottom of her dress for the first time and just how badly tattered it was. While it still looked stunning on her, he suspected that it might be all that she had. Her story had been incredibly sad, and, having suffered loss himself, he could imagine how deeply Flats hurt inside. But the thought of her dress made Frenchy's heart hurt worse than anything else, and he wished somehow that he could at least right that one painful wrong.

When Flats came back down, Elvis, oblivious to the deep feelings the other two Ruffians were experiencing, forged right ahead with his line of questioning.

"So how did you end up stuck in this pickle jar with me and French Fry? And, if I might ask, if we're successful, what's in it for you?"

"Well, I was safe at the Pole. But, my goodness, that place is frigid, as are most of its people. I think that Santa must have sensed that my heart had frozen over. That I needed a fresh start. So he gave me this opportunity, and, just like you guys, I'm counting on my wish."

Frenchy stood there listening, and watching her, enchanted. Momentarily losing track of the fact that Elvis was standing right there as well, he felt himself drawn a couple steps closer to Flats, close enough now that he could smell her strawberry scent. At that singular moment his world closed out everything except her, and something magical happened: Frenchy went from merely being smitten to a state far more transcendent.

"And what's your wish?" he asked, his tone way dreamier than he might have intended for Elvis' ears.

Flats smiled. "That's an easy one," she said. "A new life, one entirely of my own choosing, starting with a nicely thawed out heart."

Frenchy returned the smile and nodded. He loved the sound of that, believing he stood a chance to somehow fit into that plan. In fact, *he knew he did*.

"Goodness, I just realized that I need to get going," Flats said suddenly. "Santa wanted me to let him know as soon as we got our plan in place. But I'll be back again real soon, certainly no later than Goetta Day. In the meantime, good luck. I can only imagine how much work you have ahead of you!"

"To be honest, this really ain't going to be all that heavy of a lift," Elvis boasted. "Victory is as good as ours, baby!"

"Just keep this in mind, in the event of failure," Flats said, jokingly extending her claw out toward Elvis, causing him to jump back and raise his hands protectively. "And you'd be wise to heed the lessons of Icarus!" she added.

Frenchy and Elvis looked at each other, puzzled.

"Is that a rock band?" asked Elvis.

"Goodness, you just might actually be a caveman," Flats replied. "No, Icarus was the kid from Greek mythology with wax wings. He got cocky and flew too close to the sun. The wings melted, and he plummeted to his death. You see the analogy?"

Frenchy nodded knowingly, at least pretending to be following along. But Elvis shook his head back and forth, not wanting to give Flats the satisfaction of thinking she had actually taught him something.

"Sounds like a bunch of highfalutin bullshit if you ask me," he said, laughing. "Miss Brainy Chick, name-dropping Greek gods. The only one of them stories I want to hear about is Uranus!"

Flats, blushing, lowered her head and pinched her nose, concealing her laughter. Frenchy, meanwhile, cracked up in spite of himself.

His laughter trailing off, Frenchy drifted even closer to Flats, locking eyes with her. "Hey, I picked out a cool place for your sleeping quarters, high up in the tower. You'll have a really pretty view of the river valley, and the sunsets are beautiful up there. I'll have it all cleaned up for you before you return."

Flats reached out and clutched his hand, in part a handshake but also in part *holding hands*, with Frenchy certainly considering it to be the latter.

"Thanks, Frenchy," she said warmly. "That's very sweet of you."

Their hands parted, and Flats backed up, preparing for her takeoff.

"I'll see you boys in a few days. Good luck preparing for Goetta Day!" she said.

And off she flew, drawing Frenchy's eyes up with her. He stood totally transfixed, staring up until the very last second, when she had drifted completely out of view.

Elvis studied his new partner. It was apparent that Frenchy's motives were quite unique from his own, because while Elvis was largely in this for himself, the path Frenchy was on was something altogether different. He just hoped they were in sync enough to get them all to the finish line together. "Yo, French Fry, listen, this is our shot, so I gotta hear it one more time. Are you in this with all your heart?"

Frenchy looked Elvis squarely in the eyes. "Trust me, dude," he said. "My heart couldn't possibly be more fully into something!"

Elvis knew exactly what Frenchy had meant. What's more, he believed him.

Chapter Seventeen

Icarus

Frenchy awoke the next morning ready to roll, his body pumped full of adrenaline for the steep four-day hill they had to climb. Certain Elvis would already be down on the factory floor acquainting himself with his new team, Frenchy wanted to give his partner some space to do his thing. So he occupied himself until noon, biding his time drawing until he could wait no longer.

He jogged through the guest quarter wing and then out the Control Room, buzzing down the curved staircase to the first floor. There he caught the day's first glimpse of the Scandies. There were only a handful walking around, fewer still than the day before, and, remarkably, their snail-like pace had slowed even further!

"What the ffffffffff...?" Frenchy said under his breath.

Then a Scandie, his head slumped down and his eyes glued to the ground, proceeded to walk straight into Frenchy. Opening his eyes from the jolt, the Scandie took a good look at who he had just run into and passed out cold, falling to the ground like a board.

"Little guy must have been sleepwalking," Frenchy decided, still wrestling with the concept of just how much the Scandies revered him. "Who can blame him, with how quiet it is around here?"

He turned and retraced his steps, sprinting back up the stairs in search of an AWOL Elvis.

Arriving at Elvis' quarters more than a little agitated, Frenchy banged on the door. "Elvis, what are you doing? We have a ton of work to do!"

His words were met with silence.

Listening closely, he heard what sounded like applause and music coming from nearby. Heading toward the Admiral's former quarters, he pushed open the door, and the sound grew considerably louder. As Frenchy took a few apprehensive steps into the room, he saw what appeared to be a box sitting on the floor, with curved glass in front and what looked like a set of Martian antennas on top. Inside the box a rather peculiar scene was playing out. A group of three humans, dressed in strange costumes, stood side by side behind microphones, jumping up and down and carrying on like lunatics. All the while, a large crowd of many more humans sat behind the trio, wildly cheering them on.

"These humans are all freakin' nuts," Frenchy muttered to himself.

Moving closer to the box, he rounded a large, high-backed chair, and there was Elvis, lounging in one of the Admiral's silk robes, his feet propped up on an ottoman. Beside him was a tray table, upon which sat a glass of ice, a half-consumed bottle of dark elixir, and a very fat, very lit cigar.

"French Fry," Elvis exclaimed when he finally noticed him, his words loud and slurred. "You gotta watch this! It's called

Let's Make a Deal, and these idiots just can't help themselves! They get a good prize first, then they gamble it trying to get something bigger."

Frenchy eyed the box, trying to comprehend whatever it was that was happening.

Elvis slurred on. "But the funny thing is, they always end up getting crap instead, like this last bonehead that just got a live chicken in exchange for a boat! It's freakin' hilarious!"

Now catching on that Elvis was pickled, Frenchy started to grow royally pissed. "What the hell's wrong with you?" he shouted. "We've got a mountain of toys to make, and here you are flushing away our time!"

"Calm down, buzzkill," Elvis slurred. "I've told you three times now, this is kid's stuff. I need two days, three tops, to knock this out. I'll show the rats how to check the list twice, go into the storage area and get the right manual and then grab the supplies they need. Easy peasy, lemon squeezy. Now, quit your nagging and have a drink with me!"

With so much on the line, Frenchy couldn't understand what Elvis was doing. "A drink? Jesus, you had to do this now? With what we face? We gotta get to work, like, right now! So cut the crap and let's head down to the factory!"

Elvis arose from his chair and took a long drag off his cigar, then used it to gesticulate as he began pacing about. It was clear he was getting more worked up by the second, and the elixir certainly wasn't helping. "I've been stuck on a shitty sheet of ice for fifteen years, more broke than you can imagine. And all of a sudden I wake up in what for me is the lap of luxury. Heat, an actual bed, a big old fluffy chair. For just one day, I wanna kick back and feel what it's like to live like a king! One stinkin' day! Is that too much to ask?!"

"Look, I get that you want to have a good time," Frenchy replied. "But it's bullshit for you to be having it right now and, frankly, selfish as hell. I mean, all you had to do was hold off for a few days. You know, just wait!"

The comment clearly struck a nerve. "Wait?!" Elvis shouted, his voice filling with venom. He aggressively stumbled toward Frenchy, pulling up chest to chest with him. "I've spent my entire life waiting! Waiting to get a piece-of-shit used bicycle, so I wouldn't have to walk across town in the frigid cold. Never happened! Waiting to see a real human doctor to get stitches for the gash on my face so I wouldn't have this freakish zipper on my cheek! Never happened! And waiting for someone to make me a hot freakin' breakfast just one single freakin' morning over the course of my fifteen freakin' years on this planet! Just one! *And. It. Never. Happened!* So you know what? I'm done waiting! I'm on my own now, and it's time for me to start taking. And I'm gonna start by *taking* this goddamn day off! End of discussion!"

Elvis clumsily slumped back into his chair, pouring his glass full of elixir and gunning it down in one gulp. He then turned the box's volume all the way up, preemptively drowning out anything else that might have been said.

Feeling that there was nothing good that could come out of his staying even a moment longer, Frenchy left, very much rattled by what he had just witnessed.

His head filled with gunk, he couldn't help but waste the rest of the day himself, wracked with anger, confusion, and frustration. He tried to pull out of his funk by reminding himself that they still had three full days left, and Elvis had made it sound like that was more than enough time. But with his toy-making partner now so far out of control, who really knew?

So the gunk, and funk, clouded over Frenchy's head, darkening what otherwise could have been a wonderfully vibrant day, until he eventually surrendered to sleep later that night.

• • •

Excited about the opportunity for a do-over, Frenchy bounded out of bed early the next morning and headed down to the factory floor. Once again, he was shocked by the scarcity of Scandies.

"You there," he called out to the first one that walked by.

Seeing Frenchy, the Scandie froze, a distant look glazing over his eyes.

Frenchy had seen this look before, and, sensing the Scandie was about to hit the bricks, he hurried to intervene. "Hey, look, it's all good. I just need your help for a second. So please, don't faint."

It worked, and the Scandie snapped to.

"Can you go get your leader guy, you know, the one without a name?" Frenchy asked.

The Scandie nodded, then shuffled off without saying a word.

Standing there waiting, Frenchy watched the few Scandies that were scattered about. Each of them was playing with a type of toy he had never seen before. It consisted of a flat wooden paddle with a circular hole and a little square chunk of wood attached to it by a stretchy string. It became clear that the object of the game was to flip the chunk up into the air, then guide the paddle under it as it fell back to earth, trying to land it in the hole.

After watching for several minutes and not witnessing a single successful wood chunk landing, Frenchy saw the Scandie leader approaching from across the factory floor.

"Hey, man, thanks for coming!" Frenchy called out.

"Certainly, Oh Special One," the Scandie leader replied.

"Okay, first things first," Frenchy continued. "We gotta do something about the name situation around here. While I respect your no-name edict and all that, it's just sort of, how should I say this? *Awkward.* I mean, I gotta call you something. So if it's just the same to you, from now on I'm gonna call you Sam."

Sam shrugged as though the thought of having a name was neither here nor there. "You can call me whatever you like," he said. "Doesn't make it my name."

Frenchy sighed. "I get it," he said. "But please, trust me. It'll help make our conversations flow a whole lot better."

"As you wish, Oh Special One," Sam replied.

"Okay, that's another thing. I appreciate you guys thinking I'm special and all that. I happen to think so too every once in a while," Frenchy said, laughing. "But to actually be called that—again, it's, like, totally awkward. So how about we simply go by Sam and Frenchy?"

Sam nodded. "Yes, Frenchy, as you wish."

"Okay, great. So, we've got a lot of work to do, but before we get started, can I ask you something?"

"Of course. What's on your mind, Oh Special One?"

Frenchy rolled his eyes, smiling. "Well, I was wondering what that toy was that the guys in your crew are playing with?"

"Oh, that little beauty? It's called a Hole In One," Sam replied proudly. "One of my finest brainstorms. We had a big pile of spare ping-pong paddles lying around, and one day I put a hole in one."

To Frenchy's amused surprise, Sam's eyebrows waggled at the wordplay.

"Simplest thing in the world to construct," Sam went on. "Just combine stretchy string and wood, and voila, you have a toy. It's actually a diabolical little gadget, and it keeps the troops occupied for hours, as it's never occurred to even a single one of them that they're trying to land a square peg in a round hole. First guy that figures it out will probably be in line for my position someday," he concluded, laughing.

The idea of other elves aspiring to step into Sam's shoes was interestingly incongruous for a society self-styled as hierarchy-free. But further thought of the matter would have to wait for another day, as it was high time to get down to work.

"So, Sam, getting you guys started is supposed to be Elvis' job, but he's obviously not here right now. So how about you just get started on your own? I mean, there's gotta be something productive for your crew to be doing, right?"

"Wish it wasn't the case, but there's absolutely nothing for us to do. Remember the other day when I asked you about the skeleton key? It happens to open the Material and Instruction Manual Storage Area, and it's so critical to our operation that the Admiral used to wear it on a chain around his neck. That's probably where it remains, and without it, we can't access the area that holds every single thing we need in order to do our jobs."

"Holy shit!" Frenchy exclaimed. "You're telling me that the directions showing how to make all the toys—and everything necessary to make them—is in that room, and we might not be able to get in there?"

"There's no 'might' involved here, Frenchy," Sam replied. "Having tried everything, I'm telling you with absolute certainty: without that key, we're not getting in there."

Frenchy looked up at a clock hanging overhead. "Damn it,

it's past nine already! Where the hell is Elvis? Maybe he knows some type of trick to work around it…"

Sam cocked his head sideways and shrugged his shoulders, having nothing better to offer.

So, for the second time in two days, Frenchy was forced to retrace his steps.

Running straight to Elvis' quarters, he banged on the door, loudly. "Elvis, what the hell are you doing? We have a serious problem on our hands!"

It was met by a tortured moan and garbled words. "Uuuuuh-hhhhhh! Leab me awone."

"Oh no! No flippin' way!" shouted Frenchy.

Beyond exasperated, he barged through the door, finding Elvis lying in bed, a pillow pulled over his head and an open bottle of aspirin on the nightstand.

"This shit ain't happening again!" Frenchy snapped. He hurried over and snatched the pillow from Elvis, exposing his eyes to the harsh sunlight peeking in through the blinds. "Get your ass up!"

Elvis rolled over onto his side, desperate to evade the devilish light. "Oh my god, I'm so miserable. Just leave me alone to die!"

Frenchy ran down the hall to the bathroom and filled a Dixie cup with freezing water. Returning, he angrily threw it into Elvis' face, but all the icy dousing brought forth was another mournful moan.

"Goddamn it, Elvis! Nobody can get any work done because we're locked out of the storage area. You gotta come and help us. You're killing our chances before we even get started!"

Elvis rolled onto his stomach, grabbing another pillow and pulling it over his head. And that, apparently, was his final statement about the matter, because even after Frenchy stood there for several more minutes, cussing, screaming, and poking at him, he didn't make another sound.

Furious, Frenchy eventually gave up and stormed toward the door. "You're worthless," he barked, sprinting out of the room.

"Shut the door," Elvis groaned. But by then, Frenchy was long gone.

CHAPTER EIGHTEEN
Finding a Loophole

The next morning, down to a mere forty hours to somehow figure out how to crank out one thousand toys, Frenchy and Sam reconvened on the factory floor. Sam had apparently spent his time rousting his troops, as there were now roughly two thousand Scandie workers spread out across the floor, the first welcome sight for Frenchy in a couple days.

"Thanks, Sam," Frenchy began with a sigh. "This is great. If only I knew what to do with all of them."

Just then, Elvis, at long last, hustled out onto the factory floor, looking both embarrassed and contrite. "Look, dude, you have no idea how horrible I feel," he began, facing Frenchy. "So I promise, from now on—"

Frenchy threw his palm up, thrusting it right in front of Elvis' face. "Stop!" he demanded. "Just stop! There's nothing you can say to get us back the two days you just pissed away. All we can do now is try to work out of the jam we're in, and it's a flippin' big one. But believe me, we'll deal with you being an over-the-top asshole after the Goetta Day delivery is behind us."

Elvis, seeing both how angry Frenchy was and the determined look in his eyes, figured it was best to just do as he'd said. "Alright, dude," he replied, turning squarely to the future. "So, tell me, what's this big problem all about?"

"Come here and see for yourself," Frenchy said crisply, walking over to the door sealing off the material warehouse. "It's locked," he said, his tone dire.

They all looked up at the imposing metal door. A thick metal plate encircled the lock, making it seem to Frenchy that short of blasting a hole through the wall with dynamite, there was simply no way they were going to gain access.

Elvis, on the other hand, was far less cowed. "Ooooohkay," he said. "So... a locked door. Last time I checked, there's a spiffy new invention called a key that'll magically open it."

"Christ, Elvis, stop being such a goddamn smartass," Frenchy spat back. "If you'd have been here the past two days, you'd know that there is no key. I was hoping that you might have learned some special trick to get around locks back at the Academy."

"They taught us how to make toys, not how to channel our inner Houdini. So no, I won't be doing any lock-picking."

Their situation was dire indeed. Yet Elvis still, *still* found it appropriate to make wisecracks. Infuriated, Frenchy let out a wave of frustration on the warehouse door, grabbing its handle and violently jerking with all his might, at the same time ranting like a madman.

"Thanks a lot, Elvis! You've pissed away two days, one drunk and the other hungover, and you've managed to put the only thing that keeps me safe at risk. And yet, instead of being just a *little bit* humble—which would take something of a miracle,

I guess—you go right on spitting out your stupid freakin' jokes! God, I've never heard anything remotely as annoying as your voice right now! So, please, just do me a favor and *shut the hell up!*" Frenchy bellowed.

Then, turning his bubbling-over frustration toward an inanimate object, he yanked a final time on the handle, as hard as he could.

And the door popped open.

Apparently it had been stuck shut too tightly for the little Scandies to pull open, but not too tightly to thwart a seriously pissed off Frenchy.

Frenchy, Elvis, and Sam, their mouths dropping open, shared a collective sigh of relief. Then, excited to see inside, they all rushed into the warehouse.

But once inside, a sense of dread settled over them—for there wasn't a single screw or a stitch of stuffing, no batteries or ball bearings, not even a dash of denim for a dolly's dress. In fact, there wasn't a single *anything* that could be used to build any part of any toy. The only two things that remained in the cavernous room were a bunch of empty binders, each labeled with the name of a specific toy, and a large mound of ash, presumably the remains of what had once been inside those binders.

"Holy shit," Elvis muttered. "The crazy old coot torched the village on his way out. He must have been gunning for some serious revenge, because this might be the most epic f-you of all time!"

"So what do we do, Elvis?" Frenchy asked, dizzied by the bait and switch. "Like, there's gotta be a plan B, right?"

Elvis, still floored by the utter *hatred* that must have

consumed the Admiral, could only shake his head. "No, to be honest, I don't have one," he said quietly.

Both boys shifted into the exact same pose, like that of a kid watching his balloon unexpectedly drifting away, their hands on their heads, their mouths agape.

Standing there like that, envisioning their dreams slipping away, Elvis couldn't help but notice what was going on out across the factory floor: every single one of the assembled Scandies was busily consumed with nothing but the simplest of toys.

"Look at them," Elvis said ruefully, the weight of regret for his behavior over the last two days now falling fully upon him. "Amused by a toy straight out of the Middle Ages!"

Frenchy's ears perked up. "Hey, Sam," he called out excitedly. "Can you guys build your Hole In Ones without an instruction manual?"

Sam laughed. "Of course! It's those pretentious Polies that introduced the instruction binders. Our people have always made toys the old-school way: We just hold up the last one we made and make it again. Having made thousands of Hole In Ones, a few more will be no problem."

Frenchy smiled. "Another species that doesn't like those Polie guys! So what about materials? Would you have everything you'd need to build them?"

"Well, they're mostly wood, which we have more of around the river valley than you can shake a stick at. And, of course, the most important part." Sam pointed over to an enormous spool of string, towering up over the factory floor. "Stretchy string," he proudly proclaimed. "I found a perfect batch of it a few years ago, so I bought the entire thing. Strong enough to take a good stretching, but bouncy enough to snap the wood chunk back as fast as lightning."

Frenchy, his mind racing, turned to Elvis. "Do all the toys for Goetta Day need to exactly match Flats' list? Or can we substitute different ones?"

"What, so you're in the toy business all of a sudden?" Elvis cracked.

Frenchy chested up to Elvis and calmly put his hand on his shoulder, the whites of his eyes on full display. "I'm in the business of getting our asses out of this mess. Now, answer my goddamn question!"

Elvis nodded, seeing that Frenchy was in no mood for anything but a straight answer. "Well, for Christmas, the list has to be kept pristine. If a kid asks for something, they get exactly that. But for a crappy local holiday like Goetta Day, there's no quality control. One of Santa's flunkies will come down, do a quick count, then take back off with whatever we give him. Hell, he'll probably just toss the toys out of his sleigh as he flies over the kids' houses. So I guess we can pretty much make whatever we want to make."

"And what about if a kid gets all pissed off for not getting what they asked for and they rat us out?" Frenchy asked.

Elvis laughed. "Dude, this is the North Pole we're talking about. They don't even have phones up there, so it's not like there's a complaint line!"

Frenchy paused, weighing what Flats' reaction might be when she found out that they had basically gamed the system. But that concern quickly got nudged aside by another: their failure would put her in harm's way just the same as for him and Elvis. So, what else could he do? He decided they would go for it.

"Well, in that case, Elvis, let me introduce you to the world's greatest toy inventor and the savior of Goetta Day 1978: Scandie Sam!"

"May I?" Frenchy asked, reaching out to grab Sam's Hole In One.

Frenchy steadied the wood chunk on the paddle, then thrust it upward with a quick, abrupt flick of his wrist. The chunk shot up, reaching the full extent of the stretchy string in a flash, then boomeranged and shot right back down, landing squarely in the hole.

A big celebratory whoop went up from across the factory floor.

Sam, smiling broadly and shaking his head, couldn't believe it. He had truly thought the feat to be impossible. "To twist a little phrase from the final chapter of the Prophecy: *as though by magic,*" he said with a knowing wink.

Frenchy excitedly turned back to Elvis. "So, one thousand Hole In Ones. That would officially count as us reaching our goal, right?"

Elvis shrugged. "A toy's a freakin' toy. So, it sure as hell sounds like it to me!"

Then one more time back to Sam: "And Sam, are you and your crew good with this?"

"Oh Special One... Sorry—Frenchy. For you, it would be an honor," he replied.

Frenchy nodded, sensing the confidence radiating off Sam. For the first time, he could see a pathway to the goal line. It was about time.

Elvis, suddenly keenly aware that there was a good bit of work to be done, ham-handedly attempted to get the Scandies moving. "Alright, guys, enough yacking. Let's get to work. One thousand paddle things it is!"

And not a single Scandie moved a muscle.

Frenchy shook his head, amused by Elvis' lack of rapport with the Scandies. "Dude, watch how it's done."

He turned out toward the factory floor. "Guys, first of all, thank you," he said, raising his voice for all to hear. "This really means a lot to me! And please understand that just by trying, you've already earned a special spot in my heart!"

The Scandies let out a crazy roar. Then, filling with a frenzied, almost manic energy, they began to move about like hyper little toy-making machines, albeit more than a bit out of control.

Frenchy and Elvis watched the chaos for a few minutes, with the Scandies looking like they were conducting a blindfolded, boozy fire drill in the dark.

"Frenchy, I have an idea," Elvis offered, having sized up the situation. "I'll get them organized, and, since they clearly respond to you, how about you keep them all revved up? It's going to be hard for them to keep up their crazy pace for the next forty hours, but that's what we're going to need in order for us to make it!"

"You got it, man!" Frenchy replied.

The boys slapped five and then went about their jobs.

In fact, they both got into the same frenzied trance as the Scandies over the next thirty-nineish hours, with Elvis keeping the ship heading in the right direction and Frenchy keeping its crew pumped up. Not once even looking up to check on their progress, they simply kept their heads down and worked, trusting that the other guy was doing the exact same thing. In the end, they would have to count on each other.

Time had flown by, and now, less than an hour before the midnight deadline, an incredible number of Hole In Ones had been amassed, their golden brown hue coloring the factory floor, and their earthen, woody aroma filling its air. It was quite clear that this unique item was currently the only thing this particular toy factory was in the business of cranking out.

Amongst this world of wood and stretchy string, Flats returned, strutting directly out onto the factory floor.

"Hmm. Looks to be a big old bunch of the exact same thing. Odd, and certainly not reflective of the list that I recall dropping off," she said to the first Scandie she encountered. "Just what on earth have these boys been up to?"

She walked over to the holding pen, a huge wooden cube containing all the completed Hole In Ones that had not yet been wrapped, and picked one up. Taking her time, she carefully examined it.

Frenchy and Elvis, far across the factory floor, were closely studying her reaction. Subconsciously, they had both partially ducked behind a thick support column, not exactly hiding but not exactly rushing to be seen, either.

They watched as Flats' eyes first gauged the enormity of the holding pen and then as they scanned down the assembly line, brimming with hundreds of the exact same toy. Suddenly, those same eyes were fixed fully upon their own. Feeling the intensity of the gaze, both boys instinctively ducked all the way behind the column, then quickly popped back out, realizing that it probably wasn't a very good look.

Sensing that some serious toy-making monkey-business had gone down, Flats' eyes widened and sparked to life, the little flames within them glowing brightly, visible all the way across the factory floor.

"Oh shit," both boys muttered at the exact same time.

CHAPTER NINETEEN
The Confession

Her anger stoked, Flats bent her knees, then powerfully sprang forward. Thrusting out her wings, she soared parallel to the factory floor at a tremendous speed, a flash later dropping down toe to toe with Elvis.

"You conniving little con man!" she screamed into Elvis' face, one of the harsher phrases to ever grace Flats' lips. "Please tell me that you knuckleheads didn't just make the exact same toy for every kid in Loveland!" she barked, half talking and half shouting. "Or, assuming my eyes aren't lying to me and you actually *did* do such an asinine thing, then tell me that it's 100 percent legit and that it isn't going to cause our fragile little scheme to come crashing down!"

"Look, we had no choice. And just so you know, it was both of our ideas," Elvis blurted out, thinking that if he reined Frenchy in as a co-conspirator, Flats might soften to their approach.

"We got thrown curveball after curveball!" he went on. "Starting with a locked material storage warehouse, which cost us a bunch of time and then turned out to be totally empty. With no supplies to work with, we wracked our brains until French Fry came up with this loophole. We jumped right through it, and, as far as I know, yeah, it's totally cool!"

Elvis eyed Flats, assessing if he should say what he was considering saying next. "Plus, nobody will ever know."

He probably should have kept that last part to himself.

"Damn it, Elvis!" Flats belted out. "You don't make choices based on whether or not you think you'll get caught! So let me ask you, Mr. Toy-making Hotshot, how long did you spend mulling over other solutions after you discovered that the warehouse was empty?"

Elvis didn't see the trap being set for him. "Oh, as soon as we saw that we had a problem on our hands, we shifted gears," he boasted. "Frenchy came up with his idea within just a few minutes, and we've all worked around the clock since then."

"I see," Flats said. "So let me make sure I'm clear on your timeline. I'd imagine that getting into the warehouse was your highest priority, which means that you would have done it right away, like at the crack of dawn on the very first morning. Did I get that right?" She paused, closely studying Elvis' eyes, which started to dart about the factory like ping-pong balls.

He nodded yes, sort of, as though his brain was trying to move forward with the line of baloney but his body didn't want to have anything to do with it.

"And then you discovered it was empty, and you immediately shifted to Frenchy's plan," Flats continued. "And since then, everyone has worked nonstop on the same toy for four straight days. So is that the whole story, or is there anything you'd like to change? Because eventually I'm going to ask every single one of those rats for *their* version of the story. And remember, their kind doesn't exactly have a reputation for going down with the ship."

Elvis, now wedged between a lie and a full-blown confession, looked down to the floor. "I'm not exactly sure when we first went in there, but it wasn't too long after you left," he mumbled in reply—which, while maybe not *technically* a lie, was still a good ways from the truth.

Flats' eyes shot over to Frenchy, searching for affirmation, but she wasn't going to find it there, as his eyes were now glued to the floor as well. It was his turn to be squeezed between two bad options, not wanting to mislead Flats in any way, but also not wanting to potentially place Elvis' throat in grave danger.

So Frenchy tried to wait it out, his eyes not coming up for what seemed like an eternity. And there they stood, with Flats silently staring at what looked like two naughty schoolchildren, their breathing, and a nearby clock ticking off the seconds, providing the only sound.

Finally, sensing Flats' gaze on the top of his head and not liking how it made him feel, something bubbled up inside Frenchy. It was time to get all the cards out on the table.

Channeling his best inner Elvis, he let it rip. "Sometimes you just gotta freakin' do what you gotta freakin' do!"

Frenchy and Flats locked eyes, both taken aback by the comment.

"You weren't here," Frenchy continued, much more measuredly. "We were. And nothing was working. So Elvis and I had to do the best we could and fight through it together as one. Just like you said we should."

Frenchy's body language was a curious mixture of vulnerability and resolve, his damaged hand tucked into his vest as far as it would go, his back arched, and his head held high.

His stance melted all the anger right out of Flats. "Okay," she said softly. "Just for the record, I know something fishy went down here. But I don't know what exactly, and I don't want to waste what precious time we have left trying to figure it out. So let's just keep on going and make sure we finish on time. But Elvis, I'm telling you loud and clear, if you lied to me and I find out before you cop to it, you're going to wish you hadn't!"

Elvis had one thought and one thought only: to get the hell out of there before he had to answer any more questions. "Alrighty then. Yep, like Flats said, let's just keep moving forward, full speed ahead."

He slapped five with Frenchy, and they exchanged a knowing look. Then Elvis darted off, making a quick getaway.

Frenchy fanned out as well, resuming his role as all-around Scandie morale booster. As he roamed down the assembly line providing encouragement, he couldn't help but be impressed by the organizational expertise Elvis had brought to the team. Every sequence of the work was flowing seamlessly, with a series of simple, distinct tasks taken on by the various groups of Scandies. Once each task was completed, the work product would be passed on up the line, stretching from the lumberyard all the way through to the holding pen. Starting with the wood wranglers, who artfully honed thick logs down into thin sheets and little square blocks, then on to the paddle shapers, and finally over to the stretchy string staplers, everything moved like a well-oiled machine. It was quite an impressive feat, from tree to toy in no time at all.

The last hour went by even more quickly than the previous thirty-nine had. Now, just a few minutes before the North Pole driver's midnight arrival, Frenchy, Flats, and

Elvis reconvened on the factory floor, eagerly watching the Scandies wrap the last couple of gifts. With a flourish, Sam proudly tossed the last Hole In One into the Exit Bin, letting out a little whoop as he watched it settle down in.

"Number one thousand!" he exclaimed triumphantly, and the entire factory erupted in a crazy, high-pitched cheer.

Sensing that a party was about to break out, Frenchy set off out of the castle, venturing deep into the Black Forest. Nearing the Festhaus, he blasted his airhorn four times, and moments later the Commandant appeared, smiling.

"Sir Commandant, might you be able to spare three bottles of ale?" Frenchy asked as he held an imaginary bottle to his mouth and mimed taking a slug from it.

The Commandant laughed. "But of course, mein friend."

A brief moment later, celebratory ale in hand, Frenchy turned and headed back to the castle.

Upon returning, Frenchy found Flats up in the Control Room. He set the ale in the fridge, and then, noticing that she was studying a flat, black disc, he walked over to join her.

Holding the disk out, she read from the label. "'Stumblin' In.' Oh my gosh, I totally love that song. We could pick up something called Armed Forces Radio up at the Pole, and it just cracked their Top Ten. Have you heard it?"

"Heard it?" Frenchy said, laughing. "For the entire twelve or so hours I shared the castle with the Admiral, he played it on continual repeat at full volume! Believe me, that song is never leaving my brain!"

Flats motioned to what appeared to be some sort of music machine that made the discs come to life. "Do you know how this thing works?"

"I think so," Frenchy replied. "I saw it in action the morning the Admiral left. You put a stack of those discs onto the little metal pin that's sticking up, then you slide that lever on the side forward. Somehow, the platter at the bottom will start spinning, the first disc will drop down, an arm will slide over on top of it, and the music will start to play. It's really pretty cool."

Flats did just as Frenchy had spelled out, opting for the first song to be by someone named Elvis Presley, a nod to their fellow Ruffian. And, sure enough, a jangly mashup of guitars, piano, drums, and vocals soon kicked in, filling the Control Room with a sound unlike anything either of them had ever heard before.

They looked at each other, smiling and bopping their heads.

"That sounds so freakin' awesome!" Frenchy said.

"It really does!" Flats agreed cheerfully. Then her demeanor abruptly shifted, as though a difficult thought had suddenly popped back into her head. "Frenchy, please, will you level with me about what happened here when I was gone? I mean, something just doesn't…"

She stopped at the sound of Elvis walking into the room, deliberately clearing his throat to get the others' attention. He didn't seem like his usual self. It was as though someone had adjusted his dials to the wrong speed, like he was a 45 RPM record playing at 33.

"I've got something to say to you guys. I held it inside until I was sure we reached our goal, but it's eating my guts up, so I gotta get it out." His words were way softer than usual and not tinted with their usual bravado. "And you both gotta promise to not get mad at me."

Frenchy and Flats, very much wondering what he was going to say, both nodded.

"Of course, dude," Frenchy said.

"Um, Flats, first of all, I lied to you earlier. Or at least I wasn't truthful. Because, for the first two days after you left, I was a selfish jackass, and I wasn't around to help Frenchy. In fact, I was totally worthless. It's just that I mess up sometimes and fall a bit too deeply into the elixir," Elvis said, haltingly. Then he began to tear up.

Frenchy watched him, not believing that this was the same kid who, until now, hadn't seemed to be afraid of anything.

"No, wait a minute. That's bullshit!" Elvis continued, summoning his strength. "To be honest, way too often, I fall fully into it. All the way in over my head. I caught it from my mom, I think. And the last two days I realized, it's one thing when I hurt myself—I mean, nobody's ever really given a shit about that. But I can't stand the thought that I did something that could've hurt you guys. So I can promise you this, it won't happen again, and until midnight on Christmas Eve, I'll stay away from the stuff. And, um, I'm really sorry for letting you both down."

With his head slumped and his body shaking, Elvis looked like a lost little boy.

Flats rushed over to hug him, wrapping the soft inner parts of her arms around Elvis' back. Frenchy followed suit, throwing his webbed hands around the two of them and squeezing tightly. They held on like that for several long seconds, a knowing warmth pulsating between the three of them, with each of them feeling like nothing else needed to be said. The healing power of forgiveness had spoken loudly and clearly, and also quite beautifully.

Then the mood in the room shifted abruptly once again, this time spurred on by upbeat sounds now coming out of the music machine, as "Stumblin' In" had come to life.

Turning to face one another, Frenchy and Flats began to rhythmically bounce about, instinctively moving in the way that the music compelled them to move. With both of them knowing every word by heart, they began to take turns mouthing the lyrics, pointing at one another and hamming it up more and more as the song picked up steam.

Drawing close, they leaned in to a pretend microphone and mouthed a verse as one, as though they were rock stars performing their famous duet together.

Laughing, they collapsed into each other's arms, their faces touching, almost fully stumbling onto the floor.

Elvis watched the couple smiling and looking into each other's eyes, and, out of nowhere, a huge bolt of envy flashed through him. Two kids frozen in their moment, *they just looked so happy*.

"Christ, I gotta meet a chick!" he blurted out.

The statement hung awkwardly in the air, bringing the couple's embrace to a halt, as Frenchy and Flats were once again drawn to hear whatever was going to come out of Elvis' mouth next.

He didn't disappoint. "I mean, I'm almost sixteen freakin' years old, and I've only seen two human females in the flesh. One was my mom, which definitely doesn't count, and the other was Mrs. Claus, and she's like a hundred and twenty years old. So, like, ewww, that doesn't count either."

Frenchy's and Flats' eyes grew as big as saucers.

"Seen… in the flesh?" Frenchy said. "Dude, you mean, like, you saw them *naked?!*"

Elvis covered his eyes with his hands. "Oh, my god! What's wrong with you?" he asked, astonished. "Don't be disgusting! I mean 'seen' as in they were in the same room as me, fully clothed, and I saw them! My point being, there ain't any accessible human hotties up at the Pole. All that's up there are Polie chicks, and every one of them is an ice queen, and Clauses, who are entirely off-limits to those of us from across the tracks. But there's gotta be a ton of human girls around here. I can just feel it. And I want to try and meet the cutest, blondest one I can. No, scratch that, I just *have* to meet her."

Frenchy and Flats were listening to what Elvis was saying, but they didn't know what he expected them to do about it, for they definitely didn't intend to go out looking for humans.

"Sorry, man, but I think you might have to fly solo on this one," Frenchy replied. "I'm not risking tangling with those monsters again. They don't seem very, um, *tolerant* of my uniqueness, and it doesn't sound like they are for Flats' type, either."

Elvis smiled. "Well, I thought about that. There's one night of the year where you guys won't look any different from the humans. Because on this particular night—Halloween night— *everybody* looks different. You two will blend right in, and I can go as my own princely self, looking for a damsel in distress. All we gotta do is figure out where they'll be and how to get there. So, what do you say? You guys in?"

Frenchy and Flats looked at each other. Deep down, they were both quite curious to be out amongst the humans, a part of them wanting to believe that there was some good to be found in them, or at least in some of them. So they both nodded, tentatively electing to take the plunge.

"If we can figure out how to keep everyone safe, we're in," Frenchy said.

"Goodness, gracious, great balls of fire!" Elvis exclaimed,

clapping his hands together. "Oh Cupid, winged messenger of the heavens, get your sweet ass down here and dial me up some curves!"

Frenchy and Flats laughed, reveling in Elvis' ability to twist a phrase. He definitely proved to be a most difficult guy to stay mad at.

Chapter Twenty
The Dance

With the Ruffians still up in the Control Room, the clock inched toward midnight. Looking out into the courtyard, Elvis caught a glimpse of a large sleigh approaching in the distance, just about to clear the compound's walls.

"Yo, guys, gotta jump out for a minute and make sure they get everything loaded up. Carry on, and don't do anything I wouldn't do," he said, laughing as he shot out through the Control Room's door.

The mood of the room changed again the instant Elvis left.

Frenchy, seizing the moment, reached into his back pocket and pulled out his folded-up drawing of Flats and himself. He looked it over for a second, then handed it to her.

"Here, I drew this for you. I think it says things better than I can with words. It's crazy how fitting it is after what Elvis just brought up about the Halloween party."

Flats studied the drawing. "Oh my goodness, me and you? That's so sweet, Frenchy! And who are these guys?" she asked, pointing to a few shadowy figures standing nearby the pair as they danced.

"Those are the humans, but good ones, free of hate. We have no fear of them nor they of us. I really think Elvis might be onto something with the Halloween idea. I mean, how crazy would that be, us not being considered different because everyone else is pretending to be?!"

Flats smiled, then drew the drawing to her lips, leaving a subtle lipstick imprint on the page. Then she carefully folded it back up and slipped it into her pocket. "Frenchy, this means the world to me. I'm going to keep it in the most special of places."

Flats moved toward him, and at the same moment a new record dropped onto the turntable, this one a slow, beautiful ballad. It longingly told of giving hope when there was none to be found and providing a path to safety when trouble raged. Frenchy and Flats instinctively drew together, and, unlike their previous fast dance, this time they intertwined tightly like licorice pieces, without the slightest hint of space between them. They rocked like that for a long, wonderful moment, a time during which nothing else in the world mattered except the two of them and their enchanted embrace.

Meanwhile, down on the factory floor, the Scandies were counting down the last ticks leading up to midnight. With a few left to go, Elvis gave the thumbs-up signal to the sleigh driver, who steadied the reindeer's reins, ready to get them back on their way. But just before he whipped his team good and hard for liftoff, something drew the driver's attention up to the Control Room, and he caught a clear-eyed view of Frenchy and Flats locked in their magical moment.

Then, with a quick flip of his wrist, the sleigh lurched forward, off to deliver its goods.

Back in the Control Room, the licorice dance continued,

and Frenchy wished that he could forever freeze time precisely in that moment. That is, until his thoughts turned to kissing Flats, something he suddenly realized could quite possibly happen at any moment. But how, he wondered, did one initiate such a mysterious undertaking?

His thoughts distracted, Frenchy ever so softly stepped on Flats' toe, bringing a sweet smile to her face and causing her head to lift just a little. With her lips just inches from his own, he leaned forward, readying to touch them together.

But he didn't. Instead, he paused, and his mind began tumbling awkwardly, like a load of laundry bouncing around in the dryer. The questions charged into his head at lightning speed, uninvited: What if he didn't kiss her right? A reasonable concern, since he had never kissed a girl before. And what if Flats didn't even want him to kiss her? Then he'd come off like a total creep. And what if...?

The pause had broken their magical spell, and a new disc, this one snappy and fast, dropped onto the turntable. Flats pulled back, reaching down and grabbing both of Frenchy's hands, and she smiled, though it was now tinted with the tiniest hint of regret. Then, leaning in, she laid upon Frenchy the aspiring suitor's kiss of death: the ever-dreaded friendly peck on the cheek.

"When the time is right, we'll both know it," she whispered. Then Flats started to fast dance once again, her lips now a million miles away.

Frenchy sighed, knowing he'd reasoned away something about which he'd been absolutely certain. An opportunity lost, he could now only hope that it wouldn't be his last.

CHAPTER TWENTY-ONE
A Fatal Attraction

October 30, 1978 - North Pole

Within an ornately furnished boardroom, twelve green-shirted Polies, a bratty crew that included Spiro, sat slouched around a long table, each of them giving off a vibe that they weren't at all happy to be there.

At the table's head, Sir Nick Claus, a rotund twenty-one-year-old human, keenly felt his audience's disinterest. As first in line to the House of Claus throne, he was a heartbeat away from becoming just the eighteenth Santa Claus in history, a position that brought with it a level of worshipful reverence from most of the world. But to these Polies he knew it didn't mean a damn thing, as they harbored a deep disdain for all things Claus.

And, being a Claus, he held the exact same disdain for the Polies.

Same as it ever was.

Sir Nick

But regardless of the bad blood, they also remained fully intertwined with one another, forced to navigate through the unique division of responsibilities that the currently reigning Santa had put in place some three decades ago. It was a simple, non-negotiable bargain: the Polies made the toys, and the leader of the Clauses delivered them. That the Polies toiled three hundred and sixty-four days a year more than any Santa ever had and, in return, received none of the worldwide love and adulation forever heaped upon the Claus leader—well, that was an issue for another day. This day was about one thing only: making sure that the toys would be ready, every single one of them, right on time.

"So, gentlemen, shall we begin?" said Sir Nick. "I know that none of you want to be here any longer than I do, so at least we share that in common this morning. And as a little bribe to keep the discourse flowing quickly, once the proceedings conclude, you can welcome yourselves to the spread of cookies in the back of the room."

Every eye in the room shot around to the massive mound of cookies amassed behind them.

"So, we gather once again for our annual conference of Territorial Observers," Sir Nick continued. "As in the past, my primary interest is in making sure you guys are on target to meet your Christmas Eve quotas. Wouldn't want my father to be left empty-handed, now would we?" He threw his head back and let rip the Claus' signature laugh, loud enough to rattle the walls.

"Ho! Ho! Ho!"

Not a single Polie so much as cracked a smile.

With Sir Nick's eyes pointed upward, Spiro saw his opportunity. Launching a paper airplane toward the front of the room, it flew looping through the air, up until its pointy tip crash-landed right into Sir Nick's bulbous belly.

The Polies certainly found *this* amusing, with each breaking out into uproarious laughter.

Sir Nick's laughter came to an abrupt halt. He bent down and snatched up the plane, angrily crumbling it up into a little ball. "Spoiled little twits," he muttered under his breath.

He went over and slammed the crumpled-up plane into the wastebasket. "Fine, down to business it is. We'll get into the individual Territories and where you guys stand on your quotas in a minute. But first, I need updates on a couple lingering issues. Bartholomew, I received word that a potential uprising was sparking in France. Is there anything to be concerned about down there?"

Bartholomew, a slight elf with perfectly parted blond hair,

was slouched low in his seat, his mind elsewhere. He casually glanced down at a notepad for several long seconds, deliberately positioning it just so on the table. "Nope," he eventually replied, before letting out an obnoxious, wide-mouthed yawn.

Sir Nick walked around the table, coming up behind the boy and bending over so that his mouth was right behind his ear. "Elaborate!" he barked suddenly. Outweighing the elf by a good four to one, he used his physicality to his advantage, making it abundantly clear that he wasn't at all pleased with the response.

Bartholomew jumped up in his seat. Apparently having gotten the message, his posture straightened, and his cadence quickened. "Well, the French Administrator had threatened a strike, demanding a new castle. Evidently twenty-five guest quarters weren't enough for him, so I replaced him with an Administrator who found the accommodations quite suitable." Bartholomew's eyes then went back down to his notepad, as though that was that.

Sir Nick threw his hands out to his sides. "Damn it, boy, go on! Tell me how it went down!"

"Christ! What, are you writing a book? I transferred the original troublemaker to the most god-awful place on earth, a frozen Russian Territory called Siberia. Then I hung a photograph of that desolate wasteland in the French castle for the new guy to stare at when he arrived, and wouldn't you know it, I never heard a single peep of discord out of him."

Sir Nick shook his head. "You guys certainly have a unique way of dealing with your personnel," he said, laughing derisively. "Jam your heavy-handed ways down their throats until they either digest them or choke to death. So, skipping over to the Americas, Spiro, what's going on in New England? Are there still difficulties there?"

Spiro, as equally disengaged as Bartholomew, was busy doodling, and he offered his reply without even bothering to look up. "Don't know what business it is of yours."

Sir Nick now cut a quick path over to the back of Spiro's chair. "You need to remember your place, boy. But if you've forgotten just what that place is, I'd be happy to have my father provide a reminder. And as to what is or isn't my business, my family has been spreading joy to every corner of this globe for centuries. So I consider everything on it as my business. Now, I suggest you get busy answering whatever it is that I ask of you, and be quick about it!" Sir Nick snapped, his tone foretelling that his patience was wearing thin.

Spiro allowed the words to hang in the air for a good, long while, letting it be known that he wasn't going to roll over for Sir Nick. "Ohhhkaaaayy," he said finally. "Yes, sir, busy I shall be, just like a good little eager beaver. New England—the land of loudmouths unable to properly pronounce their r's—those louts have been bitching about something or other since your daddy first imposed the Territorial structure back in 1946. Yap, yap, yap. I finally grew tired of it, so I had the one with the biggest mouth tarred and feathered. You know, it sure seemed to do the trick, as I haven't heard a peep from any of the others."

Sir Nick winced, and he stared disapprovingly at Spiro for several seconds, shaking his head. "Why does it always come down to violence with you?" he asked, rhetorically. "For crying out loud, those people are on your team, and yet you insist on treating them as indentured servants. But, goodness me, I dare not meddle in the methods of the vaunted Polie toy-making dynasty, lest your leaders get their undergarments in a bunch."

He shook his head in disgust, then took a deep breath, biting his tongue to keep from saying more. Walking back to the head of the table, he ruffled through his paperwork, coming to a note that Santa had slipped him earlier that morning: "*Be certain to inquire about Ohio.*"

"Oh, yes," Sir Nick said aloud. "So, Spiro, what's going on in Ohio?"

Spiro stopped doodling, his eyes darting straight over to Sir Nick. "What of it?" he shot back tersely.

Sir Nick knew right away that he had hit a nerve. "Well, we're all aware of its unique, shall we say, leadership situation. So how have the recent measures we've taken been received?"

"And by measures, are you referring to the mess that you and your father threw in our lap without so much as asking? It's going great, I guess, if you consider having a fifteen-year-old hotheaded drunk in charge to be a wise course of action. Amazingly, he somehow managed to successfully complete a trial run of one thousand units the other day. But it goes without saying that Christmas will be another ballgame entirely, ramping up the load to over a million units, just a tidy little thousandfold increase. So let the chips fall where they may, and hopefully you and the Fat Man will be happy sleeping in the bed that you made!"

Sir Nick's face reddening, he swept his arm across the table in front of him, sending a cloud of papers flying up into the air. "Damn it!" he bellowed, his voice booming. "You know, I let a lot of crap slide with you Polies, but I will not stand idly by and let you disrespect a sitting Santa. He shall be addressed as

THE FROGMAN OF LOVELAND

Santa Claus or, if you feel a little extra respectful, Saint Nicolas. And, just to be clear, I'm not asking you, son, I'm telling you!"

Sir Nick and Spiro stared at each other for several long, tense seconds, with neither of them blinking.

Eventually, a sly smile crossed Sir Nick's face. "And what of the Frogman?" he asked jauntily.

Recognizing now that he was being baited, Spiro's posture stiffened, and he grabbed the edge of the table with both hands, trying his best to not let Sir Nick know he was getting to him.

"I'm not really sure what to say about it," Spiro began. "From what I can gather, it's still there, since the winged girl didn't bring back word that it'd fled. Well, at least not that I heard. But know this: if that beast causes even a moment's disruption to our operation, I will make sure it doesn't see the dawn of another day!"

Sir Nick responded in an instant. "And I shall once again remind you that you're to give all those there a very wide berth, and those words come directly from my father himself. Your business there begins and ends with your quota, and you shall let all other matters be!"

"Oh, goodness, believe you me, the esteemed Saint Nicolas the Seventeenth has made his point very clear to me on the matter," Spiro replied, wringing his hands red under the table.

Sensing he was on the verge of a full-blown Spiro meltdown, Sir Nick couldn't resist throwing one more log onto the fire. "And speaking of the, ehem, winged girl, as you say, how is Flats doing?"

Spiro slammed his fist on the table, sending shockwaves through the room. "How the hell am I to know!" he shouted. "With thousands under my command, am I to keep a watchful eye over every last one of them, even down to a common runner?"

Sir Nick had experienced Spiro's temper several times throughout the years, but this was different, far more combustible and urgent than ever before. "You know, lad, instead of allowing your emotions to rule your actions, you'd be better served letting your brain cells call the shots. After all, it is still upon you to make sure every Territory delivers in seven weeks, including this one. Frankly, if it were me, I'd be giving serious consideration as to whether an observational visit to Ohio would be in order, to gauge if their trial run success was the real deal or but a fluke."

"Go all that way just to babysit the Claus' pets? Ain't happening!" Spiro shot back.

Sir Nick threw his head back and groaned. "This isn't about them! Or you! It's strictly about you doing your job and making sure they're in the best possible position to meet their quota. But however you decide to handle it, I want to make one thing abundantly clear: the expectation of results—*of your results*—remains unwavering!"

Now fully worked up, Sir Nick headed toward the room's exit, needing to distance himself from Spiro and his first-class pigheadedness. "C'est la vie, the wise man lets it be," he said. "Now, if you gentlemen would excuse me for a moment, I shall be off to clear my head of some recently accumulated gunk. In my absence, please gorge yourselves on some sugar. Maybe it will sweeten a few of you up a bit."

He exited, and the Polies descended like locusts upon the spread of cookies.

Spiro made a dash over to the cookies himself, grabbing up a handful. As he turned to escape with his haul, Bartholomew

THE FROGMAN OF LOVELAND

ran up to him, barely able to contain his excitement. "Dude, what's going on with your girlfriend?"

Spiro put his hands up. "Hang on! If you're referring to Flats, it's ex-girlfriend, and I'm not even sure that's an accurate description, since I was never really that into her. But anyway, what the hell are you talking about?"

Clearly relishing the opportunity to smack Spiro across the face with some juicy gossip, Bartholomew laid it on thick. "Word on the street is that one of Santa's drivers caught a good look at Flats and the Frogman. He said they were practically doing it, with his hands on her ass and her tongue down his throat!"

Anger and panic pulsing through his veins, Spiro tossed his cookies onto the floor and frantically took off out of the room. Running down the hallway at full speed, he barged into the bathroom, coming up right behind Sir Nick as he stood at a urinal. Panting, he spoke to what could delicately be described as Sir Nick's lower back.

"Sorry to disturb you, but I gave it a second thought. I'm going to make a run down to Ohio, you know, just to make sure that everybody's doing what they're supposed to be doing."

Sensing the urgency in Spiro's voice, and given the fact that the matter had suddenly risen to such importance that it had to be addressed *here,* Sir Nick once more offered guidance. "Very well. But hear me again: tread most softly in this matter."

"Oh, yes, of course, sir," Spiro replied. "I shall tread as softly as a marshmallow…"

He then turned and walked out of the bathroom, finishing his sentence as the door closed behind him: "… right before it burns!"

CHAPTER TWENTY-TWO
Fully Amongst the Humans

October 31, 1978 - Back in Loveland

On a cold, damp Halloween evening, Frenchy, Flats, and Elvis stood at the courtyard gates, fidgeting uncomfortably. They were joined by two Wurstie guards, both of whom seemed to relish staring down Elvis, with one of them occasionally pounding his fist into his opposite palm.

"Are you sure this taxi guy is legit, Frenchy?" Flats asked, breaking the silence. "And how'd you even find out about him—or this dance, for that matter?"

Frenchy smiled proudly. "*Loveland After Dark*! It's the greatest newspaper ever. The Admiral had a stack of them in his room right next to his girlie magazines, and they ran a story a couple issues ago about the big Halloween dance. They also have ads in the back for all sorts of cool stuff, like the indoor plant-growing lamp I ordered the other day. So the guy that's driving us, he advertises that he'll get you all around town, anywhere, for five bucks. Here, check it out."

Frenchy fished a newspaper clipping from his pocket and unfolded it for the others to see.

Flats' and Elvis' jaws dropped when they looked at the ad, which featured a wild-eyed cab driver clutching fistfuls of dollar bills. He was surrounded by four scantily clad women also flush with cash, with theirs held in place by their bikini straps.

Equally eye-catching was the tagline: "*Five bucks to and fro. Your old lady will never know!*"

Elvis' eyes widened. "Holy shit! Rolling in style with the town nudie bar wrangler! I hope you brought along some singles, French Fry!" he said, laughing.

Just then, a car horn sounded on the other side of the gate.

"Let's go," declared Frenchy.

One to a door, the Wursties pulled the gates open, and the Ruffians were off on their adventure.

A yellow-checkered cab with no license plates sat idling just outside the compound's wall. As Frenchy yanked the back door open, the loud wail of a saxophone hit him, vibrating up his arm and throughout the rest of his body. The crew traded concerned looks, and then they collectively made the leap, piling into the backseat.

The driver turned around, and disconcertingly, his eyes remained fully hidden behind his sunglasses, which were tinted so darkly that they actually appeared to be painted black. A waterfall of hair flopped down in front of his face, further impeding his view, and additional bushes of hair burst out every which way, making it look like the man had a full-on mop resting atop his head.

Joe Le Taxi

The entire taxi bounced to the beat of brass instruments and rhythmic drums, the words sung in a language that none of them understood, but one that sounded quite cool, as though the voices were simply another musical instrument joining in on the mix.

But the most interesting thing about the taxi was how it smelled, like spices from a faraway, mysterious place.

Frenchy spoke up as loudly as he could, shouted, actually, and asked a question that probably didn't really need asking. "So, are you Joe Le Taxi?!"

"Whoa, lordy, lordy, would ya get a load of that! The jivest turkey in town just flew right into my taxi! Boy, how many flippin' freebirdin' cabbies you see trollin' round down here in Fantasyland, chauffeuring about the likes of you crazy-assed costumed cats? Now, before any more nonsense comes outta your mouth, you best toss me up some cabbage!"

Cabbage-less, Frenchy instead offered all that he had brought. "So, Mr. Le Taxi, we don't have any money. Or cabbage. But would you take four bottles of ale instead?"

"Well, dude, depends on where you little trick-or-treating perverts are going."

"Um, Loveland High School, sir," replied Frenchy.

Joe pondered the bargain, setting his head about to bobbing. "Joe thinks it's a fair trade, man. Yeah, perfectly righteous, actually. But dudes, ten minutes inside, tops—just enough time to score whatever it is you're scoring or wet whatever whistles you're lookin' to be wetting. A second longer and I promise you, I'm ditchin' your freaky asses. Now, fork over that bubbly!"

Puzzled, Frenchy froze for a second and glanced over at Flats. Fortunately, she was able to translate Joe's pirate-like patois, motioning for Frenchy to hand up the ale.

Joe immediately tore into the first bottle, twisting it open and chugging its contents so quickly that they seemed to go down in one gulp and then, just as fast, doing the same with the second. He burped loudly and laughed, then popped open the third and fourth and guzzled them down in the exact same manner.

Holding an imaginary microphone to his mouth, he turned toward the backseat, flashing a crazed grin. "Ladies and gentlemen, this is your captain speaking. The fasten seat belt sign has been turned on! There's rough skies ahead!"

Joe hit the gas, and the taxi blasted off like a rocket ship, pinning Frenchy, Flats, and Elvis against the backseat. They scrambled to grab onto whatever they could find, including each other, and fumbled for seatbelts, which were nowhere to be found. Startlingly, Joe seemed to actually speed up around the bends, taking them at such breakneck clips that the kids were thrown about from side to side, strange forces pulling on them against their will. They looked at each other and bizarrely *burst out laughing*, reveling in the intoxicatingly thrilling mixture of exhilaration and terror, a life-affirming free fall that could only be enjoyed by the young, those without yet the scar tissue to know that they shouldn't.

And then, just as quickly as it had started, it was over.

Tires screeching, they pulled up to a large brick structure decorated with signs and streamers, a banner overtop heralding Loveland High's 1978 Halloween Dance. Light peeked out a propped-open door, a beacon summoning the crew to their date with the humans.

"Ticktock, ticktock. The trippy trio's on the clock!" Joe called out as the group scurried out of the cab.

As they passed through the door, the Ruffians separated, with Frenchy and Flats going off toward a bright, lively area and Elvis heading straight to where he sensed danger might be lurking.

Frenchy and Flats approached a large group of teen-age humans, seemingly separated into two distinct camps. Some of the assorted astronauts and Indians, goblins and ghouls appeared to be drifting about aimlessly under the gym's bright lights, feigning cool indifference toward members of the opposite sex. But as the couple looked out across the dance floor over to where the lights grew dimmer, they noticed a different group, those paired off and dancing closely. *Very closely*. This crew exuded no indifference whatsoever.

A voice rang out from a series of speakers up in the gym's rafters. "Alright, all you cool cats and diamond dogs, time to break out those slow-dancing shoes! We're going on a little space odyssey with none other than Mr. Ziggy Stardust, looking for 'Life on Mars.'"

A beautiful, haunting song began to play over the gym's speakers.

Frenchy and Flats started to walk across the dance floor, now fully amongst the humans, their steps apprehensive, tightly grasping onto the other's hand for courage. At that moment, the same thought crossed each of their minds: if their ruse was discovered by even a single one of the humans, there was a good chance they wouldn't escape the building alive.

And then something magical happened. The humans began to part and form a pathway, allowing the new kids a chance to display their far-out cosmic costumes all by themselves. Walking on, floating really, Flats and Frenchy couldn't believe it. The human kids were smiling warmly at them, some even clapping, not just simply accepting them as feeling beings but actually seeming to *admire* them.

They both allowed themselves a deep breath, and then they caught eyes, sharing a special, knowing glance.

Fully Amongst the Humans

A perky human girl ran up to the couple, startling them. "I've never seen you guys before. Do you go to Loveland?" she asked excitedly.

Drawing upon the two human occupations to which he'd recently been exposed, Frenchy did his best to come up with a cover story. "Um, no, we don't actually go to school. I drive people around in a yellow car all day long in exchange for cabbage, and my friend Flats here dances on a stage in her bikini and people give her singles. Hard work, but it sure beats being forced to sit around reading a bunch of boring old books," he concluded.

"Well, I just had to tell you, your makeup is so groovy! And you, your wings, oh my god, they're the coolest!" the girl gushed. "You look like you can actually fly! You guys are totally going to win the cutest couple contest!"

Frenchy and Flats smiled and thanked her, then resumed their walk through the crowd, over to where the lights dimmed. There they carved out their own little island, resuming the dance they had started a few weeks earlier. The kids surrounding them were all doing the same, a mass of bodies lumped together, every single one of them somehow oblivious to everything beyond what they held in their arms.

As Frenchy and Flats embraced, the magical spark they had experienced the last time fully returned. With their eyes locked together, Frenchy was determined to seize the moment, not about to let his brain trip him up this time. He leaned in, so close he could feel her breath on his face, and lined his lips up with hers.

Closing his eyes, he leaned forward to bridge the last little remaining gap.

And just like that, she was gone. Frenchy felt Flats slip from his embrace, and he opened his eyes to see her hovering ever so slightly off the ground, sliding a few feet away from him so subtly that no one else noticed a thing.

Frenchy threw his arms out to his sides, expressing a wide range of emotions, including concern that he had totally misread Flats' feelings. But really, he had no idea what to think.

Aware that she had sent mixed signals, Flats drew closer again, grabbing his hands and holding them softly. Then, making certain that none of the couples dancing nearby could overhear her, she brought her lips to Frenchy's ear, speaking in a whisper.

"Frenchy, you haven't left my thoughts since the very first moment we met. Now, while that's a really good thing, it's also bad, because nothing less than our survival hinges on us being successful over the next two months. Elvis' survival, too. So we have to put our mission first, and we can't complicate things right now. I'm really sorry, but we need to wait."

Wait. Having waited for what seemed like his entire life to have his empty heart filled, Frenchy didn't want to go even another second without exploring where this connection could take them. And goodness, two long months?

"That sounds like an eternity," he said. "The only thing I know is, I just want to be with you, like, all the time. And I want to start right now. To do any different seems to be letting good time go to waste!"

Flats smiled. "Far from it. Think of that time as insurance that we'll at least have a chance for a future together. And if we're really, really lucky, and we hit it off like we both think we will, then that future will turn into forever. So, please, you're just going to have to trust me on this."

Frenchy nodded and smiled softly, not at all happy with the

THE FROGMAN OF LOVELAND

verdict, but sensing that it was nonnegotiable. Flats returned to his arms and their dance continued, but all the while her head remained sideways on his shoulder, her lips far away.

Elvis, meanwhile, was on a romantic quest of his own.

A pretty girl, one with a seriously rough edge, had caught his eye. She wore high-laced black boots, their color matching her slicked-back hair, and a white T-shirt, with one of its tight sleeves nestling a little rectangular box against her bicep. With her jeans shredded just so, her cool bearing made her seem a good bit older than the other kids at the dance—as well as thoroughly and completely unapproachable.

Like a heat-seeking missile, Elvis mustered up every ounce of swagger he had, marching right up to her.

The girl's face lit up as she watched Elvis approach, digging his greaser duds. "Hey, looks like we're costume twins," she said.

The comment went right over Elvis' head, which was currently fixated on other things. "What's up, beautiful?" he said. "So, first time here?"

The girl rolled her eyes and laughed. "Yikes! That's gotta be the worst pickup line I've ever heard. But let me do my best to wade through it. So, if you're asking me if I've ever been to this building before, well, that would be a yes because, um, I go to school here. But if you're actually asking if I've been to the Halloween dance before, well, then that would be a yes too because, duh, I'm a junior. So, how about we start over: you tell me your name and then throw me out a new line—but this time, make it a good one."

"Okay, so the first part, I'm Elvis," he said. "And a new pickup line, huh? Alright, here's one sure to sweep even the choosiest of ladies right off their feet." He cleared his throat. "Your charm and world-class beauty just made a certain part of my body feel like the capital of Ireland. Because as soon as I caught sight of you, my wiener was Dublin!"

The girl cracked up. "Oh my god! That's the single worst thing I've ever heard, and I love it! So you're not just cute but funny, too. I'm Candy. Want to go to the dark side of the gym?"

Elvis had no idea what that meant, which made it sound all the better. "Hell yeah!" he blurted out.

Candy grabbed Elvis' hand and pulled him along over to the darkest corner of the room.

Here, over on the dark side of the gym, things were different. In this world, the paired-off boys and girls were attached at the lips, hanging onto one another for dear life. The mating ritual seemed to go about unnoticed until it crossed some type of imaginary line, at which point one of the adult humans would walk over and smack the boys on the backs of their necks with a yardstick, looking to cool off any overheated lovebirds.

Elvis and Candy dove into each other and quickly started dancing, but not really, as their movements resembled proper dancing only insomuch that they remained somewhat vertical. What they were really engaged in was a full-blown make-out session, complete with kissing, grinding, and hands roaming up and down the other's back.

Not long after they'd gotten down to business, a man with a flashlight walked up behind Elvis and whacked him on the back of his neck with a stick. Undeterred, Elvis simply raised his hand up to guard the sensitive area. When the amorous couple didn't let up, the man took it as a personal challenge to get them to part, and he began beating Elvis' knuckles like a kid trying to crack open a piñata. Though it hurt like hell, Elvis didn't flinch, and with the couple continuing unfazed, the man eventually doddered away in defeat.

A few moments later, an out of breath Frenchy and Flats ran up to the couple. Quickly leaping into action, they had much better luck breaking the pair apart, with each of them grabbing one of Elvis' arms and pulling him several feet backwards.

"Dude, it's lucky that we found you," Frenchy said excitedly. "Our ten minutes is almost up, and we're totally screwed if Joe Le Taxi takes off without us."

With a fellow Ruffian hanging onto each of his shoulders, Elvis jokingly tried to break away, stretching out for Candy's hand.

"My fair maiden, parting is such sweet sorrow! But I vow to see you again, if only I knew how to call upon you?"

Candy laughed. "Here," she said, sliding her hand into her jean pockets and fishing out a little silver tube. Pushing his jacket sleeve up a few inches, she then wrote her name and phone number in bright red lipstick on his forearm.

Seeing an opening, Elvis dove back in for one last kiss.

Frenchy and Flats, groaning, were forced once again to pull him off, and this time they didn't dare loosen their grips.

"Damn it, Elvis, we gotta go!" Frenchy snapped.

With that, they dragged him, kicking and screaming, all the way out to Joe's taxi.

Climbing back into the car, the trio noticed that Joe Le Taxi was different than earlier. He had turned quiet, subdued even, the madman from earlier having been replaced by a calm, extremely chilled-out version of himself.

Elvis plopped down in the front seat, happy to keep to himself, the thoughts of Candy and their awesome make-out session still rattling around in his head. Knowing now what being with a human girl really felt like and absolutely loving it, he relished the thought of future adventures.

Meanwhile, Frenchy and Flats were nestled in the back, holding hands and occasionally exchanging little glances at one another. As the miles clicked by, Frenchy, thinking of their earlier conversation, leaned over and whispered in Flats' ear.

"So, when can we, what was that dumb term you used, 'complicate things'?"

Flats smiled sweetly, whispering back. "Let's just say I've always had a soft spot for Christmas morning."

Frenchy nodded and returned the smile. "Wow, that'll sure be one magical morning. Starting our futures together at the same time as getting my wish to secure the castle, a kingdom for those futures to unfold. All on the same day! Damn, I can hardly wait!"

Flats turned her face to the window, not wanting to give a hint as to what she was feeling inside. But, truth be told, her stomach was in knots. For not only did the mountainous task of meeting the toy quota remain, but so too did the uncertainty of Santa delivering on his end.

Knowing she must, she coaxed her mood positive, telling herself that their book of days would have a happy ending. Somehow. Turning back to Frenchy, she flashed the most carefree smile she could muster. "Yes, that would definitely be most magical."

Frenchy's smile widened, for everything was taking shape. And while the start of his journey with Flats was going to be set back a little bit, he took solace in knowing that it was now just a matter of time.

CHAPTER TWENTY-THREE
The Interloper

On a gray, dismally overcast early November afternoon, Frenchy was out in the courtyard, hard at work foraging for food to feed the factory's furnace. In addition to his initial role as team spirit rabble-rouser, he'd also become the keeper of the literal fire, making sure Elvis and his team of Scandies stayed warm while they toiled day and night, cranking out their mountains of toys.

After the success of the Goetta Day delivery, knowing that they sure as heck couldn't make a million Hole In Ones for the real deal, the guys had made it a priority to thoroughly search for any traces of toy-making materials. They hadn't been disappointed. Turned out, the compound's vast network of nooks and crannies contained several huge caches of hidden supplies, stuff the Admiral apparently hadn't gotten around to burning before he left. It now seemed possible that the knockout blow he'd intended for the North Pole wouldn't pack the punch he'd thought it would.

Elvis came out of the factory and joined Frenchy, bringing some news of the progress inside. "Yo, French Fry," he called out. "It's hotter than a witch's brew in there, dude, which is exactly what we need. Keeps those Scandies moving good and fast. So check this out: we passed the fifty thousand mark this morning! All the usual things, you know, like footballs and dolls, the stuff that gets asked for every year. Plus, I found another big stash of supplies this morning, over by where the giants live. So I think we have pretty much everything we'll need to make whatever the Pole's list throws our way. Hell, at the pace we're on, we'll be at over a hundred thousand by mid-December. I mean, come on, *one hundred thousand toys*? There's no way there's that many kids in this stinkin' Territory!"

Frenchy shrugged and smiled, having no concept of what the numbers Elvis was throwing around meant. "Well, it all sounds good, man. So keep up the good work, I guess."

"You got it. And thanks again for keeping us cooking!" Elvis said, slipping Frenchy some skin. Then, noticing an ominous black cloud rolling in, Elvis turned and headed back into the factory.

A few minutes later, Frenchy noticed a large flying object approaching from out in the distance, at first quite high in the sky but now descending at a rapid clip. He watched as the object sailed right over the compound's protective walls.

The spectacle was nothing short of astonishing: two boys seated in a carriage-type vessel were being propelled through the air by four flying reindeer. But it was also equally concerning, for they had so easily breached the security barrier that Frenchy had regarded as impenetrable. Up until now.

The boy handling the reindeer's reins lowered the team ever so carefully, gingerly coming to a rest in the middle of the castle's courtyard. He threw a ladder over the side and hurriedly descended, carrying with him an enormous suitcase,

THE FROGMAN OF LOVELAND

and then he stood at the bottom with his arms outstretched, fully at the ready to catch the other boy should he take a spill.

A moment later, the carriage's princely passenger had both his feet safely on the ground, and Spiro Donahue Buckingham III was on Loveland, Ohio, soil for the very first time.

He looked around, furrowing his brow at the surroundings, one part fairytale castle, one part dump, like a beautiful old Tudor home that had been taken over by frat boys.

Noticing what appeared to be a yard hand gathering fallen tree limbs, Spiro called out to him. "You there, boy, how about dropping that rubbish and grabbing my bag?"

Frenchy took a long moment looking Spiro over, letting the question hang in the air. "Yo, I'm kinda busy, chief," he eventually replied. "So you and your bag are on your own."

Spiro gasped, unaccustomed to being spoken to in such a manner. "Now, what kind of an attitude is that? Do you have any idea who you're addressing?"

Frenchy slowly walked over to Spiro. "Who I'm *addressing?* Well, it would seem I'm addressing someone who thinks quite highly of himself."

Spiro noticed Frenchy's green hue for the first time. "Oh, now I see! Fortunate me, I have made the acquaintance of the one they call the Frogman. I must say, I'm impressed that you can form words. I had imagined something more along the lines of 'ribbet, ribbet'!"

Frenchy took another step forward, moving so close to Spiro that the tree limbs in his arms were now the only things separating the two. "Look, I don't know who you are and I really don't give a damn, but you've dropped into my place, and I sure as hell didn't invite you. So how about you load your scrawny ass back into that fancy flying machine of yours and get lost?"

Spiro threw his head back and laughed. "Your place?!" he said. "This place, and every speck of soil upon it, is the official property of the Polie Empire."

"Ah! So you're one of those Polie guys? I gotta say, at least you come as advertised. And sorry, sporto, the Admiral officially gave this place to me, and I got a signed legal document that says so!"

He dropped his armful of tree limbs, making sure they landed squarely on Spiro's boots, then reached into his pocket and pulled out the Admiral's scribbled note. Regarding the document as 100 percent legally binding and knowing that Flats believed the same, he was certain it protected his interests.

"How ya like them apples?" Frenchy said, thrusting the note in front of Spiro's face.

Spiro, in return, didn't even glance at it, instead taking his hand and lowering the document out of his sightline. "The Admiral was, to put it mildly, *nuts*. Otherwise, he'd have had the good sense to know that all property of the Empire is totally and unequivocally nontransferable. Which, in *my* legal opinion, makes you nothing but a common squatter. But enough wasted breath on the matter, because at some point I'll just have my people take it back by might if you insist on perpetuating this little sham of yours."

Frenchy had heard well enough from the mouthy stranger, who in short order had not only invaded his space but was now threatening to snatch it from him. "You wanta see might?" he asked. "How about we dance, right here and now?"

"Take your best shot, Froggy," Spiro replied.

Incensed, Frenchy leapt forward, grabbing a handful of green Polie shirt up by the elf's shoulder, at the same time pulling his other fist back, readying to deliver a shot to Spiro's jaw. But just a second before he let it fly, he heard Elvis calling out frantically.

"Whoa! Stop! No! No! No! Frenchy, no!"

Frenchy lowered his arm, and Elvis ran over, strategically sliding himself in between the two would-be combatants.

Rattled, Elvis sized up the situation and quickly went to work on damage control. "Oh, hey there. Welcome to Loveland. From the looks of your sleigh and your Polie patch, I'd imagine that you're the Territorial Observer."

"A brilliant deduction. Tis good to see that perhaps not everyone here is an uncivilized boob," Spiro replied. "Yes, you would be correct. The name is Spiro, and I oversee this Territory along with a great many others. And you must be Elvis, Santa's little reclamation project."

"Uh, yes, that's right, Elvis Parker," he said, pushing down the urge to chirp back at the 'reclamation' crack. "Here, let me show you to the guest quarters. I'm sure you could use some rest after such a long journey."

Elvis hoisted up Spiro's suitcase and motioned for him to follow, at the same time putting his feet in fast motion. He knew that the three of them standing around chatting was bound to lead to nothing but trouble.

As they turned and headed off toward the castle, Spiro twisted around and shot Frenchy the dirtiest look he could muster, to which Frenchy responded with a double-barreled single-finger salute.

They weren't even ten seconds into their stroll when Spiro lobbed Elvis a question straight out of left field: "So, I understand the winged girl is staying here at the moment. I'm just curious, does she have her own fixed quarters, or does she sort of flop around from place to place, like she's only here in passing?"

Elvis cocked his head, astonished. Of the millions of things that a Territorial Observer, responsible for an entire continent of toy production, could ask, that was Spiro's first question? Elvis began to connect the dots, and a scary realization quickly came together in his head: This was the kid he had heard the crazy stories about, the one with the unhealthy obsession with the winged girl. Hell, how could Spiro not have even the tiniest suspicion that everyone at the Pole knew about his creepy infatuation with Flats? Or, more chillingly, what if he did know, and he just didn't care?

"You're talking about Flats, right?" Elvis asked.

"Yes, that's her name. *Flats.*"

"Yeah, of course she has her own room. It's up there," Elvis said, pointing straight up to a pair of large, swinging windows, high atop the castle watchtower. "If you don't mind me asking, how do you know her?"

"Oh, she always had a big crush on me back at the Pole," Spiro replied. "But I'm not one for slumming, if you know what I mean. Like they say, plenty of chicks in the sea."

"Um, I think it's fish," Elvis said, which Spiro didn't acknowledge.

The pair resumed their walk through the courtyard, and Elvis, feeling a bit hungry, pulled a baggie full of chocolate candies from his pocket, popping a few into his mouth.

"Hey there, fellow," Spiro said. "I've been in the air all day without so much as a bloody bag of peanuts, and you're holding out on me? Handeth that over!"

Spiro obnoxiously snatched the bag out of Elvis' hand,

pouring every single piece into his mouth and chomping down on them. "They've got a weird taste," he declared. "What's in those, spoiled raisins?"

"Flies," Elvis said, laughing. "Frenchy made them!"

Spiro bent over, retching and spitting, trying to summon the remnants of fly wings out from the back of his throat, his regal bearing long gone. "That's freakin' disgusting! Who in god's name is this wretched Frenchy character?"

"That dude you just met."

"The Frogman?! Wait, you've given it a name? What is he, like your pet?"

"Oh, good god, no!" Elvis shot back. "Frenchy's super cool, and he takes care of a lot around here, like keeping the place cooking."

Spiro shook his head, not believing what he had just heard. "You talk of it like it's your friend!"

"Because he is! And a damn good one, too," Elvis snapped, the crispness of his words meant to indicate that there wasn't the slightest hint of ambiguity about them.

"Unbelievable!" Spiro declared. "You really don't get it, do you, Parker? First, the Admiral has a nervous breakdown at the worst possible time of the year. And then Santa goes out on a limb for your ass, lord knows why, and puts you in charge of guiding this shithole Territory through the Christmas Eve rush. You're involved in some important business, son, and yet here you are fiddling around with a freaky frogman?! Seriously, man, what's going on in your head?"

Elvis thought for a second. "Well, I think my head's in the right place. Flats' plan from the very beginning glued the three of us together, kinda like a package deal. Then me and Frenchy happened to totally hit it off. You know, that never happened to me in over ten years at the Academy, not even once. So we're a team, and we're gonna ride this thing out together, wherever it takes us."

"Suit yourself," Spiro replied. "But if I were you, I'd be careful of relying too much on friends. After all, people are like the pieces on a chessboard, and you need to protect the ones that carry the most value. Success and power, those things endure, but friendship? Well, there's a reason why you start the game with eight pawns. It makes them expendable."

A chill went down Elvis' spine as it occurred to him that the guy who was essentially his boss had a very different world-view from his own. Thinking it best to shift gears, he turned to what surely must have been the reason for Spiro's visit. "So, maybe we approach things a little bit differently. But I know one thing: I bet our goals on hitting the freakin' quota are exactly the same. Speaking of which, I'm guessing the main reason you're here is to give us the list and then you'll be on to your next stop, right?"

"Well, yes, part of why I'm here is to hand off the list," Spiro replied. "That said, I suppose we should just check that one off while it's fresh on our minds." He reached down and zipped open his bag, pulling out an enormously thick binder. "Here," he said, handing the document over to Elvis.

Taking in its extraordinary weight, Elvis' eyes widened.

"And as far as my next stop, we'll see," Spiro continued. "I was planning on staying here at least a couple days, maybe even three, in order to get a good sense of what everyone is up to. And, of course, I'll be popping in from time to time leading up to the Eve."

Elvis filled with dread, now knowing that this wasn't going to be the lightning-quick pit stop he had hoped it to be, nor the last. Yet Spiro couldn't possibly have any *official* business in Loveland that warranted more than a quick pop-in....

Their journey continuing, they cut through the Control Room and headed down the hallway leading to the various sleeping quarters. The warm summer scene that Frenchy had walked through on his first trip down the magical hallway had changed to something altogether different, and the boys now found themselves stepping through a chilly late autumn day.

Elvis, thinking that finding even a small crumb of something in common with Spiro might set their relationship off on better footing, tried one more conversational shift, name-dropping his bastardly nemesis from the Academy, someone *everybody* hated. "Christ, it's colder than a witch's bosom in here. And, speaking of cold, how are things back at the Pole? I'm guessing they haven't put that dickless old goat the Elder out to pasture yet, have they?" Elvis asked, laughing.

"Oh, you mean my father?" Spiro replied coolly. "And no. Trust me, nobody would dare to even consider 'putting' him anywhere."

If the earth had suddenly split, opening a bottomless crevice stretching straight down into the fiery pits of hell, Elvis most certainly would have jumped right in. It was unbelievable: Spiro had been there all of three minutes, insulting Frenchy to the point of almost getting clobbered, talking über creepily about Flats, doubling back to Frenchy, actually referring to him as 'it' several times, and then claiming the person Elvis hated most in the entire world as his father. In three minutes! With a good forty-five days left until Christmas Eve, how much havoc could Spiro wreck if he decided to wade deeply into their business?

"Oh, um, yes. Well, lordy, would you look at that, we've made it to your room," Elvis stammered, tossing the room key over to Spiro. "So, enjoy your stay.…" he concluded, the words trailing off as he made a quick getaway, his pace ramping up to a jog as he headed back through the castle and out into the courtyard.

Once outside, he stopped to scrutinize *the list,* the all-powerful document dictating the exact number of toys that would be expected from them and, by extension, ruling over their lives from now until the Christmas Eve deadline.

He sized up the number of pages and then flipped through a few, trying to gauge approximately how many listings were on each. Seeing that there were a helluva lot of them jammed on every page, Elvis began to sense that he may have under-estimated the anticipated quota, er, *somewhat.* With his nerves starting to tingle and his forehead dampening with sweat, he needed to end the suspense, like, now. So he jumped ahead to the very last page.

When he saw the listing for the very last toy, a hockey stick earmarked for a child named Zarley Zalapski, his jaw dropped. It was identified as toy number *one million!*

"Oh my god," Elvis uttered. "What on earth have we gotten ourselves into?!"

CHAPTER TWENTY-FOUR
Dirty Tricks

On day two of his visit, Spiro was up in the Control Room, watching Frenchy and Elvis on the factory floor below. He made sure they knew he was up there, too, turning on all the lights so that they had a good, clear view of him.

Frenchy and Elvis, on the other hand, were attempting to do the exact opposite, working to keep their minds off Spiro and squarely on their suddenly mountainous task at hand. Elvis had briefed Frenchy about the million-toy demand, and though he didn't come right out and say their mission was impossible, he did suggest that it would take something of a miracle to successfully pull it off.

Unfortunately, the pull of Spiro was proving too great, distracting Frenchy from their would-be strategy session and leading him instead to the very place he had wanted to avoid.

"He said something about me making ribbit sounds! And Christ, he freakin' called me *Froggy*! Ten more seconds and I would have seriously kicked his ass, and I still might. Why do we even have to put up with that asshole, Elvis? I mean, from the way Flats sold this plan, it seemed like we were going to be answering to Santa."

Elvis paused, searching for a simple explanation to a most complex matter, one for which he lacked perspective. After all, how could a fifteen-year-old kid wrap his mind around tensions that had been simmering for thirty-two years?

"Well, technically Flats does answer to Santa. As for me, I suppose at the moment I'm tucked under the Polie umbrella, though it was Santa that did the tucking. And you, well, you just happen to own a critical piece of what used to be part of the Polie Empire—at least, as far as I'm concerned. So, bottom line, I think we have to keep both Santa and the Polies happy, which in part means putting up with the asshole. And then in the end, we have to deliver the goods. That's the only way we stay in control of this mess."

Elvis reached over and grabbed Frenchy's shoulder. "And please, Frenchy, I know this is gonna be hard, but you have to promise me you won't lay a hand on him. That would be a total disaster! I mean, you have to remember the Polies actually have their own army, a damn big one, and if you kick Spiro's ass badly enough, they just might send it down here."

Frenchy shook his head, letting the words settle in. Though he wasn't thrilled with Elvis' request, he understood the importance of it. "Look, man," he said. "I won't touch the dweeb provided he keeps to himself, and stays away from the f-word!"

Elvis cocked his head sideways. "Wait a second, how'd you know about—"

But Frenchy cut him off. "And by that I mean the seven-letter one."

They both managed a smile, with Elvis' born mostly out of relief. Of course Frenchy didn't know about Spiro's obsession with Flats—how could he? And, knowing it would make the "no ass-kicking" rule all but impossible for his friend to obey, Elvis intended to keep it that way.

The moment of relief was cut short, however, whisked aside by a most unexpected sight, that of Flats joining Spiro up in the Control Room.

"Why the hell would she be talking to that jerk?" Frenchy asked.

"I don't know," Elvis replied, inwardly cursing. "I mean… Look, I wasn't going to mention anything because I was never really involved in Polie gossip bullshit. But there were always rumors floating around about Spiro and Flats. They all pretty much centered around him harassing her, but honestly, I have no idea if there was anything to it beyond that."

He decided to leave it at that, selectively editing out Spiro's crack the previous day about the "winged girl."

They both stood still, watching the scene unfold up above. With neither of them able to read lips, they were both in the dark, leaving the interaction of those they were watching largely open to interpretation.

Upstairs, having walked into the Control Room, Flats took comfort in the fact that it enjoyed a 360-degree view of the world below and, by extension, the world enjoyed the same view right back. If ever there was a place offering total transparency, it was here.

"Thanks for coming, Flats," Spiro began. "I've been dying to talk to you. Did you get the flowers and Polaroids I left up by your door?"

Flats' creep meter kicked on, and she positioned herself with her back over by the large bank of windows, knowing that anyone down on the factory floor would have a clear view of her. "I'm glad you brought that up right away, because no, I left them right where you put them. Look, Spiro, we've been through this like, what, five times? I don't want anything from you. It's creepy, and leaving pictures of yourself without a shirt on is just downright gross. So please, stop it. Let's just focus on our jobs and our common goal, pulling this Territory out of the weeds enough to somehow meet its quota."

"Ah, yes," Spiro replied. "Our common goal."

He took a few steps toward Flats, encroaching into her personal space. She in turn took a step backwards, now finding herself pressed tightly up against the windows.

"So about that goal. It's been brought to my attention that you've been doing a great job down here, and I'd like to make sure your hard work gets rewarded."

"Geez, Spiro," Flats replied. "Thanks, I guess, but really, it isn't necessary."

Spiro forged ahead. "No, no. Star performers deserve special treatment. And, as I'm sure you know, I run Territories all over this continent, places much warmer and prettier than this dump. So if you'd like to make a move, just say the word. And maybe be a little bit nicer to me."

He moved a half step closer still, now literally rubbing up against her.

Frenchy and Elvis were frozen, unable to tell if they were peeking in on a consensual affair or on the early stages of an assault. Torn over what to do, if anything, they did nothing. Rather, they simply continued to watch.

Meanwhile, Flats couldn't move without aggressively pushing Spiro back, which she feared might ignite his ferocious temper. So she instead tried to talk her way out.

"You know, Spiro, I'm fine here," she said as pleasantly as

she could muster. "My plan is that we ace the Eve, and then I can begin a whole new chapter of my life. But that's a matter for another day and one that I very much look forward to taking up with Santa."

Spiro snuck one more glance down at Frenchy and Elvis, and he could see that he still had their close attention.

"Well, if you change your mind, I can give you what you want," he hissed. Then he grabbed Flats by the back of her head and pulled their faces together, planting a hard and painful kiss onto her lips.

Back down below, Frenchy couldn't believe what he was witnessing. "What the hell are they doing?!" he shouted. "Now I'm kicking his ass for sure!"

Frenchy began to run toward the stairs, but Elvis hurried out and got in front of him, blocking his way.

"French Fry, look, don't take this the wrong way, because I promise, I really don't know what's going on here. But consider just for a second that Flats and the asshole might have liked each other, like, a long time ago, and maybe things weren't always weird between the two of them. I mean, what do you really know about her or her life at the Pole, for that matter?"

Elvis felt sickened just saying the words, as his fondness for Flats equaled his freshly discovered disdain for Spiro. But he was also trying to provide an alternative, measured view of the situation—as well as possibly avert a serious beatdown.

"No," Frenchy said, emphatically shaking his head. "No freakin' way! She would never even go near that asshole, let alone like him. And besides, she likes me—I think. Goddamn it! I don't know what to think, but I'm sure as hell getting to the bottom of it!"

He pushed Elvis aside and sprinted up the steps leading up

to the Control Room, his anger fueling his speed. Knowing a disaster was about to unfold, Elvis took off as well, trailing Frenchy by a few steps.

Reaching the Control Room door seconds later, Frenchy busted through, with Elvis right on his heels. Flats was gone, and Spiro was awkwardly hunched over as though he was looking for something on the floor.

The Polie rose up, not letting on that his stomach was in serious pain, and turned fully to Frenchy. "Bitch gave me a little love tap!" he said, wheezing out a creepy little laugh. "I guess maybe she thinks I'm not paying enough attention to her or something. But what's she want from me? I'm a busy man."

Frenchy stormed right up to him, his eyes blazing. "Maybe she doesn't like you. Did you ever think of that?"

"Like?" Spiro said, snickering. "What's 'like' have to do with it? I have a hookup in every Territory, and I doubt any of them like me all that much. It's all part of the game. The ones that go the extra mile move up, and the ones that don't, don't. Way I look at it, I can promote whoever I choose, so why shouldn't the ones that give a little extra advance? Like Flats."

Frenchy was beside himself, a bubbling stew of confusion, anger, and betrayal all boiling over in his head, steaming out any rational thought. "You're disgusting" was all he could think to say.

"Perhaps," Spiro smugly replied. "Then so be it. I'm a disgusting Territorial Observer with tons of power and a boatload of chicks. I'll take that any day over being a green-faced loser that probably hasn't ever even gotten to first base!"

Elvis knew that his friend was about ready to blast off, so he positioned himself to where Frenchy would have to go through him to get to Spiro. Good thing, because Frenchy launched just a second later. Elvis stopped his initial momentum and grabbed onto him with all his strength, doing his best to restrain him until he could at least try to restore some order.

"Dude, stop!" Elvis yelled. "It's not worth it! Let's just get the hell out of here and grab some air. Christ, don't do something that we're all going to regret."

A fragile peace ensued, with Elvis keeping his best hold of Frenchy and Frenchy's eyes on the verge of bulging out of his head. All the while, Spiro just smirked. They stood frozen like that for several tense seconds until Spiro simply couldn't help himself.

"Look at the bright side, Frogman. I'll be out of here tomorrow, and you'll be left alone to take your best shot with her. Heck, she might even be loose enough to give it up to a loser like you. But remember, whatever base you end up getting to with her, I was on top of it first."

Frenchy came unglued. Spinning from Elvis' grasp, he ran over and delivered a vicious right-handed haymaker into Spiro's eye. Then, pinning Spiro up against the wall by his throat, he issued a dire warning. "Someday, when all of this is over, no more toys and no more Polie bullshit, we'll cross paths again. And, as surely as I stand here, I will finish you!"

Letting go of Spiro's throat, Frenchy stormed out of the Control Room.

Spiro, gasping for breath and once again hunched over, forced out his words. "That monster just signed his own death certificate."

CHAPTER TWENTY-FIVE
The Fight

Flats was outside in the courtyard, pacing near the spot where she had first dropped in on Frenchy a month earlier. Elvis had already checked on her, making sure she was okay with whatever had gone down in the Control Room. He'd also given her a quick rundown of what had happened between Frenchy and Spiro.

"I did everything I could to stop it," Elvis had said guiltily.

"I believe you," she'd replied. "And while 'okay' isn't exactly the right word, I'm fine."

When really, her mind was quite messy at the moment. How could she simultaneously be so smitten with someone and fully ready to knock their block off? After all, what on earth had Frenchy been thinking? Threatening to kill someone as high up in the Polie Empire as Spiro stood to blow their entire fragile plan to pieces.

She was also still boiling mad about being kissed against her will by Spiro and wondering whether or not she should report it. And if so, to whom? Spiro ran the entire North American operation, so if she went to the Polie administration, she'd have to go straight to the Elder. Being a lowly runner, not to mention one loyal to Santa, the odds of her finding an objective audience in the likes of Spiro's father were slim.

The only decent option seemed to be going to Santa. But that had a downside as well, as it would mean dumping yet another issue onto the lap of the most important person in the world at precisely his busiest time of the year. An issue, Flats was well aware, that would likely rise to heightened significance in the ever-sensitive Claus-Polie Cold War.

So, for the time being, she decided to simply swallow the emotions, taking consolation in the fact that she had at least gotten in a little vengeance by leaving the creep with a serious stomachache.

Cue Frenchy—and perhaps the worst timing in the history of boy/girl fights.

Stuck fully in his own mind, he marched up to Flats, his arms flailing agitatedly. "I might not be the smartest guy in the world, but I figured out one thing. The reason you and I being together would complicate things is that you're already the property of King Polie Dipshit! I guess lying down with the guy in charge can't be too bad for your 'work.'"

It was the little air quotes around the word 'work' that did it.

Flats pulled back and drilled Frenchy with a swift left jab, landing a bullseye right between his eyes. She held back a little so as to not break his nose but still got her point across loudly and clearly.

Frenchy staggered back a couple steps, clutching his nose, a good bit of blood already spewing out. "Christ," he said weakly, the word totally void of the venom dripping from his previous comments.

"Sorry," Flats blurted. "But you deserved it. You're having quite a day, asshole! You totally let that little mole get under your skin, and your brilliant, measured response is to first clobber him, then *threaten to kill him!* So not only did you just commit a felony, you also happened to put every single thing we're trying to protect here in jeopardy. Elvis' wish, my fresh start, your castle—consider them all to be on thin ice simply because you can't see when you're being baited. So just sit back and wait for the over-the-top response from the Pole, because you can bet your hotheaded ass that a twisted mind is already dreaming it up!"

Frenchy lowered his head, the gravity of what he had done sinking in.

Flats' voice grew softer, her inflection shifting from one of anger to one infused with pain. "But by far the worst part of all this is what just came out of your mouth, accusing me of sleeping with the boss in order to get ahead. That's just about the most disgusting, hurtful thing you could have ever said to me." She stared at the ground in disbelief, now almost whispering. "There's still plenty of day left. Want to see if you can cross any more asinine, insensitive things off your to-do list?"

She shook her head and started to walk off but then stopped on a dime and turned back, coming within inches of Frenchy. "And ask yourself this: How did he look when you ran in there? Like someone who just enjoyed a little game of kissy-face? Or like a creep that just got punched in the gut? Because that's exactly what happened!"

Frenchy's nose was now spewing blood, the two lines heading straight down into his mouth, reddening his teeth and making him look like something from a monster movie. "Damn! I mean, it's kind of hard to erase what my eyes just saw from down on the factory floor," he said, the words pained and garbled.

Flats, looking at Frenchy's red teeth and pained eyes, began to soften. She grabbed his shoulders, gently shaking him as she spoke. "Are you listening? That's because you only saw one part of the story. You didn't see the part before that, which was me trying like hell to avoid him—not just here but for the entire time I was at the Pole. And you didn't see the part after it, either, when I socked him for forcing himself on me. You saw a teeny, tiny part of the story, and then you went all into macho boy mode, letting your stupid pride and ego fill in the rest. It would've meant a lot to me if you'd have asked me to fill it in instead."

Frenchy's voice was hushed now, like that of a small child. "So, you were never, like, um, his girlfriend?"

Flats adamantly shook her head. "Oh my goodness, no! Frenchy, the humans have a word for what he is: stalker. He makes my blood curl."

Frenchy let the words bounce around in his head. He wished he could just press a giant rewind button, but, knowing life didn't offer such an option, he moved forward the best he could. "Look, I'm really sorry. I should have come to you first, with trust in my heart. But I didn't. All I can do now is promise to do better next time."

Flats removed a soft piece of cloth from her pocket and gently wiped the blood off his lips. "I forgive you," she softly replied. "Because as knuckleheaded as your stunt was, trust me, I know firsthand that he can bring out the worst in people. Even those of us who aren't silly, hotheaded boys."

Flats smiled sweetly, draping her arms over Frenchy's

shoulders. "Look, Thanksgiving's in a few weeks, and then it's a four-week sprint to Christmas Eve. Creepo's going back to the Pole tomorrow, which'll buy us some time, but trust me, this isn't over with Spiro. Or the Polies as a whole. I imagine it's not every day that a Territorial Observer gets socked not once but twice, so I can see some people getting really worked up about it. Which is all the more reason to focus like crazy on our mission, because that's the only way we're going to see our way through this madness."

She looked deeply into Frenchy's eyes. "One more thing, just to put your head to rest. I've had feelings for exactly one person in my life. You. And I promise, after we get to the finish line together, seconds after midnight on Christmas morning, I'll meet you at this very spot and we'll see where this crazy path takes us."

They hugged, holding on for several special seconds, and then Flats kissed Frenchy tenderly on the cheek. This time, it seemed like much more than a friendly little peck.

CHAPTER TWENTY-SIX
Creating a Monster

Thanksgiving 1978 - North Pole

Spiro and the Elder sat at opposite ends of a long dining room table, a lavish spread of assorted fruits, cheeses, and nuts laid out before them. With the finest linen draping across the floor-to-ceiling windows, it allowed just the right amount of late afternoon light to peek in. Mid-table, a huge turkey rested, surrounded by a summer's worth of produce painstakingly preserved through the frosty autumn days of the northern Arctic.

The Elder admired the spread, but he remained puzzled as to its genesis. "Always nice to have some time with you, my boy, but remind me again why we chose this day, a workday, no less, to partake in such a bountiful feast."

Not really sure himself, Spiro smiled. "Honestly, I have no idea *why*. But I've noticed the humans down in the Americas taking part in it through the years. They call it 'Thanksgiving,' and, as far as I can tell, it gives them an excuse to stay home, eating and drinking everything they can get their hands on.

I thought it sounded like a pretty good idea, one of the very few coming from the humans, so I borrowed it!"

The Elder, laughing, nodded approvingly, appreciating the cleverness behind initiating a hearty feast for no apparent reason. But then he suddenly noticed his mug had gone empty, causing his brow to furrow and his disposition to turn on a dime. "You there," the old elf snapped, pointing at a Polie Hardship Exemption standing at the rear of the room.

Stepping forward, the boy averted his gaze down to his scuffed-up shoes, as eye contact with the Elder was strictly forbidden for the Hardships.

"Replenish my ale, and be quick about it!"

The boy did as told and then furtively walked back to his original position, his eyes never once drifting upward.

The Elder looked across the table to Spiro, noticing a slight heaviness to his son's demeanor. So he set the conversation in motion, speaking in tones made a good bit louder by the ale. "Laddie, I sense that the weight of the world is resting upon you. Please share with me word of your troubles, for perhaps I can help lighten the load."

Spiro fidgeted. "Well, sir, overall things are fine. From a toy quota perspective, it looks as though all the Territories are going to be in good shape for the Eve. I think."

The Elder eyed him. "It sounds quite clearly, my good man, that a sneaky little devil named However is knocking at the door. So you might just as well usher him in."

Spiro nodded. "Yes, sir, you're right. However, a matter remains, a most troubling one. The Frogman, down in Ohio, it's still there, and it's becoming more of a problem by the day."

The Elder's eyes widened and his mind roamed, filling with conjured up images of this otherworldly creature, knowing he was on the cusp of hearing his very own firsthand account of what the beast was really like. "Ohio, where I cast the bastard Parker boy to, tis it not?" he asked, tickled to be able to connect his own little twist to the tale.

"It is," Spiro continued. "He's there, as is the monster. I had sought it out, actually, as I wanted to see if perhaps there might be a place at the table for it. But alas, there is not, for it clearly resides solely in a world of force and violence. Though I had come in peace, it lashed out, unprovoked, and savagely attacked me, vowing to kill not just me but all those like me."

The Elder gasped.

Spiro continued his tall tale. "I fear it's only a matter of time before such a bloodthirsty menace is eventually discovered by the humans, bringing with it a flurry of unwanted scrutiny into our way of doing things. Because you can bet your bottom dollar that our carefully honed image—that of a quaint North Pole workshop with its happy little elves—will be utterly blown to bits, all by that wretched creature getting himself captured. I mean, the breathless investigations that would surely follow would make Watergate look like child's play. There's simply too much to lose, and he must go."

The Elder was listening closely, carefully weighing the words. Then, perversely, he began to laugh in a chilling, menacingly scheming sort of way.

"What is it that you find amusing, Father?" Spiro asked.

"Not amusing. Serendipitous!" the Elder replied, clapping his hands together for effect. "The Parker boy has also been rumbling around my head of late, and I suppose by extension that Territory as well. Perhaps we can solve your monster problem at the same time as solving a nagging problem of my own, piercing two birds with one arrow."

The Elder took a good, long gulp of his ale, then clapped again, this time twice, summoning the Hardship back over. "At once, pour my boy a hearty mug full of ale."

The Elder paused, waiting for the mug to be filled. Then he motioned the Hardship out of the room as though he was trying to rid himself of an annoying fly. "Drink up, my boy. Your loins should best be girded for the tale I'm about to tell!"

Spiro did as told, downing a good bit of his ale in a couple big slugs.

Pumped up full of himself, the Elder rose to his feet. "For over three decades, we Polies have done all the work, yet all we're given is the scraps after the Fat Man has had his fill. Just slaves in nice quarters, really. I feel the time is nigh to change that, and your little burg down in Ohio might be just the place to plant our flag. The last straw was six weeks ago, when that bloated egomaniac summoned me only to dress me down and make it clear that our entire society meant about as much to him as his team of stableboys. Equally replaceable. Since then, one thought has consumed my mind: in the year 1978, with every single civilized part of this globe having its own reliable postal service, if anyone is replaceable, it's the *delivery boy*."

Spiro sat straight up in his chair, his mind ablaze, barely able to believe that he was listening to his father, the second-most powerful man at the North Pole, perhaps contemplating a scheme to overthrow the first.

"But why Ohio?" he asked. "What does the Frogman have to do with Santa?"

The Elder dropped back into his chair with a thud. "Ooof. No, no, the focus isn't the Frogman. Though it'll have to be dealt with as well, just to make sure it doesn't get in the way.

I'm talking about the bastard boy, the key to knocking Santa off his high horse."

The murky picture was slowly starting to come into focus for Spiro. "Does this have something to do with those rumors you told me, about how Santa might have actually sired Elvis?" Glancing over, he noticed a sly smile crossing his father's face.

"Now, now," replied the Elder, laughing wryly. "I'm not one to walk in the gray shadows of rumor and innuendo. No, I bask in the light of truth, so in recent days I set about to find it. Turns out that Santa and the missus went through a little rough patch about sixteen years ago, and let's just say that the Fat Man was known to have spread quite a bit of his Christmas cheer around. It was also pretty well-known that the timing of the Parker boy's mother's story never really added up. It seems her hubby ran off well over a year before the boy came into the world. And, of course, with him clearly being a human, certainly no Polie could be accused of doing the dirty deed."

The Elder paused to draw upon his ale. "Now, I suppose one could also consider immaculate conception as a possibility. However, I'd have to imagine that Tracy Parker was quite a goodly distance away from being free of original sin!"

They both shared a hearty laugh at the crack.

"But all of this is just hearsay, and I needed it converted to fact. So I went to the Claus' hospital. It turns out the humans are actually quite open about identifying those responsible for bringing their newest members into the world. I simply went to the front desk and requested something called a birth certificate for the Parker boy, and sure enough, it listed as his father none other than K. Kringle. So it is hearsay no more: the anointed one, Saint Nicholas the Seventeenth himself, once upon a time strayed across the tracks and fell down with some trailer trash!"

Spiro and the Elder reveled over the thought, laughing and letting it sink in for a good long time. But when the laughter subsided and the Elder continued, his mood had suddenly shifted, turning quite serious, angry even, spurred on by the ale.

"It all makes sense now. Santa shoved the Parker boy down our throats because he's the heir apparent. And if he's able to succeed with that train wreck of a Territory, *one that a first-generation Polie deserted*, Santa will look like a genius while at the same time giving birth to his son's legend. Of course, our people will be depicted as fools, and that red-nosed rascal will bask in the adulation all by himself just like he always does!"

The Elder, feeling himself getting all worked up, paused, taking another gulp of his ale. "So, I had a devilish little thought: How about we turn the entire situation on its head, causing the boy to not only fail, but fail miserably, triggering a shutdown of the entire year's toy delivery all the way from Ohio westward? It will be such lovely poetic justice, teaching Santa a harsh lesson about ever again stepping beyond his boundaries!"

Spiro let the gravity of the words sink in. "And how do you think we should go about that, ensuring that he fails?" he asked.

The Elder fished a folded note from his pocket and slid it across the table. "A little reading material sent in by a child who was clearly unamused by Mr. Parker's efforts during the Goetta Day delivery. Smells to me like a treasonous act against the Empire, one worthy of at least a few days in the dungeon. But what say you?"

Spiro eyed the note carefully. Then he nodded emphatically.

The Elder rose to his feet once again, now teetering back and forth, clearly a good bit wobbly in the boot. "Take the army down and, once the Parker boy is out of the way, have them destroy every last toy they've managed to build. And remember, the bigger the mess, the worse Santa will look for having created it. Dreaming for a moment, if the Parker boy implodes so dramatically that Santa could never see beyond the wreckage, then his soft spot for the little snot will harden. And if that were to occur, the entire line of succession would then end at Sir Nick, which means it's as good as finished. Because I can't imagine that dim bulb even knows where it is that babies come from!" The Elder drained his mug and slammed it to the table, then fixed his eyes on Spiro. "But the first step is slaying the Frogman," he finished icily.

Spiro's eyes glowed. Taking out the Frogman was a deed with which he was most at ease and one that he had given much thought. "And I know just how to do it, all the while keeping the Empire's hands clean!"

He hopped up from the table, pacing around excitedly. "It's simple. I shall whisper a tale as old as time itself into the ear of the most slippery of humans, a television man, telling of a bloodthirsty demon besetting upon their village. Of course, the bloodiest of tales spread the fastest, and soon the villagers will begin to shout over one another, seeing who can most loudly disavow the beast. Over time, with fears stoked unabated, who will stand up and question if the beast is really so bloodthirsty after all? No one. Because, fact or not, it's always easier to simply join the mob than to buck up against it."

"Ah! So you supply the monster, and the villagers supply

the pitchforks! Yes, why not let the humans get off their asses for a change? An idea so brilliant, my son, that I'm surprised I didn't concoct it," the Elder decided, nodding.

"Why, thank you, sir," Spiro replied, holding his father's gaze from across the room.

The Elder, even though his vision was beginning to cloud over from the toxic mixture of ale and hubris, was certain he had caught something in Spiro's eyes, as though the flames were burning just a bit too brightly behind them. And he had a suspicion about what was fueling the fire. "It occurs to me that a certain being has remained unmentioned. So, I might ask, how do you see the winged girl fitting into all of this?"

Spiro feigned being caught off guard by the question. "Oh, goodness, I haven't really given it any thought. But now that you've asked, I guess she'll have two options. She can either run off and be left to wander this cruel world alone, or she can subjugate herself to ol' Spiro and beg to be allowed back up. It'll really be up to her."

Clearly quite satisfied with themselves, Spiro and the Elder turned their attentions to their feast, diving in robustly. Their plan's perfectly evil symmetry made them both smile, for they would be ridding themselves of two foes, bringing a third to her knees, and setting Santa squarely in his place.

They raised their empty glasses, and the Elder offered a toast.

"To a thousand years of Polie rule! And when history looks back upon this moment, let it be forever remembered that it all started in... oh, goodness, what's the bloody name of the place?"

"Um, Ohio?" mumbled Spiro.

"No, no. Not the Territory," the Elder replied. "The town.

The actual place where our line will be permanently etched in the sand."

"Oh, it's called Loveland, sir. Loveland, Ohio."

The Elder shook his head. "Oh my stars! A true embodiment of the Clauses, at once both cloying and starved for adoration. So as soon as we call all the shots, let our first order of business be changing the blasted name of the place!"

Then he laughed his wheezy laugh, just as void of humor as ever.

CHAPTER TWENTY-SEVEN
Monster Hunters

December 21, 1978 - Back in Loveland

Facing the enormous challenge of an ominous and quickly approaching Christmas morning deadline, the four weeks following Thanksgiving had flown by for the Ruffians. Thankfully, Spiro had left them alone after all, enabling them to focus on making a huge dent in their toy quota. That very quota was at the forefront of Frenchy's and Elvis' minds this morning, as it was pretty much around the clock these days.

"Looks like we're just about one hundred thousand short at this point," Elvis said, glancing down at a clipboard with a long list of children's names and their toys of choice.

"So is that good or bad, Elvis?" Frenchy asked, unable to put such an enormous number into any kind of perspective.

Elvis wanted to frame his response in the best light possible. "Well, I wouldn't call it good, but it ain't impossible, either. We've been averaging about twelve thousand toys a day, so we're going to need to double that over the next four days. It'll

THE FROGMAN OF LOVELAND

take everyone working around the clock—but if everything goes perfect, we have a shot."

This made sense to Frenchy, and after all the twists and turns their saga had taken, a crazy, mad dash to the finish line seemed only natural. "Just tell me what I can do to help, dude."

Elvis nodded. "It'd be great if you could crank the furnace up to as hot as it can go and keep it that way until midnight on the twenty-fourth. The Scandies really seem to go into that extra gear when they're good and toasty. You up for that?"

"Hell yeah, man! Consider it done!" Frenchy said, already setting off on his way to scrounge for more wood to feed the furnace.

• • •

Later that night, having been on the go nonstop for a good twelve hours, Frenchy took a much needed break. Sitting alone in his room and dipping some cookies into a glass of milk, he absentmindedly fiddled with the remote control. As channel after channel whizzed by, the television randomly landed on a show about surviving in the woods. Woods, it turns out, that looked very familiar to Frenchy. He watched as the host, brandishing a menacing-looking hunting bow, patrolled the Little Miami riverside as though staking out an enemy.

"This is Renaldo Guevarra," the host said to the camera. "On this week's episode of *Monster Hunters*, we are tracking a specter so terrifying, we've been given special orders from Governor Rhodes' office to not just capture the beast but take it down on sight! But, before we proceed, I have to warn viewers that what's about to go down may turn shocking—and quite possibly deadly. So I'll give those with heart conditions a few seconds to change the channel." He paused a moment for dramatic effect. "Alright. You've been duly warned!"

A crudely drawn image appeared onscreen, that of a creature with the misshapen body of a human and the head of a lizard, wearing ill-fitting clothes and a hat adorned with an *F*. Blood dripped from the corners of its mouth, and in its webbed hand was the severed arm of a small child. The arm was missing a bite-sized chunk.

"What the ffffff…?" Frenchy said aloud, his eyes as wide as saucers.

"This is the Loveland Frogman," Renaldo continued. "Terrorizing the hills of southwest Ohio, it has reportedly murdered at least twenty children over the past two months, sickeningly grinding their soft, pink flesh into sausages, which I've been told it washes down with copious amounts of ale."

The image on the screen cut to a gruesome close-up shot of a horrific scar going up the entire length of a man's stomach. Then the shot panned back, exposing the man as the weed harvester who had cut Frenchy's pinky off.

"This gentleman, who asked to remain anonymous, is one of only two people to have had an encounter with the frogmonster and survived to tell about it," Renaldo continued.

"Ya see this scar?" the man asked, somewhat redundantly, as the camera was two feet away and pointing directly at it. "That frogman knocked me down and zippered right up my belly with its razor-like teeth. Must a sucked a good ten pints of blood outta me before my buddies were able to chase it off with their chainsaws! You boys gotta get it before it strikes again!"

The screen then cut to Officer Ray Shockey, the policeman who weeks earlier had shot at Frenchy at The Monkey Bar, as Renaldo's voiceover introduced him.

"And, even more shockingly, it seems that its campaign of gore is only getting started. Let's meet Officer Ray Shockey, a veteran of the Loveland Police Department and the only public official to date who has not only seen the monster, but also survived to actually log an official written report about the terrifying encounter."

"Yep, I seen that frog creature with my own two eyes," he started off excitedly. "It's as green as grass, that's for sure, and its got giant webbed hands. It's a thief, too! The day I seen it, it was swipin' a couple cases of brew right from underneath the nose of the Monkey himself. I fired off a couple of rounds, you know, just to let it know to get a move on. It worked, too, 'cuz ain't nobody seen it since. But trust me, it'll be back. Because once them cryptid types get that taste for human blood, there's only one way for 'em to satisfy their urges, and that's by killin'. And from what I heard, this one likes 'em young. Even babies!"

The shot cut back to Renaldo dramatically shaking his head as if to rid his mind of such a horrific thought. Then he started speaking excitedly, his words growing more intense as they tumbled out: "We'll follow our standard format, limiting ourselves to a seventy-two-hour hunt and, as always, using only the weaponry available in the eighteenth century. A seemingly daunting task, we've been aided by an anonymous tip that gave us the general proximity of where the creature has been bedding down. So join us over the next three exhilarating nights as we battle to slay the beast, knowing that until we do, it's still lurking out there amongst you. Alright, fellow sportsmen, buckle up for this edition of *Monster Hunters*. The clock starts right now!"

Frenchy sat straight up in his bed. "Holy shit!" was all he could think to say.

He went over to his window and pulled the drapes apart just a tiny bit. To his astonishment, across the river valley there were more archers on horseback than he could count. One in particular had his bow string pulled taut, his arrow pointing directly at Frenchy's window.

In an instant, the arrow crashed through the windowpane and soared just inches over the top of Frenchy's head. As he stood there frozen with fear, several more archers pulled arrows from their quivers and loaded up their bows, leveling them right at him. Before Frenchy could even think, the distinct twang of several bowstrings being let go reached his ear, unfreezing him and sending him instinctively diving down to the floor.

Lying helpless as more and more arrows burst through the window above, Frenchy made a deal with himself. He had to get out of the castle and fade into the hillside for the three days the Monster Hunters would be around—because if they brought their hunt inside the compound's walls, they'd expose not only him but the others as well. The Wursties and Elvis, with their human forms, would probably be okay, as would the harmless Scandies. But Flats, like himself, would be a certain goner, viewed as one more trophy for the warped show's collection. He could never let that happen.

Just as he started to ponder how in the world he could safely sneak out of the castle, there was a knock at the door. Crawling across the floor and rising only when he was sure the archers couldn't see him, Frenchy checked the peephole. Oddly, there was no one there. Carefully cracking open the door, he saw a little Scandie standing a good foot below the peephole's scope.

The Scandie handed Frenchy a drawing. It showed what looked like the interior of a cave, complete with a bed, radio, snacks, and several girlie posters. At the bottom was a simple caption: "IT IS TIME."

Frenchy surmised that the Scandies had been watching the very same television show and that they had already concocted a plan for his safety. Pretty smart thinking, but a critical question remained. "Do you guys have a plan to get me there?" he asked. "There's no way I can be out in the river valley, not with the bullseye I have on my back."

The Scandie shook his head, his face saddening as he realized his people had overlooked such an important part of the plan.

"It's okay, we'll figure something out," Frenchy said, reassuringly tousling the Scandie's hair. He paced around, thinking. "Wait a second," he said suddenly. "I got it!"

Frenchy sat down, grabbing a pen and paper and dashing off a sketch of what looked like a long box with a hinged lid. "Please round up all your buddies and have them get to work building this. I'll meet you guys down in the factory in ten minutes." He gave the Scandie the sketch, then turned him in the direction of the exit, giving him a gentle push in order to get his feet moving at a robust pace.

Racing against time, Frenchy was then off to sneak in two very important goodbyes.

He first ran over to the Control Room, knowing he'd find Elvis monitoring the workflow from up there. Rushing in, Frenchy slipped Elvis some skin and then launched into a quick explanation about his predicament.

"Look, man, these lunatics are coming after me, and they're going to keep coming until they kill me. The Wursties might be able to hold them off for a little while but not for three whole days. So I'm going into hiding."

"Sucks, dude," Elvis said. "I did a little stint in the joint once at the Pole. It ain't fun, but you'll get through it."

"Yo, Cool Hand Luke, who the hell said I'm going to jail!?" Frenchy asked, quite taken aback by the insinuation.

Elvis shrugged. "Well, you're being forced to go somewhere you don't want to go, and you can't come out for a set amount of time. Sounds like jail to me. Just remember the three things that turn hard time easy: good chow, some righteous tunes, and a bunch of girlie posters."

"Jesus," Frenchy said, fully bothered by the thought. "Imprisoned for the crime of being who I am. Well, that's a metaphysical whopper I'll have three days to chew on, but for now I gotta run. Are you going to be okay without me as far as keeping the furnace going? I think I've stockpiled enough wood to get us to Christmas, so you'll just have to ask the Wursties to chuck some in every once in a while."

"Yeah, man, we'll be fine," Elvis replied. "It'll actually be the Eve when you get out, so you'll be able to help us with the sprint to the goal line. In the meantime, be safe, bud!"

They engaged in a bro hug, shaking hands while pulling one another forward and slapping the other guy firmly on the back.

"Keep an eye on Flats for me, dude," Frenchy said, turning to make a dash for the exit.

"You got it, man," Elvis called out behind him.

Flats, meanwhile, was high up in the castle's tower, something of a prisoner herself, confined to her room by the constant sound of arrows clanking about in every direction. Terrified, she instinctively knew that the arrows had to be intended for either herself or Frenchy, and she anxiously awaited word from him.

She paced about her quarters, which were cast in her own

194

image, its solid stone walls covered in soft white lace that blew gently in the breeze. Vivaldi's "Spring" was playing in her head, as it often did during trying times, its message of hope always seeming to provide a little shelter from whatever storm she was going through.

There was a soft knock on her door. "Hey, it's me, can I come in?"

"Of course, Frenchy," she said, hurrying over to unlock the door.

As soon as she saw him, Flats could tell he was very shaken. "Oh my goodness, what are all these arrows about?" she asked.

"They're about me and ending my days. Shot by some sickos from a twisted television show that hunts those like you and me for sport. The bad news is there's a lot of them, and they seem to have an endless supply of arrows. The good news is that their mission has a ticking clock, which gives them only three days to get me. So I gotta disappear and stay hidden, and hopefully they'll simply run out of time."

Flats absorbed the weight of what he'd just said. "Goodness, leaving the compound all by yourself? That sounds really dangerous."

"Well, it's better than waiting around here like a sitting duck. The Scandies have lined up a hiding place for me, and I think we have a pretty solid plan to get me there safely, which, by the way, involves me dying, but not really."

Flats gasped. "Dying? What on earth do you mean by that?"

"Oh, geez, sorry. Yeah, I guess my purported resurrection is in the rearview mirror. This is gonna be more like playing possum. To the outside world, I'm going to be a total goner, complete with a coffin and a full-blown funeral. But rest assured, I'll be back as good as new."

"I understand the trickery involved," Flats said. "And I'm sure you guys have it all planned out. It's just, I don't like the thought of you being out there all alone."

Frenchy smiled. While he in no way wanted to cause Flats to worry, he couldn't deny that the thought of someone caring about him warmed his insides. And not just any someone. *Her.*

"But I won't be alone," he said. "You'll be with me, in my heart, which will make it all go as right as rain. So let's just bide our time for three short days, sending those lunatics back to whatever wretched place they came from, and I'll be back before you even realize I left."

They embraced, holding onto one another for several long seconds. As they pulled apart, they grasped onto each other's hand, two very unique appendages fitting perfectly together as one.

As much as he hated it, Frenchy knew the time to make his escape was growing shorter, so he started to let go. But Flats wouldn't allow it, pulling him sharply back to her.

"My goodness, I just got a really bad chill," she said. "You have to promise me that you'll be okay and that you'll come back safely."

Frenchy made a crossing motion with his hand. "I promise."

They leaned in even closer, their lips readying to touch.

Just then, an arrow whizzed in through the open window, slicing right between their faces and embedding into the wall directly behind them. They looked at it quivering an inch from both their noses, then quickly pulled apart from one another.

Frenchy crouched down and began to duckwalk toward the door.

Turning, he called out behind him. "Stay in here. Keep the door locked and don't let anyone in. I promise, we'll pick up right where we left off the next time we see each other! You promise too?"

"Yes, Frenchy," Flats said, her smile both sad and brave. "I promise too."

Frenchy returned the smile, then took off running as fast as he could down to the factory floor.

CHAPTER TWENTY-EIGHT
The Funeral

Bursting into the factory, Frenchy right away encountered a group of twelve Scandies standing around a box with hammers and nails, apparently readying to nail it shut. But as he got closer, Frenchy could see that it wasn't just any box but rather his sketch already brought to life: a real live casket, i.e. his wooden mobile home for the upcoming stretch of his journey.

Further, the Scandies had taken an extra step to make that journey a little smoother, decking the casket out with a huge supply of sodas and snacks.

"Thanks for the chow, guys. Here goes nothing, I guess...."

Frenchy took a deep breath and climbed in, finding it more than a little spooky to be hopping into a casket under one's own power. It definitely wasn't going to be first-class travel, either, as the confines were quite claustrophobic, giving off the overall feeling of, well, being shut in a coffin. But most concerning, as Frenchy began to notice the second the Scandies flung the lid shut, was that he couldn't breathe.

Panicked, he started banging hard on the lid, hoping to be heard before any of the nails could seal it shut. "Get me out of this death trap!" he shouted. "Christ, I can't breathe, and it's darker than doom in here!"

Sam instructed the crew to pull open the lid and then calmly addressed Frenchy. "Oh Special One, we are so sorry for your discomfort," he said. "We shall alter your cocoon to make it more to your satisfaction."

"Sam, it's Frenchy, remember? All I need is to be able to flippin' breathe. And to have just a tiny bit of light coming in."

"Consider it done, Frenchy."

They both smiled as Frenchy climbed back out to enjoy his last moments of freedom. Meantime, Sam politely issued a couple of orders to his team, directing them on how to make the necessary improvements to the casket. Just a few minutes later, it was ready.

Frenchy climbed back in, noticing that his travel capsule was now equipped with a snorkel and a clear plastic windshield fashioned out of a child's scuba mask, expertly cut flush into the lid's surface. He nodded, giving the Scandies the signal to once again close the lid, this time for good.

Frenchy listened as nail after nail was hammered home, each one sealing his fate ever more securely, and he couldn't help but to recognize that his life was now fully in the hands of the Scandies. Starting to again feel a tinge of panic, he peered up through his little windshield, his eyes searching for something to steel his nerves.

At the same moment, Sam leaned over the windshield, locking eyes with Frenchy.

Something transpired in that moment. Perhaps it was just the beautiful symmetry, with both parties having brought more to the other than they had ever sought in return. Whatever it was, it worked, providing Frenchy with the courage and peace he needed to ride out the journey ahead, come whatever may, and also for the Scandies to proceed free of fear.

Sharing a nod, they both acknowledged that the mission was a go.

On Sam's directive, the Scandie crew lifted up the casket, carrying it out of the factory, across the courtyard, and down to the compound's gates. There they set it down and paused to get into character, filling their spirits with nothing but woe and working themselves into a mourning sadness so palpable as to take on a physical form.

A pair of Wursties swung open the gates, and it was show-time: a full-blown funeral processional was about to unfold right under the watchful eyes of the Monster Hunters.

Leading the charge, the first two Scandies came out playing bagpipes, a mournful Irish tune. They were followed by a third Scandie holding an elongated pole, the top of which displayed a large, framed portrait of a cartoonish, demented-looking lizard-human creature, with "R.I.P. FROGMAN" in big bold letters at the bottom.

Then came six pallbearers, each carrying their share of Frenchy's weight as they wailed mournfully—and quite convincingly.

But the stars of the show were the last three Scandies. These guys were in hysterics, shirtless, and wild-eyed, flogging their own backs with very real whips, creating streams of very real blood. Giving their all for Frenchy, their performances were worthy of the finest stage.

The entire crew continued to bravely proceed across the river valley, never once wavering. Nearing the point where they were just about to disappear out of view, the poster-bearer planted his pole into the ground. It gave Frenchy's "killers" a

THE FROGMAN OF LOVELAND

nice, clear view of the treacherous beast they had just slayed, soon to be laid six feet closer to whatever underworld awaited it.

As the processional turned, any anxiety Frenchy felt began to dissipate, for he knew that each successful step brought them closer to their final destination. Looking up through his windshield in an attempt to gauge where they were on the hillside, he couldn't help but notice that the sky was totally devoid of flying creatures. It was as though they'd all been tipped off that something evil lurked down below.

As the funeral procession drifted fully out of view, the Monster Hunters applauded, having fallen for the performance, hook, line, and sinker. Then they began to raise hearty toasts of ale in celebration of their conquest, the first quick pops making their eyes fuzzy and the ruse seem all the more believable.

With the bagpipes fading and the Scandies disappearing out of view, Renaldo addressed the camera to wrap up the proceedings. "Watching the funeral procession of the one known as the Loveland Frogman, we couldn't help but think of all those innocent little children he so lustily ate. And though our heroics in this sleepy little village won't bring them back, we can at least take solace in knowing that justice has been served. But our job is never done, and you can rest assured that we'll be back again next week to rid the world of yet another horrifying beast. Until then, this is Renaldo Guevarra, saying, 'Sudsy foam, down the hatch. Another monster has met its match!'"

At that same moment back at the castle, Elvis walked by the Admiral's quarters. Its television set was still on, blaring, and it happened to be showing the program. Even though he knew the whole casket thing was a ruse, he felt a deep sense of pain for Frenchy, as well as Flats, as it hit him squarely for the first time that many of his own race really did regard them as monsters—monsters they'd go to great lengths to rid from their world. And why, because they happened to look a little different?

"Damn, I'm so sorry, guys!" he whispered as the show faded to commercial, a couple of tears sneaking their way out.

A few minutes later, the Scandies arrived at their destination, finally able to ditch their air of despair. They pried the casket open, and Frenchy bounded out, never happier to be fully surrounded by fresh air.

Looking out at the twelve Scandies that had made the journey, Frenchy couldn't help but notice that not only were they glowing, but they were actually glowing *green*. Their bravery and reverence humbled Frenchy, filling him with incredible respect for the little critters. "Guys," he said softly. "You saved me. How can I ever repay you?"

Sam stepped forward, smiling. "Saved…? Your question drips with an irony sweeter than honey, Oh Special One, for it is you who saved us. We have simply endeavored to pay back a tiny sliver of the favor in return. But if I can be so bold as to make a request, it is that you meet me back at this very spot in three days, safe and healthy, and I promise I shall bring with me the widest of smiles!"

Frenchy nodded, returning the smile and then grabbing Sam in a firm embrace. "It's a deal. But only if you flippin' call me Frenchy!"

They enjoyed a good laugh, and then Frenchy took several minutes to hug every one of the Scandies, lingering with each as though none of them wanted the moment to end. But alas, they all knew the time was upon them, the time for Frenchy to be hidden away. So he gave one last wave, took a deep breath, and walked into the cave's darkness. Then the Scandies pushed a huge boulder in front, fully sealing Frenchy off from the rest of the world.

From beyond the stone, he thought he could faintly hear Sam. Sensing his little friend was touching the other side of the boulder, Frenchy did the same, putting his palm firmly up against it. Feeling a warmth, he knew that Sam was there.

Through muffled tones, he worked to make out Sam's words: "Be well, Oh Special One. Very soon, you and the Angel shall be together at last!"

Rattled, Frenchy licked his finger and then ran it back and forth across his forehead. "Am I cracking up already, hearing voices foretelling tales of things not yet seen? Damn, what am I even saying? I just hope he's right!"

He then turned to check out his new quarters, but instead he found himself staring into nothing but depthless darkness.

• • •

As the Scandies turned to begin their trek back, four reindeer pulling Spiro's sleigh flew over the river valley, slowing down as they prepared to land in the castle courtyard. Glancing over, Spiro got a good view of the Frogman's "In Memoriam" poster standing tall upon the hillside.

Smiling, he feigned washing his hands, then giggled icily whilst making a proclamation. "I am innocent of the blood of this just creature," he said, knowing full well just how stained those hands really were.

Chapter Twenty-Nine
The Inquisition

December 22, 1978

Spiro barked out an order for his driver as he exited the sleigh. "I'm going to hang out here a little while to make sure things get handled to my liking. So bed down your reindeer and prepare to stay a couple of days. And then make yourself scarce, as the army is going to be arriving en masse any second now!"

The driver did as he was told, leading his team over to an out-of-the-way spot across the courtyard. Spiro looked around for signs of Elvis, and, seeing a light on up in the Control Room, he headed that way.

Bounding into the room with a spring in his step, Spiro called out cheerfully, "Hey there, Elvis. How's it going?"

Elvis' nervous system went into a full-tilt tingle. Not only had Spiro just shown up three days before Christmas, but he had a certain spark about him, exuding something almost approximating warmth. This wasn't good.

"Um, it's going fine, Spiro," Elvis said. "And it's good to see you again, but I definitely wasn't expecting it, especially with the big push on. So what brings you here?"

"Oh, just making some last-minute checks on all the Territories, you know, to offer support and all that stuff. Nothing to be alarmed about, I can assure you."

Elvis studied Spiro closely, looking for any hint as to why he was really there, but he came up empty.

"Sounds good," Elvis said, his words rushed and quite the opposite of what he was thinking. "So, here's a quick update: We're damn tight, but I think we're actually going to make it if everything goes exactly as planned. Now, as I'm sure you can imagine, I'm really pressed for time at the moment, so if there's anything specific you'd like to go over, just holler."

"Geez, that's great!" Spiro said distractedly, setting off at a good pace toward the stairs leading down to the factory floor. "Let's go have a look, shall we?"

Elvis' stomach was doing summersaults, and he sure as hell didn't want to waste time peeking in on what he had been closely monitoring for weeks. But, seeing little in the way of options, he joined Spiro and headed down the steps, off to check on lord knows what.

"Yeah, sounds great," Elvis said out loud. Then, mumbling under his breath, he let his real thoughts be known: "Couldn't change anything at this point even if we wanted to.…"

As they approached the factory floor, two things became very apparent. First, it was as hot as hell. Seemed that some of the Wursties, having not been tipped off to Frenchy's faux death, had become distraught, and their means of honoring his memory was to throw everything they could get their hands on into the furnace, including fully grown live trees.

And second, the overheated Scandies were clearly on a roll, moving with extraordinary speed and making serious progress toward meeting their quota.

Their contribution was lost on Spiro. "I'd bet you that if you added all those rats' IQs together, it still wouldn't reach one hundred," he said. "Come on, Elvis, are you really entrusting your future to this crew?"

Elvis paused a long second, studying the list of toys yet to be built and then checking the calendar, confirming that they had over two full workdays left. "Damn right, I am!" he said. "These guys have been giving it hell for over a month straight. They work their asses off, and they're much smarter than they look. So, yeah, I'm betting on them, and, like I said, I think we're going to make it. Assuming we're left alone for the next couple of days."

"Oh, you're going to be left alone, alright," Spiro replied, a creepy, cold smile breaking out across his face.

He took a look at Elvis' list for himself, quickly coming to the realization that, unfettered, they stood a very real shot of pulling their mission off. "Wow, I have to hand it to you. Looks like you and your little band of freaks are really going to make it," he said. "Come on, you've got a little time to spare. Let's go get a breath of air."

As Spiro turned to walk off, Elvis groaned, rolling his eyes in frustration.

Partway into their journey out to the courtyard, Spiro caught sight of a large portrait of Frenchy that one of the Scandies had painted towering high over the factory floor. His face brightening, he stopped in his tracks and pivoted toward Elvis.

"Methinks part of your tale has been left untold. So, out with it. Is everything really going as planned here, or has there been some sort of unfortunate mishap?"

Elvis was puzzled. Having been so immersed in his toy-making quest, he hadn't even thought to continue Frenchy's burial ruse for Spiro's eyes. "What are you talking about? No, there haven't been any mishaps."

Spiro's hand extended slowly upward. Then he pointed at Frenchy's portrait with a flourish, a big smile crossing his face at the same time. "I heard your pet met his untimely demise and thus has been sent back to whence he came!"

Elvis' eyes shot up to the portrait, locking onto those of Frenchy. Feeling the very real emotion of Frenchy being gone— and of hearing the slimeball standing before him actually *gloat about it*—his temper sparked. But, knowing that tearing into Spiro would stand to ruin all that they had worked for, Elvis did everything in his power to shove the emotions back down. "Oh, yeah, some psychos killed him for nothing but sport. Totally, totally sucks that some people can be such callous pieces of shit!"

"Boy, I can only imagine," Spiro replied, unable to refrain from rubbing salt in the perceived wound even for a second. "Oh, well. The days of the unholy are marked as soon as they're formed, so the Frogman probably did better than most. At least he was able to share the air with us normal beings, if but for a brief time."

"For Chrissake, Spiro!" Elvis blurted out, unable to help himself. "Why the hell did you have such a problem with Frenchy right from the moment you first met him?"

"*Problem?*" Spiro replied. "Let's talk about *your* problem. Starting with the fact that you always insisted on calling it by a name and treating it like an equal."

"Because he is!" Elvis shouted in Spiro's face, his anger getting the better of him. But then he calmed himself once again. "I mean, because he was."

"Yeah, that's right," Spiro said. "It's gone. So, I'll tell you what. Why don't you just fall in line and disavow it? Trust me, it'll be a cinch, and then we won't ever have to speak of it again. And, in doing so, you'll show me that there's some hope of you eventually becoming a team player, which will go a long way toward getting you back into the Academy. I do know those in high places, remember."

Elvis cleared his throat, and he moved his face within inches of Spiro's, his eyes widening and his head cocked sideways. "I want to make three things crystal clear. One: not a single cell of me wants back into that putrid little dweeb factory you call the Academy. Two: get out of my way, and we'll deliver this stinkin' quota, which will serve all of us well. And three: I won't be disavowing Frenchy. Not now, not ever!"

"My goodness. Well, so be it. At least we each know where the other stands," Spiro said, his dispassionate bearing the polar opposite of Elvis'. He seemed to be checking off strange, unseen boxes that only he knew about.

An odd truce ensued. After a brief staredown, the pair proceeded to walk out of the factory and into the courtyard. It was there that Elvis first laid his eyes on the hundreds of armed Polie soldiers resplendently dressed and lined up in crisp formation.

Floored, he turned to Spiro. "What the hell's going on?" he asked.

As the words were coming out, two Polie soldiers advanced upon Elvis' backside, sneaking right up and fixing the blades of their bayonet rifles upon him, one behind each ear.

THE FROGMAN OF LOVELAND

"You had best start explaining what's going on here, boy," Elvis sneered.

Spiro laughed. "You and that hot little head of yours. It would serve you to learn to watch your mouth, as I imagine those soft, rounded ears of yours won't fare too well with sharpened steel jammed into them. Sentry, give the boy a taste of what's in store if he elects to keep spouting off."

With one of the soldiers holding his bayonet blade steady, the other took the butt end of his rifle and drove it into Elvis' stomach, causing him to double over in pain.

Elvis moaned. Then, fighting through the agony, he forced his way back to a standing position. "Spiro, you have no idea how much trouble you're going to be in over whatever bullshit you're pulling here! Santa's gonna go berserk when he finds out!"

Spiro laughed, then emphatically spat on the ground. "Well, I sure don't see his fat ass anywhere around here, and I suspect that by the next time you see it, your fate will be well sealed. But while we're on the subject of trouble, let me read you a little something, and then we can decide whose future has storm clouds on its horizon."

Spiro fished the folded-up note from his shirt pocket that the Elder had given him back on Thanksgiving. "And keep in mind, Elvis, our actions have consequences!"

Enjoying the moment, Spiro began to read the note aloud, word for deliberate word:

> *"Santa, you are nothing but a big fat faker. My name is Linda Kehoe. I'm in first grade at Loveland Elementary School. I asked for an Easy-Bake Oven last Goetta Day, but all I got*

209

was a crappy wood thing with a hole in it. All my friends got the same stupid thing. So I tell you what. If I don't get all the toys on my list at Christmas, I'm sending a letter to President Carter. And the newspaper. I mean it! Signed, Linda Kehoe. P.S. I've been very good this year, and I don't deserve this crap!'"

Spiro returned the note to his pocket. "Fortunately for us and unfortunately for you, that note got routed over to the Polie's mail room instead of Santa's. For, had it gone to him, it would still be in the giant stack of unopened mail that his lazy ass never seems to get to. But with it having fallen into the right hands, we were able to take action, hopefully keeping you from ever putting our Empire in jeopardy again."

"Jeopardy, from one kid's complaint?! Spiro, you're so freakin' full of it! We did what was asked of us, and we got a toy into every kid's hands under terrible circumstances. Hell, I think I should have gotten some type of award. But here you are making it sound like I committed a crime!"

"Bingo!" Spiro exclaimed. "Probably the first bright thing you've said since I met you. In fact, as a Territorial Administrator with powers over such matters, let me be a little more specific: I hereby declare you guilty of committing fraudulent and deceptive acts against the Polie Empire. Accordingly, you shall be sentenced to three days in the dungeon, to be served immediately!"

Elvis could feel his temper spiking again, and he struggled to hold it at bay, knowing that he needed to keep his wits if he was to have any shot at escaping this bind. "Why the hell are you doing this, Spiro? *We're so close.* Shit, we can make it if you just leave us alone. And if it's Frenchy you're hung up on, I don't know why he'd be an issue any longer. Christ, he's freakin' gone!"

"There you go again!" Spiro shouted, his anger now the one on the rise. "Couldn't go five minutes without bringing that creature up. But I'll tell you what, I'll give you one last chance. Renounce it and call it what it really is, a freak of nature, and I'll let you go free just before Santa gets here on Christmas Eve. That way, at least you can slink out of here and avoid seeing the crushed look in his eyes. But if not, you can rot in the dungeon until the rats and maggots have at you. And what would it really matter? I mean, would anybody really care?"

Elvis lunged at Spiro, causing one of the sentries to cut in front of him and reposition the cold tip of his bayonet blade right between his eyes.

"You're a conniving little prick, Spiro," Elvis spat. "One last time, there's no way I would ever renounce Frenchy! He's the best friend I ever had, and he had more balls in his cut-off pinky than you have in your entire body. So you can stick it up your pretentious Polie ass!"

"Balls? Perhaps. But certainly not survival skills! From what I heard, it didn't last an hour against that pesky crew of Monster Hunters," Spiro concluded. "Geez, come to think of it, they sure seemed to have an easy time finding the beast, almost like someone let slip where it was hiding out. Ha, if you ask me, *that's* the person who deserves some type of award."

Elvis couldn't hold back. He knocked away the blade aimed at his forehead and lunged forward, ferociously punching Spiro in the gut. As he pulled his fist back to level another shot, he felt a white-hot lightning bolt of pain enter his right shoulder, then exit.

Turning around, Elvis saw the bloody bayonet blade, now pulled back to the sentry's side, poised to be deployed again. As he went to sidestep to avoid another jab, everything went black, and Elvis collapsed into a quickly expanding pool of his own blood.

"Drag him to the dungeon," Spiro, still doubled over in pain, barked to the sentries.

• • •

Some several hours later, Elvis was awakened by a series of loud bangs, as though someone was smacking a trashcan lid with a hammer. His faculties slowly returning, he scanned the four dank, cold concrete walls that surrounded him, noticing that there wasn't a single window, and then the ceiling, leaking with a putrid brown water. Scanning over further to where a faint light shined in, he discovered the source of the noise: Spiro banging a metal jug of ale against the locked steel bar door of his cell.

"I'd offer you a sip to dull the pain," Spiro slurred. "But I heard that once your kind starts with the stuff, there's no stopping. So perhaps better to not."

His injured shoulder throbbing, Elvis nevertheless ran hard toward the door, lowering his good one and bashing into it. But to no avail. For as badly as he wanted to get at Spiro, he wasn't going to power his way through bars of steel. "You're pure evil, Spiro!"

"Ha! Left with nothing but your temper to keep you company," Spiro said smugly. "I was entertaining myself, trying to figure out who's going to be more disappointed by this whole ordeal. The millions of kids in Ohio waking up to empty Christmas trees? Or Santa Claus, realizing that his pet welfare

THE FROGMAN OF LOVELAND

project turned out to be the headcase everyone else always knew him to be? I just hope it was all well worth it for you, Parker. Seems like a good trade-off, throwing away a life's opportunity to hitch your star to a dead frogman."

"I don't know how, but somehow, some way, I'm going to get you for all this, you slimy little snake!" Elvis vowed, rattling his cell door as he spit the words out.

Spiro, enjoying the moment, couldn't resist getting in one last jab. "Oh, and in twenty years or so, when people are bowing down to me as the modern-day Father Christmas, come see me for a position. One can never have too many boot-shines."

"You, in charge of Christmas?" Elvis shot back. "Don't make me laugh. You must have forgotten that little part about spreading love. Not one of you Polies has any of it in you, and it's not something that can be bought."

Spiro's eyes lit up. "Ah, yes, sounding just like Santa himself, forever extolling the virtues of love, the last bastion of the weak and the clingy. As it's been said, the apple doesn't fall far from the tree."

With Elvis' head so clouded by anger, the comment went right over it.

Then, without so much as giving it another thought, Spiro departed, whistling "Blue Christmas" as he strolled off.

Chapter Thirty
A Most Prescient Dream

Frenchy hadn't thought through just how hard this was going to be. The Scandies apparently hadn't either, because if they had, they most certainly would've outfitted the cave with at least some form of light. Something as small as even a single candle would've made all the difference in the world. As it stood now, all he had were his thoughts, a movie playing over and over in his head, its scenes growing increasingly darker the more times they played.

Having no way to mark time or even tell if the day had changed to night, Frenchy gutted through what he thought was the first day. But who was to say if time was really passing at all? Crunched up on his cot, Frenchy could feel his mind descending into the gray dungeon. "This is a prison of my own creation," he muttered. "Movement. I need movement."

He rose up and started to pace around the cave, which calmed him a little since it required concentration to navigate through the darkness. Having even a tiny something occupying his mind was certainly better than having nothing.

However, after pacing about for a brief time, Frenchy stumbled over what felt like a six-pack of cans, presumably left on the ground by the Scandies. Instinctively he threw his hands out in front of himself, stopping his head's momentum a split second before it crashed into one of the cave's unforgiving stone walls.

So, that was it for the pacing.

Frenchy made his way back to the bed and climbed in, frightened to think of where his thoughts might lead him next. But eventually he passed out into a restless sleep, a sleep that, unfortunately, brought him anything but peace.

His dream was one he had often, and it started like it always did: with Frenchy the frog back at the orphanage, hiding in a panic as Tante Frog, broom in hand, stalked him. The story evolved as usual, with the old woman quickly discovering his hiding spot and then raising her broom overhead, readying to whack Frenchy over the head with it. In all the previous versions, she would get her licks in good, whacking away at Frenchy until the blows awakened him with an abrupt jolt.

But this time, it went differently.

Just before the broom fell, a beautiful owl swooped in, grabbing Frenchy by the back of his shirt and gracefully lifting him high up into the sky with her. Then they peacefully flew over the river valley for several wonderful minutes, the unfamiliar sensation of soaring through the air absolutely exhilarating, as though life was supposed to be lived at such great heights.

Up in the distance on the hillside, Frenchy made out what appeared to be an encampment of humans, with a little series of lean-to structures set up around a smoldering fire. Soaring straight ahead, he could tell that they were heading right for it.

Realizing he was blocking the owl's view of the humans, Frenchy attempted to yell, needing to warn her to change course. But no sound came out. Starting to panic, he squirmed about and flailed his hands out in front of him, pointing, desperately trying to get her attention.

But no matter how hard he tried, the owl didn't notice, and she continued to fly onward.

As they were just about overhead of the encampment, Frenchy could tell that the humans were hunters, and several of them had already fixed their arrows straight up over their heads. Crazed with fear, he tried one last scream, but again nothing came out.

Left with no other option, he had to provide the owl a clear view of the hunters. So, twisting and pushing off with his feet at the same time, he shook himself free and began his terrifying descent back to the earth.

Just a short second later, Frenchy heard the whistle of an arrow speeding just past his ear, then a sickening thud as it made contact with its target.

Upon the impact, Frenchy sprang awake, and he now found himself sitting straight up in bed in the darkness, screaming louder than he ever had. "The mighty mystical Special One, my ass!" he shouted. "Hiding away in here like a criminal, or worse, a coward, when everyone else is out there in harm's way. I'm getting the hell out of here right now!"

He leapt out of bed and shuffled over to the boulder blocking the cave's entrance, crouching down and pushing on it with all his might. But no matter how hard he tried, he couldn't get it to budge. "Damn it to hell!"

Desperate, and a touch delusional, Frenchy made a fateful decision.

Taking five paces backward, he readied himself to rush the boulder. Then, sprinting with all his might, he lowered his shoulder and prepared for contact. Unfortunately, though,

Frenchy couldn't see that the boulder's contour was uneven, and his first point of contact with it wasn't his shoulder, but rather his head.

Knocked fully out cold, he would spend his remaining time in the cave, however long that time was to be, in true darkness.

CHAPTER THIRTY-ONE
The Angel

Nearing Midnight, December 23, 1978

With the calendar just about to flip over to Christmas Eve, Spiro was up in the Admiral's former quarters having himself a whale of a time. With both Frenchy and Elvis out of the picture, he had the run of the place, and he was taking full advantage, beginning with a healthy sampling from the remaining bottles in the Admiral's elixir cabinet. But it was a different discovery that had really captivated his attention: a ring of keys. They'd been lying tucked beneath a tall stack of girlie magazines, and had he not painstakingly browsed through every single issue, he never would have found them.

Now it was time to see if they could open a certain locked door.

About two hundred feet straight overhead, high up in the watchtower, a sharp clap of thunder rumbled across Flats' room, jarring her fully awake from what had already been a most restless bout of tossing and turning.

Her senses on heightened alert, she heard little taps on her door, as though a varmint of some sort was scratching away at it. Startled and most unnerved, Flats felt right away that something was amiss. Going over to the door and looking through its peephole, she saw Spiro holding a dozen roses and fumbling clumsily with a set of keys.

Flats pressed one of her tiny-boned feet against the bottom of the door and then summoned her angriest voice, hoping her words would come out as tough and not frightened. "Spiro," she shouted. "What the hell are you doing?"

"I heard your little boyfriend, uh, checked out, so I thought I'd come up and see how you were doing," he said, his words slurred and nasally. "Plus, I brought you a peace offering."

"For heaven's sake, I don't know where you get the nerve to even be up here. Now, get your ass moving back down those stairs before you make this any worse on yourself."

"Worse, why, whatever do you mean?" Spiro said, laughing. "I'm having a perfectly lovely time. So what makes you think I'm looking to go anywhere except inside, to have a nice little visit with you?"

"Oh my god!" Flats exclaimed, disgusted and freaked out all at once. "Please, just get the hell out of here. If not, you're going to see what it's like when I'm really pissed off!"

"Come on, baby, you've got me all wrong. Let me in and I'll show you my good side."

"What, now you're asking? A second ago I could have sworn you were trying to break in, which is not only despicable, but it's also against the law. So the answer is a big fat no!" Flats shouted.

"Against the law?" he echoed with an ugly laugh. "To access my own empire's property, in a Territory over which I rule? Do you actually think you have any say over that which I do or don't do? But okay, you know what? I've been trying to get you to be nice to me for as long as I can remember, and I'm freakin' sick of begging!"

He rammed his shoulder hard into the door, driving right through it and destroying the deadbolt, badly injuring Flats' foot in the process. As he stumbled to the center of the room, it was now quite clear to her that he had been deeply into the elixir.

"What the hell's wrong with you?" Flats yelled, her fear and anger both intensifying along with her pain. "This is so far out of line, I can't even begin to tell you how much trouble you're going to be in!"

"You people and your infatuation with trouble!" Spiro barked. "There's not a soul in the world that even knows we're here, so who's to cause me trouble? But enough talk of that. Let's say we just start over and play nice together."

"Look, Spiro, over my dead body! I say we start by you getting the hell out of my room! You can't just barge in here like this, and you can't force yourself on me like you did before. You have no right!"

Flats took a few steps to the side, angling for a direct path to the window, which she knew she could escape out and Spiro could not.

Spiro, as though engaging in a twisted game, mimicked her, sliding over the same distance and blocking her path. "No right? Who are you to grant rights to me? You are but a runner, not yet even on the first rung of the Empire's ladder. Yet I rest atop it. So if anyone shall be doing any granting, it shall be me."

Flats worked to keep her wits, trying once more to create a clear path to the window. But the move was again countered

THE FROGMAN OF LOVELAND

by Spiro, and this time he moved diagonally, drawing closer to her.

"Look," Spiro said, his drunken mind thinking he could somehow charm Flats even in the midst of such repulsive behavior. "The Frogman is dead, and Elvis has been locked up for crimes against the Empire. You don't want to go down with their ship, do you? So how about you thaw out, and in return I'll make sure you wind up on a nice, warm beach somewhere?"

Spiro smiled creepily, his eyes forming little slits, and he clumsily thrust the roses out against Flats' chest.

Her internal alarm blaring, Flats stiffened for a fight. But first, she'd try one more attempt at verbal jousting in the hope that she could get into his foggy head. "Look, Spiro, as I told you before, I'm not looking to go anywhere. And I don't see how me treating you differently has anything to do with it. But let's go back to first things first, which is you getting the hell out of my room! And let me be crystal clear: the next time I see you, it'd better be in the workplace!"

The comment fully enraged Spiro, and he threw the roses at Flats' face, forcing her to duck. "You stuck-up little bitch! You laid down with that freaky frogman, and yet you won't even look in my direction! I'm going to show you what you've been missing!"

He lunged toward Flats, but, given his elixir-riddled state, she was able to sidestep him. He tripped on his own footing and landed face-first in the flowers, which, under a different scenario, might have actually seemed a bit comical. But as he arose and faced her, Flats knew there was nothing funny about what was happening.

His eyes ablaze, Spiro picked up a glass frame from Flats' nightstand and flung it like a razor-sharp frisbee against the wall, smashing it into a million pieces. Glancing down, Flats saw her favorite possession, Frenchy's drawing of the two of them, now lying in tatters on the floor.

Spiro, his anger continuing to grow, turned and lunged again. This time he was able to grab Flats and drive her across the room, smashing her hard up against the wall and severely damaging her wing. "I'll show you who's in charge here, baby," Spiro slurred into her ear.

There was no way Flats was going to go down without putting up a valiant fight. "Get off of me, you slimy little creep!" she yelled, trying hard to pivot away from him even as the pain splintered down her wing and through the rest of her body.

Spiro grabbed her around the back and thrust his body fully against hers, pinning both her wings tightly down to her sides. At the same time he smashed their lips together so violently that it drew blood. "You give it up for everybody else, so I'm taking my turn," he hissed.

With flight unavailable, Flats shifted to fight, kneeing Spiro between his legs as hard as she could. Freeing herself, she coaxed the talons of her good foot up high into a crane kick stance, then slashed them down like knives, cutting four ferocious trenches into Spiro's forehead. He instinctively brought his hands up to protect his eyes, already turning red from the torrent of blood gushing into them, and Flats stayed on the offensive, slashing at him again and again, turning his face into a bloody, pulpy mess.

Addled, weakened, and blinded, Spiro slid to the floor.

Knowing she had sent a lasting message, Flats eventually stopped slashing. But she couldn't resist adding an exclamation point: she leaned forward and spat the grossest matter she could muster up squarely into Spiro's bloody face.

Unfortunately for Flats, this last defiant act backfired horribly, because even though Spiro still couldn't see, he could now sense where she stood by the launching point of her spit. He sprang up and forward with a roar, hitting Flats dead-on and sending her toppling out the open window.

Her escape hatch had become a death trap. With her wing damaged, Flats started spiraling uncontrollably toward the ground. Desperate, she extended both her wings to steady her descent, crying out in agony as the air pushed against the injured one, almost tearing it fully off. The effort had its desired effect, though, slowing her fall just enough, and Flats landed with a thud on an open stretch of land across the river.

A Scandie, out getting some air during a brief break from the factory floor, had witnessed Flats toppling out the window. And, from looking up into the castle tower, he had also seen the mangled face of the one that had caused this to be. The little elf knew instantly that Flats was in grave danger, for not only had she landed right across the river from where several of the Monster Hunters were still camped out, but she was also completely out in the open.

An instant later, the Scandie heard the twang of a bow's string, foretelling that one of the Monster Hunters had already fixed his sights on the sitting duck across the river. Knowing he hadn't a moment to spare, he took off, his feet revving faster than he ever imagined they could. Time slowed down, and he was able to assess the arrow's speed and trajectory, leaving him believing he stood a chance to chase down the arrow and snatch it before it reached Flats.

Quickly reaching the Little Miami, the Scandie was moving at such an astonishing speed that he actually ran atop the water, his feet skimming across the surface. Now almost to her, he made a desperate last dive, stretching out in an attempt to intercept the incoming projectile.

But he was just a second too late. Sickeningly, he was left to watch in horror as the arrow flashed right in front of his fingertips, piercing through Flats' white dress and cutting cleanly into her heart.

The Scandie fell to his knees, crawling over and nestling her tenderly in his arms. Comforting Flats as best he could, he held the gaze of her eyes, still full of soul. "It wasn't supposed to be this way," he said softly. "You and the Special One, you were supposed to walk this world forever, as tightly as just one. It has to be like that, for it says so in the Prophecy."

His voice trailed off, and he choked on his words, barely able to get them out.

He gently pushed a few strands of Flats' hair off her face, returning the shape of her otherworldly coiffure into that of a heart.

"He loved you, you know," the Scandie whispered.

She smiled sweetly. Then, with pained regret crossing her eyes, they fell softly shut.

A small, shiny circular ring appeared overtop Flats' head. She began to rise up, and the Scandie, panicking, grabbed on with all his might, desperately trying to keep her from going. But the force simply proved too great, and the uniquely beautiful creature pulled away and ascended into the sky, now powered by something beyond her wings.

"Rest well, Angelic One," he whispered.

Then he raised his voice, wracked with pain, and railed against the heavens.

The Angel

CHAPTER THIRTY-TWO
Roll Away the Stone

Deep in the Black Forest, Sam was fast in motion. Sensing that he was in grave danger, he continually glanced back over his shoulder, certain that something ghoulish was gaining on him.

The Black Forest was super creepy even on the brightest of days. Now, with a coal black sky overhead, it was spooky beyond belief. So with each hoot of an owl, or imagined hoots from evils unseen, the little Scandie leader ran all the faster.

Finally, out of breath exhausted, he came to rest in the shadows of the most infamous building in Loveland: the Festhaus.

Straight out of the Middle Ages, the huge Bavarian inn catered to the Wursties' every need, with its most prominent feature being the giant cuckoo clock rising high above the entryway. At the top of every hour, it provided those brave enough to have made the trek with a jarring peek into the Wurstie world—and, being that the second hand had just clicked onto midnight, it was showtime.

On cue, a yellow bird sprang from behind a door, chirping once then disappearing. Eight mini Wurstie figurines, each clad in traditional Bavarian attire, then took center stage, emerging from inside the clock, curtsying, and pairing off. Oompah music rang to life, sending the figurines into a joyful dance. The dancing went on for twenty seconds or so, then came to an oddly violent conclusion, with four of the Wursties giving four others solid slaps across their faces. They then hoisted large steins of ale and toasted as though everything was just as it should be.

Sam blinked, trying to digest what he had just seen, wondering what other oddities might be going on inside the imposing building he was about to enter.

Mustering all his courage, he took off, charging with a head of steam into what looked like thick, heavy front doors. But they turned out to be quite light, and he burst right through, rolling to an awkward, somersaulted stop deep inside Wurstie territory.

Sam looked around at the astonishing world he had stumbled in on.

The cavernous room had a single long table right down the center, and it was packed full of Wursties. Scattered about were tall mounds of sausages, which they grabbed at with their bare hands and dunked into vats of bubbling spicy mustard, washing the whole lot down with murky brown ale, mud-like in consistency.

In the rear of the room, in a fenced-in cube, two bloodied Wursties were bludgeoning each other in a bare-knuckled brawl, while onlookers clutching wads of dollar bills wildly cheered on their warrior of choice.

And then there was the stage, rising six feet above the Festhaus floor. Atop it were four heavily tattooed Wursties playing loud, fast polka music. Calling out to his audience, the singer periodically showered them with mouthfuls of ale, which, strangely, they seemed to enjoy.

As Sam got up and dusted himself off, the Wursties began to swarm, instinctively knowing that a non-Wurstie was among them. They encircled the elf, grunting and pointing at him as they got closer and closer, with several of them looking like they actually might take a *bite* out of the little guy.

A sharp command rang out, putting a stop to the horseplay: "Achtung!"

The Wursties sheepishly backed off, laughing, and falling into two lines of formation.

The Commandant, in sharp, full military dress as always, approached Sam, smiling. "Willkommen. Sorry about the men. They frisky after the evening ale. So, you've traveled far. There must be matter of importance."

Sam nodded. Wanting his words conveyed with perfect accuracy, he had committed them to writing. He pulled a notecard from his pocket and handed it to the Commandant.

"'Roll away the stone,'" the warrior read aloud.

Sam, filling with sadness, nodded again, then motioned for him to flip the card over.

"'The humans' arrows have killed the Angel,'" the Commandant read, his words coming out haltingly. He cleared his throat and continued. "'But the one called Spiro caused it to be.'"

He was deeply shaken by the news, and his voice drifted off like the words had come from someone else. Taking a long moment to compose himself, he then locked eyes with Sam. They both knew the heartbreaking mission they had to undertake.

They left the Festhaus running at full speed. Retracing Sam's path from earlier, they ran through the Black Forest and then toward the castle, where they intended to cut across the courtyard as a shortcut to Frenchy's cave hideout. But just as they were about to descend the steps to the courtyard, they froze.

Looking out onto a Polie army that had to number at least two hundred soldiers, the Wurstie and Scandie, usually engaging in extremely diverse speech patterns, said the exact same thing: "Holy shit!"

They stood there, stone-struck, watching the Polies march in lockstep for a few moments. Finally, shaking out of it, Sam grabbed the Commandant's sleeve and pulled him back toward the castle.

"Here, follow me," Sam said. "There's another way to get to the Special One's hiding spot. We can leave out the front door. Come, we must hurry!"

Minutes later, they arrived at Frenchy's cave, where the Commandant single-handedly set about rolling away the large stone sealing it shut.

A moonbeam cut through the darkness and met Frenchy's eye, awakening him from a foggy slumber that had lasted over two full days. His head banging, he squinted as he hobbled out, his eyes adjusting to the welcome sight of the Commandant and Sam.

But as soon as Frenchy's eyes fixed clearly upon Sam, he knew something was terribly wrong. For the wide smile Sam had promised was nowhere to be found, replaced instead by a quivering lower lip and wetted eyes.

Frenchy and the Commandant shook hands, and there was

a palpable sadness about him as well. He also seemed smaller, as though some air had been let out of his larger-than-life chest.

"Sorrow, mein friend," the Commandant began, getting right to the devastating news. "Flats, they killed her."

Frenchy didn't immediately make sense of the words, as though they had been spoken in a foreign language. He turned to Sam for help, eyeing him with a puzzled expression, but he couldn't offer anything to ease the pain, instead lowering his head mournfully.

Frenchy looked around, searching for something, *anything*. "Killed?" he said slowly, numbly. "Who would do such a thing?"

"The hunters' arrows finished the cowardly act," replied the Commandant.

Frenchy walked a good distance away, tears filling his eyes. He tucked his injured hand into his vest and drew inward, making himself as small as he could. His mind flashed to the new mail-order dress that had just arrived, his extra special Christmas surprise for Flats, and how now, she wouldn't even get to try it on.

"I am so sorrowful, Oh Special One, more sorrowful than I can tell." Sam's voice, doleful and wan, cut across Frenchy's heart-wrenching realization. "But, dare I say, there *is* hope yet. For the Prophecy does foretell—"

"You maniacs! Damn the Prophecy! Goddamn it all to hell!" Frenchy wailed. "Don't you see?! I'm not special! *Frenchy's* not special. 'Cuz if he was, he wouldn't have lost the most important thing in the world to him. The Prophecy, it's nothing… it's nothing but a fugazi."

Frenchy lowered his head and began to tremble, crying hard, shrinking himself to near nothingness.

Sam, his entire worldview having just been shaken like the

glitter within a snow globe, gasped and recoiled, then turned and took off in the direction of the castle.

The Commandant, seeing his brave friend so positively distraught, couldn't hold back a tear of his own, for though he had seen the atrocities of war, a gash in a young person's heart brought with it an altogether different type of pain. But he knew he had to compose himself, and while not a single part of him wanted to continue on with the news, he knew he had to do that as well. So he stiffened, ordering his tears to fall back into line like the disciplined soldiers he had trained them to be. Dabbing his eyes, he approached Frenchy.

"It was the hunters' arrows, but the one called Spiro caused it to be," the Commandant said crisply.

A fire sparked inside Frenchy, the anger pushing aside grief and taking over his entire being, consuming his heart, mind, and soul all at once. "Where is he!? He's a goddamn dead man!"

The Commandant tried to dissuade Frenchy, believing he'd be running headfirst into a suicide mission. "He's at das castle, but you mustn't go. He has huge army. I've seen them, over two hundred men, and you are certain to be killed!"

"Killed? Hell, supposedly I've already been dead, yet here I am. So what's to be afraid of? Besides, better dead than walking this world while that little snake is still slithering upon it!" Frenchy looked deeply into the Commandant's eyes. "Sir, would you and your men battle beside me?"

"It would be our honor," the old warrior replied.

Frenchy put his hand on the Commandant's shoulder. "No better friend, no worse enemy!"

The Commandant returned the gesture. "Screw with ein Ruffian, screw with all Ruffians!"

The men shook hands, knowing that they had just committed themselves and a small band of Wursties to take on a huge, well-trained army. But they were at peace with the decision, knowing it was really their only option.

As they made their way back toward the castle, the pair couldn't help but notice the Monster Hunters' smoldering campfires, the twisted crew having apparently moved on to make some other unique creature's life a living hell. But with that menace removed, a new one lay ahead. Even this deep in the woods, they could hear it: the drums of war, and the crisply clacking cadence of hundreds of Polie boots.

CHAPTER THIRTY-THREE
A Loveland Tale

Before crying havoc and letting slip the rabid Wurst-ies of war, Frenchy had an idea. He suggested to the Commandant that they first try some brinkmanship, attempting to break their enemy's spirit before the battle had even begun. This would first involve engaging in a pre-battle discussion with the opposing commander, who just so happened to be the highest-ranking officer in the Polie army, a four-star general.

On one side of the courtyard stood the two hundred strong Polie army. The troops cut an impeccable impression, resplendent in their crisply ironed uniforms and finely coifed hair, a smug invincibility exuding off them.

The other side of the courtyard remained empty, as the Commandant had not yet rousted his men. All that the Polies looked upon was a muddy mess of a field, which was strewn about, for some reason, with a disgusting mixture of bloody pig intestines and other assorted organs.

The Polie General and the Commandant had already arrived at the center of the courtyard, and they were just about to be joined by Frenchy, who was strolling across the grounds at his own leisure.

High up in Flats' room in the watchtower, Spiro was watching the whole scene play out through the veil of heavy bandages. A crack Polie army medic had been able to save one of his eyes, the other having fallen victim to Flats' cutting retribution, and now, seeing Frenchy very much alive, he thought that his surviving eye was betraying him.

"Jesus Christ," he muttered under his breath. "Its ghost walks amongst us." Sliding his hand up the barrel of his rifle, he smirked. "So it'll need to be entombed a second time, and this time, I shall see that it is permanent."

Back down on the courtyard, the Polie General oozed confidence. His hubris was heightened by some serious misinformation Spiro had fed him, for when he briefed the General about his Territory-destroying mission, he'd told him there would be no resistance. But how was Spiro even to know, since the only locals he'd seen during his previous visit had been Elvis, Flats, the Frogman, and a bunch of little Scandies, a motley bunch that would prove no match for the vaunted Polie army?

But, unbeknownst to the General, a crazed crew lay in wait that certainly would be.

"You're fortunate that I've taken the time to share a word with you," the General began, addressing Frenchy and the Commandant. "For we've come to engage in battle, not discourse. So if you hope words are somehow going to spare your men's blood, you had might as well save your breath."

Frenchy and the Commandant both nodded.

"We just wanted to show you something first, chief," Frenchy said, his lack of military decorum totally rankling the General.

The three of them walked over to the edge of the courtyard,

THE FROGMAN OF LOVELAND

stopping at what had previously been the gated opening in the wall. It was now freshly sealed up with concrete blocks.

"Funf minuten," the Commandant said.

"Let me translate," Frenchy added. "Five minutes. And after that, none of your men, *or you,* will be going anywhere." Frenchy stared into the General's eyes, one of which had begun to twitch. "Because after that, the mortar binding these blocks will have set to stone as hardened as the muscles on the beasts you're about to meet. And trust me, those of your men that die on this field today will be the lucky ones, spared from things that are beyond even their darkest imaginings. You're down to four and a half minutes, chief."

The Polie General, caught off guard by the all-or-nothing tactic, attempted to mask his concern. "As I said, we have come here to fight, and so we shall."

"As you wish," replied Frenchy. "Herr Commandant, please assemble the troops."

"Hammerzeit," the Commandant barked out loudly in Bavarian.

In an instant, a wild-eyed pack of forty Wursties descended from the Black Forest, led by a forerunner wielding a pig's head on a stick. The enormous beasts, in clear view of the Polie troops, dove with relish into a most jarring ritual. First rolling around in the rank mud, they then began to bash into one another, ramming their heads together so hard that the impact could be felt across the courtyard. They proceeded to work one another into a type of frenzy, becoming so ravenous that they began eating the intestines and organs, leaving demonic streams of blood trickling down their naked, hairy torsos.

But it was the final shocking act that most clearly caught the Polies' attention, when the giants began lustily licking the blood off each other, at the same time nibbling small bites of flesh for good measure.

Watching the debauchery unfold, the General glanced back to check on his men. *Every single one of them had turned ashen white.* It was as though they had seen their own ghostly futures: playing starring roles in the twisted imaginations of the Wursties.

The General looked back at the rapidly hardening wall, then checked his watch. "Okay. Please, accept our surrender."

He saluted Frenchy and the Commandant, to which they responded in kind.

The Commandant turned to face his troops. "Es ist over! Open das wall."

The Wursties let out a collective groan, having gotten all worked up and now not having a foe upon which to unleash their energy. But at least they had the wall, which they set about bashing into.

Frenchy turned to the Polie General. "Line your men up, march them out the opening one at a time, and have them surrender their weapons there. But first, tell me, where have you bastards put Elvis?"

"The dungeon," replied the General, reaching into his pocket and retrieving a key that he then handed over to Frenchy.

"Now, your sidearm," the Commandant demanded, holding out his hand.

The General gave his pistol to the Commandant, who quickly popped the clip out, emptied its bullets onto the ground, then returned it.

"One in chamber," he said. "To keep snakes in line as they slither back to hell."

Frenchy, anxious to dash off to the dungeon to release Elvis, had a directive of his own. "Let 'em all go except Spiro," he said to the Commandant. "He doesn't get to take the easy way out."

The Commandant clanked his heels together and snapped off a crisp salute, relishing the thought of detaining such a scoundrel.

Spiro, meanwhile, was calmly taking everything in from high atop the watchtower, readying to put a very different plan in motion. Squinting through his riflescope, he had a perfect view of Frenchy's beret, its crystal clear F providing an excellent guidepost. Allowing himself a little indulgence, he shifted the scope to run along Frenchy's green fingertips, held crisply to the base of his beret as he returned the Commandant's salute.

"Thrown up from the underworld, out green it came," Spiro said, laughing. He then shifted his scope four inches to the left and three inches down, fixing it right between Frenchy's eyes. But with his finger bouncing against the trigger, he paused, lowering the rifle. The money shot would have to wait, until such a time that Spiro could enjoy it from point-blank range.

CHAPTER THIRTY-FOUR
Out the Window

Having sprinted across the courtyard, Frenchy arrived down at the dungeon, carefully unlocking the door and opening it slowly so as to not shock Elvis with an abrupt blast of the outside world. "Dude, it's me," he said in a hushed tone.

Frenchy could make out Elvis' silhouette slumped down in the darkened corner. Then he saw his head rise up, a weak smile growing across his face.

"French Fry? Damn, am I glad to see you! I wasn't sure either of us would make it out of this mess."

"Man, me neither," Frenchy replied, hurrying over and helping Elvis up. He didn't yet have it in him to break the news that the other Ruffian *hadn't* made it. Hell, he still hadn't really even let the thought seep in himself.

He held Elvis by the arm as they slowly walked out of the cell, steadying him for his first few steps. Rising up out of the basement, the light cut into Elvis' eyes, blinding him for a second.

Frenchy took a good look at his friend. He was dirty, smelled pretty bad, and had bug bites all over his skin, but otherwise he looked just like the same old Elvis.

THE FROGMAN OF LOVELAND

They headed out to the courtyard, walking over to the opening in the wall where the Commandant and a handful of Wursties were still busy processing the release of the Polies. With just a few left to go, Frenchy inquired about the whereabouts of one Polie in particular.

"So where's the dirty little slimeball, Commandant?" he asked.

The Commandant rechecked his totals, then eyed the men still inside the gates, just three of them. He shook his head, confused. "Missing one man and one rifle," he said. "The slimiest snake must have slithered off."

Enraged that the target of his ire had somehow gotten away, Frenchy cocked his head to the side and raised his hand up, as if readying to make a most pissed-off point. Just then, a shot rang out. Feeling a strange tingle in his hand, Frenchy staggered and held it up, realizing that the bullet had passed right through the base of the pinkie that had been cut off two months prior. Oddly, having hit nothing but scar tissue, the bullet didn't hurt.

He scanned the area, desperate to figure out where the shot had come from. Then it was clear: Spiro, fully armed, was up in Flats' room with his rifle sighted a mere few inches away from Frenchy's head. But once again, Spiro deferred the satisfaction of taking Frenchy out, as it just seemed too impersonal from such a distance.

Instead, two shots rang out in quick succession, and the Commandant dropped to the ground, holding both his legs and grimacing in agonizing pain. Making matters even more dire, everyone in the group had a clear view of the tower, which meant that Spiro, in return, had a clear view of them. The Commandant, Elvis, and most of all Frenchy might as well have been wearing targets.

Now knowing where to find his adversary, Frenchy began sprinting toward the castle. Elvis, in a knee-jerk reaction, tackled him, landing on top and momentarily sheltering him from harm's way.

"Damn it, Frenchy, no!" he yelled. "It's an ambush! Let's just crawl behind the wall and live to fight another day."

The Commandant valiantly rose to his feet and then hunched over, motioning for Frenchy to jump on, piggyback style. "I bring you to fight!" he declared.

Frenchy got up and hopped onto the Commandant's back, squeezing around his shoulders, his freshly wounded hand now starting to radiate with pain.

The Commandant took off running, bravely galloping out into the wide-open courtyard fully within sight of Spiro's riflescope. Three more shots rang out, and Spiro proved to be a reliable marksman, striking the Commandant with each, coloring his chest and stomach with little red dots. But even the bullets didn't stop his charge, and a moment later he and Frenchy had made it to the base of the castle, falling into a heap under a ledge, hidden from the shooter.

The Commandant's body went limp as Frenchy held the fallen warrior's head in his hands.

"Sir, that was the bravest thing I've ever seen," Frenchy said. "How can I ever repay you?"

"By avenging the Angel," the Commandant quietly replied.

Frenchy stood up and saluted, then reached over and gently squeezed the Commandant's shoulder. "We will see each other again soon. I promise," Frenchy said softly.

Turning to his mission at hand, he sprinted into the castle and straight up six floors of tower steps, stopping one floor shy of Flats' room. He went over to the window, climbing out onto a tiny concrete ledge, then sidestepping across it to just below Flats' open window. Jumping up, he grabbed onto the bottom sill, which made his hand feel as though someone was driving a stake straight through it. Steadying his nerves, he knew he was making the wager of a lifetime: If he had guessed correctly, when he pulled his head up into the window, Spiro's eyes would be fully fixed on the front door. But had he guessed wrong, his head was about to be positioned squarely at the end of Spiro's rifle.

"The beast you face is never as bad as the beast you've feared," he whispered.

He pulled himself up, his view immediately clear. *Blackjack!* He was facing Spiro's backside.

Frenchy sprang through the window and charged as fast as he could. Steps from his target, he dove just as Spiro turned and squeezed off a single quick shot, barely missing Frenchy's head as he flew through the air.

He slammed into Spiro like a cannonball, hitting him with such force that he knocked the rifle from his grasp. Frenchy grabbed it and smashed the butt end hard into Spiro's mouth, knocking out several teeth. Then he pulled back and did it a second time, bashing down even harder. Several more battering ram blows later, Spiro's bandaged face had been left without a single front tooth.

When Frenchy eventually let up, Spiro crawled over to the corner.

Frenchy turned the weapon around, jamming the barrel end up against Spiro's forehead hard enough to draw blood. Breathing heavily, with his finger twitching on the trigger, he begged his brain to tell him what to do.

After several tense seconds, Frenchy lowered the rifle, then shook his head. "You're a disgusting, low-life creep!" he spat. "The world would be better off if you weren't in it!"

Spiro, having just been given the break of a lifetime, simply couldn't stop being Spiro. "Then go ahead and finish me off, Frogman. I'm certain that killing would be in keeping with your kind's nature," he hissed.

The words, as reprehensible as they were, actually had something of a stilling effect on Frenchy. "It just occurred to me, your words mean nothing. Just vile syllables, rooted in darkness. Violence isn't of my nature. It's quite the opposite, actually."

Spiro, as was *his* nature, continued. "Maybe you just don't have the guts," he pressed.

It took everything in Frenchy's power not to finish off the insufferable little snot right there. But he knew more bloodshed wouldn't bring Flats back. "If having guts equates to hurting people, then perhaps no, I don't," he said quietly. "I've experienced enough pain and death to last three lifetimes, so instead I'm letting you go. And this ends here."

Spiro, battered, bloodied, and barely a blink removed from having his life spared, somehow still managed to speak with both disdain and conceit, even through a broken mouth. "You've made the right choice, Frogman, as not even the beastly can cleanse the stain of blood from their hands!"

Frenchy sighed, and then he laughed wryly. "You know the single shared trait of every asshole the world has ever known? Not a single one of them ever realizes what they really are."

As Frenchy took a step to leave, he felt the crunch of broken glass beneath his shoe. Looking down, he saw Flats' frame lying destroyed next to his damaged drawing. Picking up the paper, he was instantly transported back. Suddenly it was once again just the two of them out on their own little island, fully amongst the humans. At the time, he'd been certain they had a lifetime guarantee of such moments, as they were just kids, and that seemed part of the bargain.

Glancing over to a mirror, Frenchy saw Spiro's slitted eyes on his back, watching him.

"I miss her too, you know," Spiro slurred.

Frenchy dropped the drawing. In an instant he lifted Spiro up by his shirt, dragging him over to the window and sending him right on out. "Damn you!" he roared after him. "All you had to do was keep your freakin' mouth shut!"

A brief second later, a thud down below sounded Spiro's fate.

Frenchy went back and picked up the drawing, studying the imprint of Flats' lips. Then he carefully folded it and placed it in his pocket, nestled right in front of his heart.

Steeling himself, he began to limp his way out of the room, his hand pulsating more savagely with every step he took. Reaching the door, he paused and looked back one last time, watching the beautiful white lace dancing in the breeze.

CHAPTER THIRTY-FIVE
True Believers

Early Afternoon, December 24, 1978

Freed from all things Polie, Frenchy joined Elvis in the Control Room, anxious to see where they stood with their million-toy quota. But Elvis had something he needed to say first.

"Dude, I can't say how sorry I am! The Commandant told me what happened to Flats, and like I said… I'm just so sorry."

Frenchy and Elvis looked at each other, and tears began involuntarily flooding out of both of them in waves. Not knowing what to do, they leaned in and hugged, giving each other a few precious seconds to coax the tears elsewhere. Then, without provocation, Frenchy gave Elvis several smacks on his upper back, at first starting out gently, then quickly escalating to some pretty hard whacks. Elvis responded in kind, giving Frenchy five good knocks of his own. They went on like that for several more rounds, channeling their raw pain into aggressive, adrenaline-inducing sparring.

The trick worked. Pulling apart, their macho walls were once again restored, holding back any additional tricky emotions that might try to sneak out. There would be no more tears.

Frenchy knew he needed to bash his mind into motion. "Look, thanks for saying something. And there'll definitely be a time to honor her. But for now we gotta get our hands around meeting this stupid freakin' quota thing," he said. "Lord knows we need our wishes more than ever. Getting mine is the only prayer I have for keeping the castle, since it's only a matter of time before they send an even bigger army to avenge Creepo's unfortunate accident. So, don't sugarcoat it: where do we stand with the numbers?"

Elvis took several minutes to assess where they were. His eyes darted first to his list, then over to the series of holding pens, then up at the clock, circling back and doing it all over again, time after time. With each rotation, he was becoming increasingly distraught, realizing how miserably behind his forced lockdown of the last three days had left them. He thumbed through the pages at the very end of the list, on which not a single one of the toys was marked as complete, and then checked the clock one more time.

"Holy shit.... We're never going to make it," he determined, his words halting.

Frenchy looked down at the scores of enormous piles of wrapped toys towering over the factory floor like skyscrapers. "You gotta be kidding me, Elvis," Frenchy replied. "So what if we miss by a few? We're pretty damn close. I mean, can't Santa just kick a few more kids on over to the Naughty List, you know, just to make the numbers work out?"

"It doesn't work like that, French Fry. First of all, there's never really been a Naughty List. That twisted concept was thought up by the adult humans, giving them a brutal enforcer to keep their little brats in line all year round. And besides, Santa always says that it's the naughtiest ones that need a toy the most. So he's never gonna skip even a single kid, and that's why coming up short is going to be so devastating. I forget the exact creed, but it's something like, 'If we can't get something to everybody, then nobody gets anything.' Which basically means we reach our full quota or we're screwed. Been that way ever since the first Santa, seventeen hundred years ago."

Their predicament began to sink in for Frenchy. "So, all these toys would just stay here?"

"Yep," Elvis replied stoically. "That's how it'll go. If the quota isn't 100 percent met, we've been trained to just turn the lights off and leave the factory dark. And I hate to say this, but if this thing comes crashing down…" He wiped his forehead with the back of his hand. "That'd be the end of me. And with Flats gone, I have no idea what Santa would do with you."

Frenchy shook his head, reeling, the sound of the words "crashing down" hitting him squarely. His mind raced, drifting back to his thoughts from just a few days before, when he was entirely certain they were going to tackle this godforsaken quota thing, bringing with it the wish that would come as a result. And how he was going to use that wish to secure his walled-off world forever, providing him and Flats with a nest in which to build a life together. Now, with such a huge part of that dream having been stripped from him, he considered if the remaining piece still really meant all that much.

Unless… what if it was really true that no force could override the power of one of Santa's wishes?

"Damn it, so that just means we gotta work all the harder to make it," Frenchy said finally, abruptly shifting his thoughts from reverse into drive, grasping for any angle they could

THE FROGMAN OF LOVELAND

rally around. "So how far off are we? I mean, we still have like twelve hours. What if I can light a serious fire underneath all those little Scandie asses?"

Elvis studied his list. "Well, on an average twelve-hour shift they can crank out like ten thousand toys, and we're almost one hundred thousand short. So, it's pretty bleak. Looks like nothing short of a miracle will get it done."

"I've seen them get all good and worked up at their gatherings," Frenchy said. "They get to where they're jumping up and down and shouting, and heck, I've even seen a few of them hit the floor and bounce around like a fish on the deck of a boat. Maybe we could channel all of that energy into making the toys."

"That's it!" Elvis exclaimed excitedly. "They believe that you're some kinda reincarnated savior sorta thing, right? So what if you played that card, maybe issuing some sort of bullshit decree or something? Like, 'Worketh thine asses off today! Free pizza for eternity!'"

Frenchy laughed. "Well maybe not that *exactly*, but I think we're onto something. A little divine intervention on Christmas Eve couldn't hurt, right?"

With no time to lose, Frenchy ran up to the Admiral's closet, quickly homing in on an outfit for his ruse. First putting on a shiny baby blue leisure suit, he then grabbed a container labeled "MR. SLICK." Reaching in and grabbing a big gob of goo, he ran it through his hair, pulling it all back nice and tight. Then he checked his flashy new look in the mirror.

He had drilled it, having turned himself into a carbon copy of the silver-tongued snake oil salesmen he had seen saving souls for sawbucks on late-night television.

His look in line, Frenchy ran back down to the factory floor and burst in, ready to spread some gospel. "Gather 'round, all ye of faith," he called out.

The Scandies, excited to be formally addressed by Frenchy, quickly did as directed, bunching in a large group at his feet.

"Truly I tell thee, word has come from on high," Frenchy began, adopting a ridiculous Southern accent, sounding a bit like a crossing of Foghorn Leghorn and Colonel Sanders. But then he paused, his eyes catching those of a Scandie sitting right up front, filled with trust and sincerity, like those of a child still believing a parent to be free from imperfection.

Frenchy felt small, realizing now that he was selling a shiny suit and a self-serving line of crap meant to get him what he needed and provide nothing in return. And it further occurred to him that the members of this clan had the purest hearts of any creatures he had ever met. Hardworking, brave, and selfless, they toiled for the greater good, never asking for a single thing in return.

"Alright, let's start over," he said, shifting back to his normal voice. "I came here this morning to tell you a tale. But it was just that, a tale, and a very tall one, with the hope that I could get you guys to do a favor for me. Then I realized I couldn't do that. You've already done so much for me, I can't ask anything more of you."

The Scandie from the front row rose up and approached Frenchy as Sam did the same at that very moment. Bumping into one another, Sam went to step forward, readying to assume his rightful position. But instead he stopped and smiled, motioning for the other Scandie to make his way forward, up to the most special of places.

"By all means, please," Sam said warmly. "And remember, he gets a little prickly if you don't refer to him as Frenchy."

The little Scandie proceeded forward quite tentatively. "Um, excuse me, Frenchy," he said, barely audible through his bashfulness.

"Holy shit! Since Sam always did all the talking, I figured he was the only one of you guys that was able to," Frenchy said, laughing. "I've only heard the rest of you guys singing."

"Well, yes, of course we can all talk," the Scandie replied. "We just very often choose not to, as we've found that the sounds in the silence have a certain beauty all to themselves. So, sir, can I address the others?"

Frenchy nodded, once again impressed by the wisdom exuding from what some had considered a most empty-headed species. "By all means, fire away."

"Thank you, sir," the Scandie replied. Then he turned to face the group. "On this twenty-fourth day of December, 1978, in the flesh, He appeared and spoke to us eye to eye, not from the mountaintop like the other gods, but as an equal. And so let us lift up our voices as one, shouting so loud as to be heard amongst the Angels!"

The entire factory floor erupted in song, its force so loud that it shook the walls:

"*Frenchy is the Special One, ate some bugs and then He grew. Now if you'll be Frenchy's special friend, you will be special, too!*"

Frenchy, choked with emotion, asked if they could do it one more time. Of course, the Scandies were more than happy to do so, and they joyfully sang out, with Frenchy joining them in full voice.

As the singing died down, the Scandie turned back to Frenchy. "Sir, if I may ask, what is it that you came to request?" he asked.

Frenchy still felt funny about requesting a favor from such

a devoted lot, but he also knew that they were in a helluva pinch. "Well, it's just that we're going to miss the toy quota by, like, a hundred thousand toys."

"Geez, why didn't you say so? That is not so great a matter," the Scandie answered. "Crank the furnace all the way up, greasing our joints and turning our feet to lightning, and for you, sir, we shall make the impossible otherwise!"

They shook hands, and then the Scandie addressed the others once more. "Gentlemen, in the eternal name of Saint Frenchy and in honor of his beloved Angel, let us rejoice!"

Another roar went up, followed by a once-in-a-lifetime burst of energy. And they proceeded to work like that, at a speed ten times their norm, for twelve hours straight, one big, amped-up force of possessed, toy-making maniacs.

Frenchy and Elvis simply stood by and watched in amazement, with Frenchy at one point taking a quick trip back to his quarters to get out of the preacher garb. Now, a few minutes before midnight, Sam approached to hand them both wrapped gifts, their tags declaring them to be numbers one million and one and one million and two. Remarkably, they had met the quota with time to spare.

"Damn, you guys pulled it off! A bona fide Christmas Eve miracle!" Frenchy called over to Sam, astonished. "So, like, what can I do to show my gratitude?!"

"Goodness, sir, we've been down this road before. Not for nothing, but you *died* for us!" Sam said, laughing. "So we certainly shan't be asking anything else of you! But, if I may offer one small but important point of clarification: What happened here today wasn't so much a miracle. Rather, it was more so a tremendous display of faith, of us believing in you and you, in turn, believing in us."

THE FROGMAN OF LOVELAND

Frenchy, Sam, and the other little Scandie, still standing nearby, smiled and shared a warm group hug, sealing their otherworldly bargain.

Elvis, still finding it quite amusing that an entire species of beings actually held his down-to-earth friend in such holy regard, couldn't help but get in a little wisecrack. "Excuse me, Oh Special One," he interjected, laughing. "Unless you're getting ready to turn some water into ale, I gotta run. I can smell a party a mile away, and a serious one's about to break out!"

Frenchy had a plan of his own, an important matter he hadn't had an opportunity to see to in the earlier craziness of the day.

"Where you going?!" Elvis exclaimed when he saw Frenchy making to leave the factory floor. "Our big moment is almost here! You don't want to flippin' miss it, do you? The wishing hour is upon us, baby!"

Frenchy stopped short. "Hell no! I'm not missing anything! I just gotta run out for a second and see the Commandant. The dude was ready to give up his life for me out there on the battlefield today. I gotta make sure he's okay."

Elvis' eyebrows arched. "Dude, you're nuts. Honorable as hell, but nuts! You know, I can't even cover for you if you're late, 'cuz the wishes aren't transferable. So you gotta make sure to get back on time!"

Frenchy eyed the clock, which now showed less than one minute until midnight. And then he eyed the skyscrapers of wrapped presents. "It's gonna take a helluva long time to load all those presents, even with the Scandies going like mad. What would you say, like a half hour?"

Elvis was growing more anxious by the second. "French Fry,

I have no idea. I've never done this before either, remember? But, come on, man, if you insist on going, get your ass moving!"

Frenchy took off in a sprint, then, against his better judgment, he stopped on a dime, his words unexpectedly springing from his mouth like Jack popping out of his box. "Elvis, look, I gotta know with 100 percent certainty. Is it true that Santa's wishes can do anything and that, like, nothing can overcome their power?"

Elvis was acutely aware of what his friend was asking—of course he'd be tempted to wonder such a thing. But a feat as extraordinary as bringing someone *back,* that wasn't even comprehensible. So he chose his words carefully, not wanting to give Frenchy false hope, as he feared he wouldn't survive another heartbreak. "Dude, I suppose there's a first time for everything. But listen, French Fry, there are some things that are just, um, I think, *impossible.*"

Frenchy threw up his hand and turned his head as though to bat the words away before they reached his ears. "Didn't hear a freakin' thing," he said softly, but with total conviction. "I'll be back no later than five after."

"Alright, man. Shit, what do I know, anyway? So go, dude. Run like the wind!"

Which Frenchy proceeded to do.

Just as he hit the exit, several Wursties began tugging on a rope, opening an enormous overhead door on the far end of the factory. Sleighbells came to life in the distance, and a brief moment later, a reindeer-guided sleigh dropped down from the sky as though guided by magic.

CHAPTER THIRTY-SIX
The Black Sheep Heir

The amped-up Scandies had made quick work of loading Santa's sleigh to its brim, and it was now all set for liftoff. Celebratory polka music blared out across the factory floor as the Big Man sat perched high above it on his towering sleigh, itching to be on his way. His hands gripping the reindeer's reins, he rose up, knowing he had a pressing matter to tend to before he could leave. "Elvis Parker, my boy, come hither and share a word," he called out in his booming voice.

Already knee-deep into his celebration, Elvis was amongst a couple of the rowdiest Wursties, who were taking turns tossing back flaming shots of elixir. Though he had given himself a pass to partake if he wished, Elvis had opted to abstain, preferring the feeling of having power over the stuff as opposed to the other way around.

The sound of Santa summoning him hit heavily, pulling him almost involuntarily in the direction of the sleigh. As he neared it, a set of stairs descended out its side, providing Elvis with a welcoming pathway by which to join Santa. And just a moment later, he found himself sitting next to the Man himself, an unbelievably rare and welcomed privilege.

"So, the Miracle Worker," Santa began. "'Tis an honor to be in your presence. Son, I can't thank you enough for your role in saving this Territory."

Elvis, humbled, spoke quietly. "You're very welcome, sir. But it's important for you to know, it was really the Scandies that did all the work. And of course Frenchy. I mean, he's the only reason we got to the finish line, so he's the real hero." Reflexively, Elvis' eyes darted across the factory floor in search of his friend, but there was no sign of him.

Closely considering the words, those of a young man giving, when it was finally his time to get, Santa nodded. "Duly noted. And I promise your friend shall have his time, as I vow to right a most heinous wrong. But this time, the time here and now, it is yours."

Santa paused, running his hand through his bushy white beard. "Mr. Parker, I have an offer for you. I've created a most important position back at the Pole, begging for a man bursting with nerve and energy, guided by humility, and informed by love. One such as you. You'll answer only to me and my son, third in command of a seventeen-hundred-year-old institution, just a couple beating hearts from becoming a Santa yourself."

Floored, Elvis could only offer a softly delivered question. "But sir, what about the Polies?"

With that, Santa, reddening, grew animated and stood up, his voice now rattling the factory's rafters. "Their book of days has reached its end!" he boomed. "Don't think news of their recent insurrection didn't make its way back to me. Trust me, it shall be their last. And their freshly deposed leader can forever live with the losses he brought upon himself, foolishly bringing hatred into a place guided by love!"

He calmed and sat back down, eyeing Elvis closely. "We're

going back to our traditional ways. 'Old school,' as you young people say. 'Tis time to place the reins of our toy-making empire squarely back into the hands of the Clauses, where they will once again be held lovingly. Starting immediately, the Polie Territories will be dismantled piece by piece, and from this point forward every single toy will be made under one of just two rooves: the one at the North Pole, where we're busily building a magical new factory, and right here, at Frenchy's place. Because what could be a more enchanting place to help give rebirth to our legacy than a beautiful little burg called *Loveland?* And do you know who shall be in charge of such a momentous undertaking?"

Santa paused, waiting for what he anticipated to be a most enthusiastic response. But Elvis, pretty much overwhelmed by the entire conversation, just sat quietly, thinking. Eventually, he simply threw his palms up and shrugged his shoulders.

"Well," Santa continued, "what if I were to tell you it was to be one Elvis Aaron Parker? Because, as a very special young lady once rightly predicted, he'd be most perfect. So, what say you to such a proposition, good fellow?"

Elvis really had no idea what to say, such a consideration so far from his grasp that it'd never even crossed his mind. He again sat quietly for several long moments. "Geez, Santa, I'm a little stuck for words. I mean, I'm crazy proud that you'd ask. And of course I'd accept any position you wanted to put me in. But I thought that to fill the shoes of Santa, one had to have some blood of the original Saint Nicholas in him. Like, wouldn't we be breaking some type of mystical family code or something? Unless, of course, uh…"

Santa smiled, holding his hand up so as to save *that* discussion for a little ways down the road. "My son, I can assure you that no codes shall be broken. But that is a story for another day. Let us this day agree to resume these words once this magical night rests behind us, perhaps at a royal feast in your honor, say, one week ahead. In the meantime, you can enjoy your time down here and revel in your accomplishments."

"That sounds awesome, Santa!" Elvis blurted out, his nerves easing and his tongue loosening up a bit. "And, um, not to be pushy, but since I won't be seeing you for a few days, can I get that wish I have coming to me?"

Santa laughed, causing the eyes of every single Scandie and Wurstie remaining on the factory floor to shoot up in the direction of the sleigh. "Ho! Ho! Ho! No, we shan't overlook that, my good man! So, tell me, what dost thine heart long for?"

"Well, it's about my mom," Elvis began. But the words got stuck in his throat, their power catching him by surprise and filling his eyes with tears. "Christ, I'm bawling in Santa Claus' sleigh! You couldn't make this shit up!"

They both laughed, a nice, warm bonding moment shared between them.

Elvis dried his eyes with his shirt and, composing himself, he tried again. "I don't understand it. It's like she's haunted by things that only she can see. Been that way ever since I was little. I know it's a tall order, but would it be possible for you to rid her of what's chasing her, so that she doesn't have to run from it anymore?"

Santa was listening intently. "Tis yet another topic for when we next speak, son, but please know that I have a special spot in my heart for Tracy, and nothing would warmeth it more than to slay that which bedevils her. Behold, and know that this is just the first step, with a specific number of others to follow."

Santa held out his crystal ball, and Elvis stared into it, astonished.

He watched as his mother, her makeup smeared, struggled to rise up from their trash-strewn trailer floor. She stumbled outside as a beautiful, powdery snow began to fall. Two doves flew to her, the corners of fine red linen in their beaks, and they delicately draped the shawl over her shoulders. She threw her hands out to her sides and began to dance, twirling in circles, her face uplifted to the heavens. As she twirled, the years began to magically melt away, more of them fading with each rotation, and her eyes turned crystal-clear blue, sparkling bright like a Christmas morning icicle. When she became still she was laughing, a demon clearly gone from within her.

Santa locked eyes with Elvis. "And that one shan't count as a wish. Consider it my duty, and something I should've paid heed to a long time ago."

Elvis took a moment to compose himself, wiping away a fresh set of tears. When he was finally able to speak, his words came out hushed, like those of a little boy.

"Santa, thank you so much, sir," Elvis replied. "But geez, I've held onto that wish for so long, it's really the only one I had. So can I have a second to think of a new one?"

"Of course, my boy," Santa replied.

Knowing that his mother was on her road to recovery brought him great peace. And the knowledge that Frenchy would have his own wish coming, no matter what, comforted him as well. But these developments also left him momentarily hard-pressed, as he hadn't really given thought to what else he might want. So he sat back for a moment, pondering.

Suddenly, a smile broke out across Elvis' face. "Oh man, I

think I got it! But I gotta ask you first. Can it be a package deal, like peanut butter and jelly? You know, two things that just go perfectly together."

Santa, smiling, nodded yes, having never before had someone negotiate their wish. Elvis' smile widened as well. Then he leaned over and whispered into Santa's ear.

The bearded man nodded and casually gestured over toward the factory entrance.

At once, Candy, the girl from the Halloween dance, cruised out onto the factory floor atop a brand-new Harley-Davidson, a big red bow stuck to its headlight. She got off and strutted over to the Wursties' party, her black leather boots clicking perfectly in time to the polka. Then she grabbed a flaming shot of elixir and shot it down without hesitation.

"So, would any of you guys happen to know where I might find a charming little cutie named Elvis?" she asked.

The Wursties, blushing like crazy, sheepishly pointed over toward Santa's sleigh.

She turned and looked up at Elvis, big smiles bursting out on each of their faces.

Elvis, laughing, shook his head. "Damn! Thanks again, Santa! So I'll be seeing you real soon, sir. Meantime, I'm gonna do my best to get to know the humans around here, you know, to understand our core customer and all!"

Elvis stood and extended his hand. Santa stood as well, gently pushing the hand off to the side and leaning in, embracing Elvis in a warm hug.

"I look forward to your safe return home, son. Have a most merry Christmas," Santa said.

"Merry Christmas to you too, sir," Elvis replied.

THE FROGMAN OF LOVELAND

With that, he headed excitedly back down the stairs, which then automatically disappeared, tucking themselves back underneath the sleigh. But just before he took off to greet Candy, Elvis turned and shouted one more question up to Santa. "Sir, can you give me a guess on how much longer you're going to be here? Frenchy guaranteed that he'd be back no later than five minutes after midnight."

Santa, shrugging, pointed up to a digital readout at the front of his sleigh, locked in at 12:00:00, and then over to a large clock hanging upon the wall, its second hand frozen as well. "In my magical little bubble, the confines of this sleigh and everything I choose to be within my purview, it remains midnight as long as I will it to be. So whilst the world outside goes right on spinning, time stands still for me, enabling me to lift a rather weighty load all at once. Just one more trick you will soon become acquainted with, Mr. Parker."

Then Santa gave the reins a full-on tug, and with another quick flip of his wrist, he was gone, off to spread his joy, love, and goodwill.

Elvis, meanwhile, took off running toward Candy. Overwhelmed by the intoxicating events of the past few minutes, it didn't dawn on him just how perilous Santa's time-freezing trick would be for Frenchy.

Chapter Thirty-Seven
The Promise

As bells rang out, heralding in midnight on this Christmas morning, Frenchy dashed out into the courtyard, desperately wanting to see how the Commandant was doing. He was also very much looking forward to meeting Santa and, of course, taking advantage of his wish of a lifetime—but he was certain that three or four brief minutes couldn't possibly hurt anything.

As he approached a long formation of Wursties in the center of the yard, he could see the Commandant down the line, seated in a chair at front and center. As Frenchy passed the first man in line, they caught eyes, and he paused, doubling back for a brief word.

The Wurstie leaned in toward Frenchy, whispering in Germ-lish. "He ist gut. But nicht walk again."

Frenchy nodded and then continued on toward the Commandant.

The larger-than-life warrior seemed at peace, joyful even, dressed in a loud red sweater with a large Christmas tree on the front. It was quite clear that Frenchy and the Commandant were thrilled to see one another again.

THE FROGMAN OF LOVELAND

"To the most honorable man I've ever known," Frenchy said, crisply saluting.

"Und though little, you are quite big-hearted yourself, mein friend," the Commandant replied, returning the salute.

Frenchy bent down and pinned a military-style ribbon he had made onto the Commandant's sweater, a cross with "The Ruffians" scrolled from left to right. They both took a moment to admire the artwork, then exchanged a heartfelt handshake.

"I'm proud for your victory," the Commandant began, quietly. "But remain so, so sorrowful for your loss."

Frenchy's head dropped sullenly, but he appreciated the words. "I am sorrowful for you as well," he said, patting the Commandant on one of his legs. "And about Flats, for sure. But, you know, I'm working hard to keep my spirits up. I gotta say, they've been given a real boost by the loop that's started playing in my head. I can see it clearly: not only do I have my wish coming from Santa, but also, according to the Scandies, two full miracles securely up my sleeve. That's a lot of cards to play. So I'm going to use whatever I can to try to—" But something held him back from voicing his deepest desire, as if speaking it out loud would somehow jinx it, preventing it from coming true.

The Commandant, understanding exactly what his friend was saying, exchanged a knowing nod. "I wish only for the light to return to you. Merry Christmas, Frenchy," he said.

"Merry Christmas, Commandant," Frenchy replied. "Here's to many more."

They shook hands again, and, feeling as though they had said all there was to say at the moment, Frenchy turned to head back into the factory, anxious to see how all this wish business really worked.

261

A few steps into his walk across the courtyard, he realized that he was on the same ground that the Commandant had so bravely dashed across earlier in the day. In fact, a series of bloody red dots still dotted the soil. Such a heroic man didn't deserve the cards he had been dealt.

Walking over to a window into the factory, Frenchy peered through. Not able to see the sleigh being loaded all the way at the far end of the building, he watched a handful of Scandies gathered in the foreground with their heads thrown back. He could tell that they were all still worked up, for they were once again glowing green and singing as though their lives depended on it.

Suddenly his gaze shifted, making the Commandant clear in the window's reflection. He watched as the old warrior gamely soldiered on, barking out orders to his legs, admonishing them to get moving and carry out their duties. But those orders went unfollowed, and one of his men had to bend down and gently shift the position of his feet just to stop them from twitching. Catching sight of such saddened eyes, Frenchy knew that this was a wrong that needed righting.

"You can do this," he said, working to coax his mind around to the task of what needed to be done, surprising himself with the audaciousness of even having the guts to try. "'*If you believe in Frenchy, you will be special, too.*' They say it's already written, and there's two more coming. So why not give it a shot?"

Frenchy turned back to face his friend. Girding himself with a steely single-mindedness, he issued a divine directive. "Sir Commandant, rise up and walk to me."

The Commandant slowly rose from the chair, and he began stepping toward Frenchy like a toddler trying to get the feel of being on their feet for the very first time. Tears filled both of their eyes.

THE FROGMAN OF LOVELAND

"Es ist *miracle!*" said the Commandant, his words choked with emotion.

"Hell yeah, it is!" Frenchy exclaimed, laughing incredulously, filling at once with equal parts pride, bewilderment, and utter disbelief.

The Commandant smiled and spread his arms wide, and Frenchy moved in, welcoming his first ever Bavarian bear hug. It proved to be wonderful, though if the Commandant had squeezed just a tiny bit tighter, he might have split Frenchy right in two.

"Thank you for walking among us," the Commandant said, releasing him. "The rat-elves, before you come back to life, they always talk of Frenchy. Und we think they crazy!"

Frenchy laughed. "No, those Scandies aren't crazy. Is their story off here and there? Who's to say for sure? But I don't think that matters. I think that at the heart of it, what really makes them glow is the *faith* they have in their story, wherever it takes them, sometimes even in the blinding absence of proof."

They traded one last nod and Frenchy was off, letting the Wursties enjoy the night's celebration in their own way, which, knowing them, was bound to be unique.

As Frenchy jogged toward the factory to finally meet Santa, he heard the faint sound of bells overhead. Puzzled, he looked up. As his eyes adjusted to the starlit sky, he watched as a behemoth of a carriage, overbrimming with wrapped presents, was pulled upward by eight magnificent flying beasts. Seeing the sleigh quickly ascend, his elation now turned to dread. Had his wish just drifted off into the midnight sky?

"Oh, shit…" he whispered.

Panicked, he sprinted back into the factory, barely able to think.

Seeing Elvis and Candy atop their roaring new Harley, shooting across the factory floor at an astonishing speed, Frenchy ran over to get their attention.

"Hey, man. Stop! I gotta ask you something," he yelled, frantically waving his hands overhead. "It's really important!"

Elvis brought the bike to an abrupt halt. "Damn, French Fry. You look like you just seen a ghost! Dude, you alright?"

"No, I'm not! I just saw Santa taking off. Do you think he might realize he forgot about me and turn back around? I mean, my entire world hinges upon it!" But even as the words came out, he sensed that it was all just, well, too late.

Elvis could see the desperation taking root in Frenchy, as though his friend was envisioning his own bloody crash on the road ahead yet could do nothing to avoid it. He felt terrible for him, but, having been knocked on his ass himself more times than he could remember, he also knew that it was *hope* that his friend needed, not sympathy. So he treaded carefully, navigating between what truly was and what was desired.

"Well, from everything I've heard, Santa usually just plows through his route with a laser focus, letting nothing knock him off course. But when I talked to him earlier, he also said something about it always being midnight to him. So, there's that. Plus, he clearly said that you would have your day and that everything would be alright!"

"Christ, Elvis, that could mean anything!" Frenchy shouted. "*Is he coming back?!*"

Elvis got off his motorcycle, ruefully shaking his head. Putting his hand on Frenchy's shoulder, he looked straight at his friend, his eyes dampening. "Dude, I'm really sorry.... But I just don't know."

Frenchy flinched, feeling the familiar sensation that

THE FROGMAN OF LOVELAND

something important was about to be snatched away from him. His panic button now fully depressed, he took off sprinting across the factory floor over to where a group of Scandies was hard at work, already charting out their plans for 1979's blessed mission. He quickly found who he was looking for.

"Sam, listen, this is critical," he began, panting. "I need to hear a passage from the Prophecy. Can you help me?"

"Of course, Frenchy," Sam confidently replied. "And perhaps you would like my interpretation of it as well, as I happen to be quite well versed in the subject matter. Some might say the *most* well versed. Would that be of interest to you?"

"No!" Frenchy snapped. "No, listen, I need you to answer my question just as asked, not offering even a single syllable of interpretation, explanation, or expectation. I need to know exactly how it's worded in the Prophecy—and only that. Do you understand?!"

Sam nodded. "Yes, I understand."

"Good. Okay. Tell me what it says about Flats and me."

Sam took a deep breath, then swallowed hard. He was about to recite something he had been reciting since he was a child, but this time, he'd be foretelling the future of the very one standing before him. "The Prophecy sayeth:

'The Special One and his Angel: both uniquely beautiful.
Though a truly royal couple, no kingdoms do they rule.
Rain bursts and rainbows, through their book of days they run.
All the while running together as tightly as just one.
A life's tapestry unveils, its winding road doth turn.
At times forlornly veering from where the sanguine heart doth yearn.
And though darkness may befall it, in time, light will shine above.
Brought back, as though by magic: the magnetic pull of love.'"

"Stop!!!" Frenchy shouted, thrusting out his palm to silence any further words. He had heard exactly what he needed to hear and only that. "Thank you very much, Sam."

With that, Frenchy turned on his heels once again and took off running, knowing that he had to get to a very specific spot. Just about to the exit, the little Scandie he had first heard speak earlier in the day stopped him.

"Hey, blessed news, Oh Special One!" he said excitedly, his words tumbling out so fast that Frenchy didn't even think to hold them at bay. "I checked Appendix M, Subsection Fifty-Seven of the Prophecy, commonly known as 'The Unabridged Rules For Determining the Validity of Miracles.' And it turns out that what went down on the factory floor earlier clearly qualifies as one. So, congratulations! Looks like number two is in the bag!"

Frenchy's eyes widened, and he swallowed hard. He nodded at the Scandie and, knowing the little guy had in no way meant to upset him, tipped his beret in his direction. Shuffling out the factory exit, he made sure the door latched good and tight behind him. Then, throwing his head back, he let out a roar that could be heard throughout the entire greater Loveland metropolitan area: "FFFFFFUUUUUCCCCCKKKK!!!!"

Then he did all he could think to do, which was to turn and run across the courtyard like crazy, heading to the special spot he had shared with Flats.

Midway across the courtyard, Frenchy looked up and caught a final fleeting glimpse of Santa's sleigh, which was now disappearing into the empty sky. Dousing any remaining hope that he could still somehow have an audience with Santa tonight, it was now unclear whether that would ever occur at all. With cold, hard reality setting in, doubt began to lay siege to Frenchy's mind, finding it a weakened sparring partner, as this particular opponent had just lost the only two weapons that had given it a puncher's chance. A harsh lesson then began to take hold: When one's punches stood to possibly be exposed as fugazies, made-up matters of miracles and making wishes, reality would always reign as the undisputed heavyweight champion of the world. And reality's blows were now coming fast and furious.

His feet started to grow heavy, with each step moving him farther from all the frenetic activity that had consumed his life over the past two months and closer to the unknown. All the newly discovered feelings, the adventures, the mountainous challenges, they all seemed to melt away, and his heart began to hurt like never before. Suddenly, all the distractive forces that had kept the painful thoughts of Flats at bay were gone.

His sprint slowing to a crawl, Frenchy arrived at the spot where he and Flats had first met, which now felt like a lifetime ago. This time, it was just him alone with his pain. Grasping at the memory of the first dance they had shared up in the Control Room, he reached out, wrapped his arms around the space in front of him, and began to slowly rock back and forth.

Then he lowered his head and started sobbing. The future he had dreamed about just a few days before was now simply *gone*. His tears, at first born of mourning, gave way to something else, something even sadder: the desperate plea of the broken one left behind.

"You promised me that they were good for anything, the wishes. It couldn't have been a lie—there's just no way, because the words came from you! Please, I can't walk through this life alone. So here I am now, full in faith, certain that my wish will be granted and that you'll come back to me anew!"

Pleading to the Heavens

Frenchy fell to his knees and looked toward the heavens.

"*I believe!*" he shouted upward, the words garbled by a mighty wave of emotion.

At that very moment, Santa, well into his world-crossing journey, glanced down at his crystal ball and saw all that he needed to see.

At once, a loud, fast flutter burst free from the heavens. And an instant later, Flats bowled into Frenchy, sending them once again rolling head over heels upon the riverbank.

"For old time's sake," she said with a laugh.

They jumped up and pulled together, embracing as tightly as two beings could.

"I saw your Pappy. He was very sweet, and he said to tell you that they weren't ready for me yet, either," Flats whispered into his ear. Then she pulled back a little, looking squarely into Frenchy's eyes. "So this is a miracle if there ever was one. Right?!"

Frenchy smiled, his eyes shining. "Perhaps, with a little Christmas magic thrown in for good measure."

They dove into one another, kissing, locked so intricately as to become one. And then Flats blasted them high up into the Christmas morning sky.

A few magical moments later, momentarily waking from the spell of the kiss, Frenchy realized they were hovering a good half mile over the Little Miami River valley.

"Goodness, have you got me!?" he asked, looking wide-eyed at Flats.

"Yes," Flats replied, smiling. "And I promise I'm never letting you go!"

THE END

CPSIA information can be obtained
at www.ICGtesting.com
Printed in the USA
BVHW051502021122
650893BV00003B/6